Outstanding Praise for *Truly, Madly*

"This clever paranormal mystery series is sure to delight fans . . . Fun characters, sparkling prose, and a twisty plot add up to a great beginning for Valentine, Inc."

—*Publishers Weekly*

"Charming and lovable . . . [a] truly irresistible mix of clever romance and wildly inventive mystery."

—*Booklist*

"Snappy and fresh—a delightful mix of intrigue and humor!"

—Jane Porter, author of *Mrs. Perfect* and *Easy on the Eyes*

"Lucy Valentine is as comic and romantic as her name implies, not to mention engaging, sexy, and smart. She has an otherworldly knack for finding lost objects, and will undoubtedly find her creator, Heather Webber, many new fans."

—Harley Jane Kozak, Agatha, Anthony & Macavity-award winning author of *A Date You Can't Refuse*

"With characters that sparkle like diamonds on the page, this is my new favorite Valentine! Heather Webber has created a bright new world, populated by quirky characters and brimming with non-stop action—I'm a fan!"

—Beth Harbison, *New York Times* bestselling author of *Shoe Addicts Anonymous* and *Hope in a Jar*

D0954866

**St. Martin's Paperbacks Titles
By Heather Webber**

Truly, Madly

Deeply, Desperately

Absolutely, Positively

Absolutely, Positively

HEATHER WEBBER

St. Martin's Paperbacks

This is a work of fiction. All of the characters, organizations, and events portrayed in this novel are either products of the author's imagination or are used fictitiously.

ABSOLUTELY, POSITIVELY

Copyright © 2011 by Heather Webber.

For information address St. Martin's Press, 175 Fifth Avenue, New York, NY 10010.

ISBN: 978-0-312-94615-9

Printed in the United States of America

St. Martin's Paperbacks edition / February 2011

St. Martin's Paperbacks are published by St. Martin's Press, 175 Fifth Avenue, New York, NY 10010.

10 9 8 7 6 5 4 3 2 1

For my family, with much love.

Acknowledgments

Although writing a book is often a solitary endeavor, producing a book is not. A big thank you to: everyone at St. Martin's Press who ensures that every Lucy Valentine novel is as good as it can be; my agent, Jessica Faust, who encourages my overactive imagination; close friends Shelley Shepard Gray, Cathy Liggett, Hilda Lindner Knepp, Sharon Short, and Wendy Lyn Watson for brainstorming sessions, reading first passes (and giving honest feedback), career advice, and being the best cheering squad when writing-related neuroses take over.

I'm also so very grateful to Jeannie Rigod for sharing her personal experiences regarding defibrillators with me, which in turn allowed me to write one of my favorite scenes in this book between Sean and Lucy. Thank you.

Finally, thanks to everyone who (like Lucy and me) believes that love does conquer all. Happy reading!

*　　*　　*

I love to hear from readers. You can reach me through my website, www.heatherwebber.com, where you can also learn a little bit more about me and sign up for my Every-Once-In-A-While e-newsletter.

1

Suzannah Ruggieri blew into Valentine, Inc., like a category five hurricane. The antique mahogany door slammed into its stopper, rattling the beveled glass panes. Her eyes were wild, her hair disheveled, her round high cheekbones flaming. Winded, she huffed, "Hurry! The Lone Ranger's back!"

Spinning, she rushed out the way she came, her heavy footsteps thudding on the cherrywood stairs leading down to Beacon Street.

Preston Bailey, roving reporter, didn't need to be told twice. She jumped up from the russet-colored love seat in the reception area, sending notes flying in all directions. She barely paused at the door to see if I was following. "Lucy, come on!"

I jumped up, hesitated. I had been manning Suz's desk while she was at lunch. If I left, no one would be here to answer the phones. I had a responsibility to the company—after all, my name was on the door. Valentine, Inc., the country's most successful matchmaking firm, had been in the family for generations. And though

I wasn't a true matchmaker like my father, I managed to have a great success rate with clients in my division of the company, Lost Loves. My father and I used our psychic gifts in very different ways.

"Lucy!" Preston bellowed up the stairs. The sound echoed up to the third floor and back down to me. "The. Lone. Ranger. Move your ass!"

Ah, hell. I grabbed my coat and followed Preston down the steps and out the thick metal door into a typical gunmetal gray February afternoon of a Boston winter.

We dodged through stopped traffic and sprinted toward the mob gathered at Boston Common. A piece of paper fluttered across the crunchy dormant grass and I stomped on it.

"You got one!" Preston cried.

I picked up the twenty-dollar bill. Others floated by, people chasing after them, pushing and shoving.

"Do you see him?" Preston stood on tiptoes, but even in heeled boots she was vertically challenged.

Standing a good five inches taller, I scanned the throbbing crowd for any sign of a masked man. "No."

"He has to be here somewhere!" She threaded her way through the masses, throwing bony elbows and hips to get people to move aside. There was no stopping a reporter on the hunt of a huge story.

The Lone Ranger had struck again.

It was the fourth time in as many weeks. No one knew where he came from or who he was. By all accounts, he simply appeared in a mask and cowboy hat and started throwing money.

Last week, the unofficial tally hit two thousand dollars. By the look of the loot still skittering across the ground, this week's total was going to be even higher. Preston, a reporter for the *South Shore Beacon,* a daily paper that mostly covered areas south of the city, had taken to trolling the Common during the day, even though she was *supposed* to be writing feature stories on my Lost Loves clients. She was dying to find the man the media had labeled the Lone Ranger and crack the reasoning behind such outlandish behavior.

A WHDH news crew arrived on the scene, and a reporter tottered across the grass to interview people clutching fistfuls of money.

As I tucked the twenty into my pocket and leaned against a tree, waiting for the crowd to thin, I glanced to my left and found a homeless man watching me intently from a nearby bench. Caught, he looked down and started fussing with a plastic garbage bag filled with his worldly goods. He held a thermos of what I hoped was coffee.

Sudden guilt flooded me. I didn't need the money, yet here I was eager to catch a few flying twenties. I tried to justify that I'd been caught up in the moment, but that excuse didn't pass muster, as I'd caught three twenties last week and used them to buy myself a cute scarf from a shop in Harvard Square.

Feeling slightly sick with shame, I pulled the twenty from my pocket, walked over, and handed it to him.

He looked up at me with a wary faded blue gaze before reaching out with gloved fingers for the cash. A holey knit cap covered his head and an oversized black Michelin Man–type coat sheltered him from icy gusts. Dirt smudges darkened pale, yellow-tinted skin. White stubble covered his chin.

"Mind if I sit?" I asked.

He nodded to the bench.

This, I thought, was the real story. This man and all the other homeless who called the Common home, even in the midst of a brutal winter.

"You didn't want in on the action?" I asked, nodding to the crowd. I spotted Preston weaving in and out, still searching. Suz was headed my way.

"Legs don't work so well anymore!" he shouted, his voice becoming louder with each word. "Can't fight off those young'uns like I used to, and it's not so bad being poor."

I jumped a bit before I adjusted to the volume. I only had vague memories of my Grandpa Henry, who died when I was five, but I remembered he used to shout, too. He'd needed a hearing aid and had been stubborn about getting one. Vanity at its finest.

"Did you see the guy who was throwing the money?" I asked loudly, doubting this man's lack of a hearing aid had anything to do with how it would look.

He took a draw from his thermos. "Masked. Hat. No horse. Tossing money this way and that."

That about summed it up. Then I smiled when I realized he was speaking (well, shouting) in rhyme.

Suz counted twenties, her eyes glowing, as she walked toward us. It just went to show how anyone could get caught up in a situation. Valentine, Inc., paid her well. Not only because she was a valued employee, but also because she was practically family. And thus, we had entrusted her with all the family secrets.

"One hundred forty! Woo-ha! I'll be treating myself to some nice wine while eating a nice big steak at The Hilltop tonight."

I jerked my head toward the guy next to me, silently asking her to make a donation.

Suz frowned as she followed the motion.

I widened my eyes and continued twitching.

She huffed, peeled off two twenties, and handed them to him. "Oh fine." She gave him the rest of the cash. "You need it more than I do."

He quickly tucked the money inside his glove and stood up.

"Ladies, I'll be on my way!" he shouted, tipping an imaginary cap. "Have yourselves a wonderful day!" He winked, turned, and hobbled off.

"For the love of Dr. Seuss, Lucy. You know he's probably just going to drink the money away," Suz said in an are-you-crazy kind of whisper.

"So were you."

She flipped her dark hair. "Touché."

I stood, searched for Preston's spiky platinum hair in the thinning crowd. "Besides, you don't know that he'll spend the money on alcohol. Maybe he's hungry. Maybe *he* wants a nice steak."

Soulful eyes narrowed. "You don't know he *won't* drink it away."

"You don't know he *will*."

"You can't be that naïve, Lucy."

I'd lost a lot of my naïveté over the last six months when I started freelancing as a consultant for the Massachusetts State Police, using my psychic ability to find lost objects to help locate missing persons. Often the cases didn't come with happily ever afters.

"I just want to believe that in every person there's a little decency. Is that wrong?" My breath formed little white clouds as I spoke. It was twenty freezing degrees, and I questioned why I'd left the warmth of the office.

Oh right. Greed.

Now I felt really queasy.

Her eyes softened. "It's dangerous to only see the good in people. You, of all people, should know that."

I tossed a look over my shoulder. The homeless man had only made it ten feet or so, shuffling along at a snail's pace. It was because I'd seen firsthand the evils of the world that I searched for the good. I had to.

"We should head back," I said.

"What about Preston?"

"I'll leave a trail of bread crumbs."

Preston and I had come a long way in our relationship. At first, I'd hated her for revealing my biggest secret in the pages of the *Boston Herald*. But as we collaborated on articles featuring my Lost Love clients, things between us had thawed a bit. I wouldn't go so far as to say we were close—I still didn't completely trust her—but I didn't want to throttle her anymore. That was saying something.

The cold was starting to seep under my skin as we climbed the steps to the second-floor office. The door to Valentine, Inc., was ajar. I cautiously peeked inside and found my grandmother, Dovie, sitting in Suz's desk chair, flipping through client files. Dovie harbored dreams of matchmaking, but since she'd married into the family, she didn't possess the ability to read auras that was genetic only to bloodline Valentines—a gift, legend declared, bestowed on my family by Cupid himself.

It had been my great-grandfather who had founded Valentine, Inc. What our clients didn't know was the company's incredible success had little to do with the long questionnaires and personality tests endured on a first appointment but everything to do with . . . color. Every person carried with them a colorful aura, which only those gifted could see. True love was predestined by pairing lovers with similar hues.

Unfortunately, I'd lost my ability at fourteen when a surge of electricity changed my life. I'd gone from living in a world surrounded by colorful people to being able to find lost objects—a quality that for a long time I thought was pretty useless. Not only because my family was in the business of making matches based on auras but also because I didn't think I could do the world any good being able to find a lost wallet or car keys or a lucky key chain.

I'd been wrong. There was more to my gift than I ever dreamed.

"What are you doing here?" I asked Dovie. My father would have himself another heart attack if he found her rifling through his files. Was she trying to make matches or looking for love herself? Her most recent relationship, with a man I'd set her up with, had only lasted three fun-filled weekends. Dovie, like all Valentines, was as commitment phobic as George Clooney. That being said, she might change her mind if he came walking through the door.

My mother came in from the back hallway, carrying two mugs of coffee. She handed one to Dovie and air-kissed my cheek, then Suz's. Mum was fairly glowing. Her hazel eyes danced, the gold specks glittering, and a smile flirted playfully at the corners of her lips.

"What's up with you?" I asked. She looked truly lovely in a purple cowl-necked sweater, dark jeans, and ballet slippers. Her pixie-style hair had just been cut and colored a golden blond. She looked younger. Happier.

"Me?" Mum waved a hand in dismissal as she sat on the love seat. "Nothing. Nothing at all."

"Something," Suz said, shooing Dovie from her desk chair. "You look great."

Mum shrugged coyly. "Been on a little diet, that's all."

"Diet?" Mum didn't diet. Ever. She firmly believed in eating what she wanted, when she wanted, and the hell with people who cared about calories and cholesterol. Living life to the fullest with Mum meant having a New York–style cheesecake in the fridge at all times. "Diet" was the worst four-letter word in her vocabulary.

"I'm getting older," Mum said. "I need to be more careful about my weight. I'm taking a Zumba class, too." Her eyes brightened. "You should come with me, LucyD!"

"A zoo what?" I asked.

Dovie laughed and launched into a cha-cha, her long legs lithe and graceful. When she was younger she danced Burlesque at a club in Manhattan—it's where she met my grandfather. After they married and secretly divorced, she continued her dance training and eventually became a choreographer. These days she mostly used her talents for local musical theater and social events, but it didn't take much for her to randomly break into dance. "Zumba. It's an exercise program featuring dancing."

"Fun!" Suz squealed. "When and where? Count me in!"

Diet *and* exercise? I stared at Mum. Who was this woman? Certainly not *my* mother. "What's going on? I mean, what's *really* going on? You're not sick, are you?" She didn't look sick, but it would take something as monumentally life-changing as a chronic illness to get her to break a lifetime of (bad) habits.

"Do I need a reason to better myself?" Her nose twitched.

Aha! She'd stumbled on the word "better." She wasn't as keen on all this diet and exercise as she let on. The nose twitch was a dead giveaway she was hiding something.

Dovie was still cha-chaing. "Oh go on, Judie. Tell her. It's past time."

Mum shot her an evil look. Good thing the two of them were the best of friends, a relationship Dad absolutely hated. His mother. His somewhat-ex wife (technically they were still married). It was a nightmare for him when they ganged up.

"What? What-what?" I pleaded.

Dovie dragged Suz into her dance. The two held hands as Dovie counted aloud, "One two three, cha cha cha." She thrust a hip and singsonged in the same cadence, "Judie has a boyfriend, cha cha cha."

I gasped. "You do? Who?"

"Just someone," Mum said.

"Spill!" I urged. Though my parents were happily separated, it had been years since Mum had anyone serious in her life. Her little on-and-off flings with my father hardly counted.

"Where's Sean today?" Mum asked.

She was referring to Sean Donahue, the supersexy PI who worked upstairs and partnered with me in Lost Loves. We were partnered in other ways, too. Just thinking about him made me go all warm and gooey inside.

For almost fifteen years my abilities had been a closely guarded family secret until a skeleton, a lost little boy, and Preston Bailey changed my life forever.

She'd "outed" me in the *Boston Herald,* and I'd been swarmed by the media. It had been quite an adjustment. But after a long talk with my father, Lost Loves was born. I now used my ability to help reunite lost loves whenever possible by using old letters, jewelry, photos. Though my gift had limitations, it had proved invaluable for some of my and Sean's tougher cases.

"Don't change the subject," I said.

"I was simply asking a question, LucyD," she said, using her pet nickname for me. My mother was a rabid Beatles fan, and I'd been named after the song "Lucy in the Sky with Diamonds." When I was very little, my mother used to call me Lucy Diamonds, but it had been further shortened over the years to LucyD.

The door crashed open. Startled, I jumped as Preston stormed in, limping.

"How can he just vanish?" she asked, throwing her hands in the air. "Poof. Gone. How? You'd think that a man who was tossing twenties like rice at a wedding wouldn't escape unnoticed. Hello," she said, taking notice of Mum and Dovie. She kissed their cheeks. My family had taken Preston under its wing—whether I liked it or not.

"The Lone Ranger?" Dovie asked.

"Struck again," Suz said, setting her desk to rights. She was fussy about what went where, and Dovie had obviously been rifling for a while before we caught her. "I had a hundred and forty dollars before Lucy made me give it all away to a homeless guy."

"He'll probably just drink it away." Mum sipped her coffee.

"That's what I said!" Suz shot me a look.

I sat on the edge of the couch. I could argue, but I was outnumbered.

"Well, I didn't get anything." Preston sighed. "Not any money, not a story, not anything. And I broke my heel." She sat next to Mum and peeled off her boot. The heel dangled sadly. "Someone had to have seen something."

"Doubtful." Dovie patted her hair to make sure it was still in place. Her stunning signature white locks had been loosely twisted into a knot at the base of her neck. "Once money starts flying, no one's going to notice anything but the green."

"I suppose you're right," Preston said, leaning back. "But there has to be a way to catch him." There was a look in her eyes I was coming to recognize. She was hatching a plan.

I checked my watch. Preston and I were meeting with a new client soon. The whole new-boyfriend conversation with Mum would have to wait until I had time for a more prepared inquisition. "Are you two in town for a little shopping?" I asked Dovie.

"Actually, no," she answered.

I tipped my head at her serious tone. "A court hearing?" She and Mum had been arrested not long ago for disturbing the peace. I thought everything had been worked out, but—

"Time served." Mum sounded like a felon who'd been locked up for decades instead of a protester sentenced to serve community service.

Dovie pulled the latest issue of the *South Shore Beacon* from the hobo bag at her feet and handed it to me. "We actually came to see Sean."

"Sean? Why?" I scanned the headline.

Local Man Still Missing

"I'm hoping you won't mind sharing," Dovie said, "because I want to hire him."

2

Macalaster Gladstone had been missing for six weeks.

Talk about poof, gone.

He'd last been seen walking his golden retriever, Rufus, along Cohasset's picturesque side streets just after the New Year. Rufus had come home; Mac had not.

The black-and-white photo on the front page showed a smiling older man with a thick shock of dark hair and full beard (who, I noticed—and not just because I was hungry—looked a lot like the Gorton's Fisherman). His arms were looped around a beautiful dog. A dark bandanna was tied around the dog's neck, and Rufus looked to be smiling, too, with his tongue lolling, his eyes bright and shiny.

Preston snatched the paper from my hand. I'm not sure why she needed to see it—she had written the story. "So sad. By all accounts they were inseparable."

"Exactly," Dovie said. "Something awful had to have happened to Mac. The police have run out of leads, so I want Sean to look into it. Fresh eyes." Her voice grew thick.

"Do you know him well?" I'd heard about the story, of course—it was hard to live in Cohasset and not. There were open conversations about what had happened to Mac at the local coffee shop, the pizza parlor, the produce department at Shaw's. I hadn't known Dovie was so invested.

"Not well," she conceded. "His wife, Betty, used to be in my Scrabble club. From what I know of Mac, he was a sweet man. One of those strong, silent types. He was a bit of a recluse, especially after Betty died, but still a big patron of the local theater and all the arts. He was an illustrator, you know."

I'd never personally met Mac, but his name was well-known in not only the South Shore community but the art world as well. His work was on par with Norman Rockwell's and J. C. Leyendecker's.

Preston handed the paper back to Dovie. "The police aren't doing much because they think he's dead."

"And that may be so, but I want to know the truth. Where's his body? What happened to him? His daughter, Jemima, isn't exactly going out of her way to get answers. She thinks he committed suicide. Ha!"

Mum tsked and sipped her coffee.

"Isn't it possible?" I asked softly, not wanting to be at the wrong end of a Dovie tirade.

"Anything is possible, but there was no note. Plus, I can't imagine Mac would willingly leave Rufus behind. From everything I've heard, that dog was Mac's best friend."

"What's the story with Jemima?" Suz asked, propping her elbows on the desk and her head in her hands.

Dovie stood, paced. "At eighteen she married a man almost twice her age, some rock star she met when she dropped out of college and became a music groupie. You can imagine how Betty and Mac felt about that."

Mum shook her head like the decision had been a fate worse than death. "Poor parents."

I was suddenly relieved my vast résumé didn't include "music groupie."

"Mac and Betty never approved," Dovie said. "Betty hinted there was something in Rick's—he's the husband—past that made them nervous, though she never said what. And of course, who wants a rock-star lifestyle for their baby girl? Unfortunately, they didn't have a say."

"Is he anyone famous?" Suz asked.

Dovie tipped her hand in a "so-so" motion. "Rick Hayes."

"*The* Rick Hayes? I'd say he was famous." Suz blinked. "Wow."

Rolling her eyes, Dovie said, "Maybe. At one time, a *long* time ago. Now he's a down-and-out aging rocker. Rumor is he's trying to put together a reality show about his family as they deal with him trying to make a comeback. He's not finding the financing, however."

"Is he broke?" Suz asked, clearly infatuated with his story.

Dovie said, "Completely. He and Jemima have been living with Mac for a while now, but he's been supporting them for years. I wouldn't doubt if they're just chomping at the bit to go to the courts and declare Mac dead so they can get their hands on his bank accounts. From what I hear, Mac had been threatening to cut them off financially if Rick didn't drop this whole reality project."

Preston, I noticed, had perked up, her broken heel all but forgotten. "I haven't heard any of this. Do you think his daughter or her husband had something to do with his disappearance?"

Arching a snow-white eyebrow, Dovie said, "I don't know, but the possibility needs to be explored."

Preston reached for her notebook. Obviously this was one angle to the story she hadn't probed. "Have you mentioned all this to the police?"

"Of course." Dovie still paced. "I believe they looked into it for precisely half a second. That's why I need Sean."

Sean. My blood thrummed at the sound of his name. We'd been dating since the fall and things were heating up and getting serious. Really serious.

Which was exciting and scared the hell out of me at the same time.

Valentines and commitment didn't exactly go together, despite the fact that we matched others for a living.

The problem was Cupid's gift to us had also come with an attached curse: Valentines could match others based on their auras, but we couldn't see our own—or one another's—color. Which made finding true love nearly impossible. Not one relationship in the Valentine family had withstood the test of time. Not. A. Single. One.

I'd grown up in two different worlds. One where true love existed, thrived. And one where my parents lived separate lives and my grandmother was left scarred by a secret divorce and delusions of happily ever afters. And though, technically, Dovie wasn't a Valentine, she often said she was cursed by association, which doomed her every relationship.

"He's due back any minute," I said.

Sean, a former firefighter, had been working as an investigator for his brother Sam's PI agency for almost a year now. Lost Loves, which had been created to reunite long lost loves by employing Sean's private investigating and my own special sleuthing abilities, was now an official division of not only Valentine, Inc., but SD Investigations as well.

Dovie plopped down in a wing chair. "We'll wait, then."

"What about using Lucy?" Suz asked, wiggling her fingers like a magician over a magic hat.

I didn't take offense, though my abilities were hardly on the hocus-pocus level.

"Wish I could," Dovie said. "Mac disappeared with only the clothes on his back. No jewelry, no cell phone, not even his wallet."

I checked my watch again. My new client was due in five minutes. "Were any of his clothes gifts?"

There were essentially two rules to how my gift of finding lost objects worked. The first being that I could only do readings on the person who owned the lost object. The other was the object couldn't be human or animal. I couldn't find lost dogs. And I couldn't find lost people. Just inanimate objects.

There was one big exception to Rule #1. Gifts. It was the only time an object had more than one owner. This exception had led to the creation of Lost Loves and explained why my work with the Massachusetts State Police had been so successful.

"I asked Jemima. She said no."

"We believe she's lying," Mum added pointedly.

Preston scribbled. "You don't think she wants him found."

Mum winked at her. "You got it."

Preston beamed. Sometimes she reminded me of a long-haired Chihuahua, with her spiky hair, eager eyes, and love of attention.

"Where is Sean? Shouldn't he be here if you have a client coming in?" Dovie asked.

"He'll be here soon. He's apartment hunting. But you don't need to wait. He's coming over tonight. We can pop in at your place."

Easy enough. I lived right next door to my grandmother, in a little beach cottage on her vast oceanside property. For my pride's sake, she allowed me to pay rent, but I knew she was putting the money aside to give back to me one day.

Everyone looked at me. "What?"

"Apartment hunting?" Suz asked. "Why not just move in with you?"

"He *does* spend a lot of time there," Dovie said, a knowing smile lurking on the corners of her lips. She was desperate for great-grandkids and was hopeful Sean and I were just one missed birth control pill away from producing one—or six.

A rush of warmth climbed my neck, settled in my cheeks. "It's too soon."

Mum said, "Nothing wrong with shacking up, LucyD."

Preston said, "You should definitely ask him."

I should have known she wouldn't take my side. "Don't you have somewhere to go?"

"You know I don't. We have a meeting in a couple of minutes. Don't get snippy with me because you have commitment issues."

"I don't have commitment issues!" I had fallen for Sean Donahue the moment I laid eyes on him—love at first sight. Wham, bam—I was a goner. As far as I was concerned, there would never be anyone else. But like everyone in a relationship, we had our issues.

Mum snorted. "Denial."

I groaned. "It's not commitment; it's Cupid's Cur—" I cut myself off, realizing I'd almost said too much. Preston didn't know about the family curse. Or the auras, either, though she was suspicious, thanks to overhearing a conversation between my brother and me at Christmastime.

My brother.

I drew in a breath. I still wasn't used to saying "my brother," even in the quiet of my own thoughts. Oliver "Cutter" McCutchan's true parentage had been kept secret for over twenty-five years, and the revelation had come as quite a shock to everyone. Mostly Cutter. His adjustment to suddenly having a whole new, somewhat dysfunctional, branch of his family tree hadn't been all that smooth, but he was trying.

We were slowly building a relationship. We spoke at least once a week, swapped e-mails, and met for drinks on occasion.

I clamped my lips closed before I revealed anything else. The decision to keep the family's psychic ability secret had been made centuries ago, around the time witches were being burned at the stake in Salem. No one in the family wanted the notoriety or the possibility of being labeled a fake or having their lives put under a microscope. The tradition of silence had been passed down from Valentine to Valentine just like the gift itself. No one dared break the secrecy, except in the rarest of situations. It was a legacy destined to continue. And a legacy Preston was dying to uncover.

"You and Sean belong together, Lucy," Mum said softly. "Living together is the next step."

"Better to sample the milk before you buy it," Dovie said. "Make sure it's not sour. And doesn't leave its socks on the floor every day."

This conversation was not happening. I was dreaming. The whole day had been one big *Dallas* episode. Where was my father when I needed him? He'd hate the idea of Sean moving in with me. Raphael, too. My father's valet and all-around right-hand man had been like a second father to me. He might be more upset than my dad.

"I thought the saying was 'why buy the milk'—"

Dovie cut me off. "Work with me, LucyD."

I was shaking my head when the buzzer chimed. "It's too soon," I repeated as Suz said, "Valentine, Inc.," into the intercom. Was I the only one with any sense?

"Meaghan Archibald here to see Lucy Valentine."

I jumped up, grateful for the reprieve as Suz buzzed Meaghan upstairs. Preston pulled on her boot.

"Can you send her back to my office, please?" I asked Suz, heading that way. Preston gimped ahead of me and turned into the little kitchenette off the hall. I gave my mother and grandmother kisses. "You two behave yourselves."

"We always do," Mum said, tucking a strand of hair behind my ears.

"Hardly."

"Shoo with you," Dovie said. As I headed down the hall, I heard her say, "Shall we throw a shacking-up party for her?"

"You're not funny!" I yelled.

"Are, too!" echoed back to me.

In my office, I set down my tote bag, pulled a pad of paper from my desk drawer. Preston limped in, carrying a coffee urn and mugs on a silver tray. She pushed back her spiky blond bangs and looked at me out of the corner of her eye.

"What?" I asked.

"You were about to say something earlier before and cut yourself off."

"Was I?"

"You're not a good liar."

Ha—I had her fooled. I was a great liar. "I have no idea what you're talking about."

She sank into a chair. "It sounded like you were about to say 'Cupid's Curse.'"

"Cupid's Curse?" I forced a laugh. "Sounds like a bad attraction at a haunted house."

"You may as well just tell me. You know I'll figure it out."

That's what I was afraid of.

3

Meaghan Archibald's pale green eyes twinkled with happiness. She looked like a siren from a vintage Herbal Essence bottle. Stunning curls spiraled through her long black hair. There was a hint of color in her cheeks, a swipe or two of mascara at most. A natural beauty. We'd already run through the particulars. She was twenty-three, a graphic designer living in an apartment near Fenway. Never married, no kids. "How old were you the first time you fell in love, Ms. Valentine?"

She'd caught me off-guard. It was the sort of thing I, as a matchmaker specializing in reuniting lost loves, might ask my client, not the other way around.

Yet the question Meaghan asked was easy. A first love was almost always imprinted in the mind—and the heart—forever.

"I was five. Gabriel Harris. Angelic eyes, down-turned lips, unruly hair, ninety-six of Crayola's finest when the rest of us only had forty-eight, and he always picked me first for Red Rover. He was the love of my life from the first day of kindergarten well into second grade. That was when during the school's Thanksgiving play I caught him trying to stick his gobbler up my best friend Em's Pilgrim's dress. I was inconsolable and cried for days on end. Soon after, I found out he'd been loaning his crayons to lots of girls in the class, not just me." I smiled. "He has triplet girls now. Karma, that's what that is."

The noise of a delivery truck in the alley below my second-floor window rumbled through the historic brick walls. Stretching out my long legs, I worked out a nagging ache in my left calf. I smoothed a crease in my gray pin-striped trousers and tried not to think about Mac Gladstone, though, to be honest, it was hard to push him from my thoughts. I was intrigued by his disappearance. I wondered what kind of information I could weasel from Detective Lieutenant Aiden Holliday, my contact with the state police.

Preston had her digital recorder running on the table. "I was eight. Matthew Dennehy. He chased me endlessly around the playground. I had a wild crush on him until the day he finally caught me—and demanded my lunch money." Her Kewpie lips pursed. "Last I heard he was a minister. Is that karma? Or predestination?"

I couldn't help but smile. Okay, sometimes Preston was tolerable. Actually, these days, she was more tolerable than not. Not that I'd ever tell her.

"Do you really believe in it?" Meaghan asked me. "Karma? Kismet?"

"Absolutely."

"I was fifteen," she said. "My first love. His name was Tristan Rourke. I want you to find him, Ms. Valentine."

"It's Lucy, please. How long has it been since you've

seen Tristan?" As I jotted the name down on a legal pad, I surreptitiously slid my gaze across my watch. I was hoping Sean would make it back in time to sit in on this meeting. He must have found a place he liked. I could easily imagine him making an offer on the spot. He was impulsive like that.

As it was, he and Thoreau, his Yorkie, had been living with Sean's brother, Sam, and his family for a few months. It wasn't until last week when Sam very unsubtly hinted that Sean and a suddenly leaky Thoreau might have worn out their welcome.

Sean had nowhere else to go but out on his own, no other family I knew of. He didn't like to talk about his past much at all. Something I was more than willing to overlook before now, as I had kept a lot of my past secret from him at first, too. But eventually, I'd told him everything—Cupid, curses, and auras, oh my—and I was still wondering when he'd open up.

My palms dampened at the thought of Sean finding a place. Because as much as I tried to convince myself otherwise, I'd love to have him live with me. Leaky dog and all.

But underneath all the want, the desire, lurked the fear. That if we moved in together the more time we'd spend together, the faster we'd end. And I didn't want it to end. Ever.

I tipped an ear to the door, hoping to hear activity in the outer office. Mum and Dovie were chatting, but so far there was no sign of Sean's return.

My dad, Oscar, the oft-proclaimed King of Love, was at a lunch meeting, which might mean he was really in a meeting or could mean he was rendezvousing with his latest girlfriend, Sabrina McCutchan—Cutter's mother.

Valentine's Day had come and gone last week, and Dad's schedule had cleared considerably. He was taking more and more time off, which he claimed was good for his damaged heart, but I suspected it had more to do with his libido. I envied other children who didn't think of, or see, their parents in such a way. To say I'd been raised unconventionally would be an understatement.

"Let's see. It's been about eight years," Meaghan finally said.

"High school sweethearts?"

"Kind of. We lived in the same house for a while. Foster children."

I saw Preston's eyes brighten. She loved a good twist to a story, and a hook like that was gold for a human-interest piece.

Leaning back in my chair, I pulled my notepad onto my lap. Meaghan twisted her hands, and the edges of her cuffs slid up her forearm. Unmistakable scars crossed both wrists.

She caught me looking. "I was young and wanted desperately to die. The doctors wanted desperately to save me. They won."

I rested the tip of my pen on the notepad. The ink bled into a widening circle. "You obviously came around to their way of thinking."

The sparkle was back in her eyes. "Thank goodness. Tristan was a big motivator, though ultimately the strength came from within."

The line sounded like something out of a therapist's mouth, but I couldn't deny Meaghan seemed happy. She fairly oozed joy.

"Did Tristan help you through recovery?" Preston asked. "Stay by your bedside and all that?"

Meaghan's lips tipped into a small smile. "Actually, no. He wasn't allowed to see me. I was placed in a psych hospital, pumped full of meds, and overwhelmed with feel-good lectures that only turned me from suicidal to homicidal." She laughed.

I hoped she *was* joking. In my other job with the state police I saw more than my share of murder.

Shimmying forward on her chair, Preston said, "Then how did Tristan motivate you?"

"Against my will some of the messages in the hospital starting seeping in. I slowly began to realize that yeah, I'd been dealt a crappy hand in life, but I still had the power to turn it around. Tristan was one thing kept me going. I wanted, I needed, to thank him for everything he'd done for me, for seeing value in me when I couldn't see it myself."

Preston opened her mouth to press, but I cut her off with a look. Meaghan would get there in her own time. "You two met as foster children?"

"We were both placed in the same house in Jamaica Plain. He had already lived there a year before I arrived. My drug-addicted mother had tried to trade me to a dealer in exchange for a fix. The dealer was an undercover cop. I was put into the system immediately."

Whoa.

"Are you okay with all this going into the article?" Preston asked, showing unexpected sensitivity.

Meaghan nodded. "Absolutely. I was actually glad to hear about the articles you're writing. If I can reach one person, change their life with my story, then sharing all the heartbreak will be worth it. The more people I can help the better. I had a happy ending, really. One of the doctors at the hospital ended up fostering me and eventually he and his wife adopted me. Archibald is their name. I used to be Meaghan Chaney. I had an instant family who loved me, was able to get my GED and go to college. It doesn't get much better. Except . . ." She trailed off.

"Tristan?" Preston supplied.

Meaghan dropped her gaze bashfully.

For once I was glad to have Preston here. I hadn't been at all happy about her writing articles about my clients, a deal concocted by her and my father, but I had to admit the pieces had been good. Really good. And Meaghan was right—if this could help one person, then all the aggravation of having Preston around constantly might be justified.

My thoughts shifted to my own upbringing. Sure, it hadn't been idyllic, but it had been safe—and I had been loved above all else. How many times had I taken that for granted?

"When I first arrived at the foster house, I'd been scared and lonely. The foster mom, Mary Ellen Spero, was nice enough. We actually still keep in touch. But it was clear Mr. Spero wasn't interested in us kids at all. Saw us as a nuisance. Tristan took me under his wing. He was two years older than me, so he was kind of like a big brother." She smiled again. It made her glow. "At first."

"Ah," I said.

"I hear a 'but,' " Preston said, eyes wide. "A big one. Like a Romeo and Juliet kind of 'but.' I mean, after all, you did try to kill yourself."

So much for that sensitivity.

"Fair enough," Meaghan said, apparently not taking offense. "Tristan asked me to go to his senior prom, but I didn't have money for the dress. And let's just say our foster father wasn't in the system to care and nurture—he wasn't about to give me any of his. So I was really surprised when Tristan came home one day with a dress I had admired."

"Awww," Preston said.

A thin, dark eyebrow arched. "The police showed up not long after."

"Uh-oh," I murmured.

"He'd shoplifted the dress. They took him away. I was devastated." She motioned to her scarred wrists. "I haven't seen him since. I really want to find him. I want to thank him. I want to—" A blush settled in her cheeks. "I want the happy ending. The fairy-tale ending."

There was moisture in Preston's eyes. She was such a romantic at heart. And though Meaghan's story tugged at my heartstrings, I had to caution her as well. Softly I said, "There is a chance we won't be able to find him."

"I know, but I feel like I have to try. It's the least I can do."

If Tristan Rourke owned property, it would be fairly easy to find him through an appraiser's office. PI 101—I was slowly learning the ins and outs of investigating. But if not, it would be trickier. "I don't suppose you remember his birthday?" I asked, trying to recall everything Sean had taught me about gathering information for the case.

"October fourteenth."

"Do you know where he was born? Or anything about his natural family? Is Rourke his family name?"

"Born here in Boston—I don't know which hospital. He never knew his real dad. His mother died when he was twelve. He had a grandmother, but she'd been too poor to take him in. That's when he went into the system."

A pinch of foreboding had me hiding a frown.

14 plus 12 is 26.

I gave myself a hard mental shake. Since I was little, I had turned to solving simple math problems in my head to alleviate stress. I was trying to break myself of the habit for a couple reasons: I figured at almost twenty-nine years old I should have better coping skills, plus I didn't like math all that much.

I tried to push the worry away—there was no cause for it. None whatsoever. Meaghan had come to me for help . . . for hope. I was a sucker for these kinds of cases. Sean called it the Love Conquers All syndrome, and I was seriously afflicted.

"I've read several articles about you and your success. I should tell you up front that your, you know," she searched for the right word, "psychicness won't help in this case."

I smiled. That was a new term for me. "Not to worry," I said. "We've had a lot of success tracking lost loves without using my abilities. We'll start looking for Tristan right away."

We went through the contracts, and she wrote a check for the retainer. I had everything I needed to get started.

"And you'll call as soon as you find him?"

Suddenly I wondered what the color of her aura might be, if it reflected her joie de vivre or held a tinge of the desperation I sensed under the surface. But I could only wonder, as my father wasn't around and he was the only one who could answer that question. I checked myself. My father . . . and my brother. Cutter also had the gift but used it in a far different way—artwork.

"Definitely," I said, "but remember my warning."

"I will." At the door, she stopped, looked back at me. "I may be able to help a little."

"How?"

"Tristan's last known address . . ."

"You know it?" Preston asked.

I reached for my notepad.

Meaghan wrung her hands and finally whispered, "Walpole State Prison."

4

"Then she just walked out?" Sean asked. He was sitting on the edge of the conference table and it was taking everything in me not to run my hand along his thigh.

"All willy-nilly," Preston said.

She was the reason for my restraint. She should have been long gone but decided to ditch her English 101 class at Quincy College once Meaghan dropped her little bombshell. Preston had just started a liberal-arts program with the intent to transfer to a four-year school eventually. Her lack of a journalism degree was holding back her career.

Sean smiled wide, his dimple popping.

My heart pittered, pattered.

"Willy-nilly?" he asked.

"It's a phrase," Preston protested.

"If you're fifty," Sean said.

"I think my grandmother uses it," I put in.

Preston crossed her arms over her chest. "You two think you're funny."

As much as we teased, "willy-nilly" had been as apt a description as any to describe the way Meaghan had dropped her news and hustled away.

Sean had found Preston and me a few minutes later, still staring at the empty doorway. He would have made it in sooner, but he'd been waylaid by my grandmother and encouraged (he really had no choice) to track down Mac Gladstone.

"What I can't understand is why Tristan Rourke would have gone to Walpole," Preston said.

Technically, Walpole State Prison had changed its name back in the eighties to Cedar Junction. However, locals still called it Walpole for the most part—a fact that continued to rankle the town's residents. It was one of Massachusetts's highest-security prisons—for the state's worst offenders.

I didn't understand, either. "He was seventeen when he was arrested. He should have gone to juvie or even been sentenced to just probation."

"Something's not adding up." Sean sat in front of my computer, typed. A second later the screen was filled with hits on Tristan Rourke.

Preston leaned in close, reading over my shoulder. "Attempted murder?"

I scanned an archived article from the *Boston Globe*. Tristan had been arrested at seventeen for attempting to strangle his foster father with a coat hanger. Because of Tristan's prior history (he apparently had a knack for stealing) and lack of remorse, he'd been tried as an adult. The trial had been brief, and Tristan was found guilty and sentenced to five years in prison.

"Check the *Herald*." I preferred its gossipy nature.

We pored over archived articles. The pieces featured

quotes from Rourke's foster parents, Anthony and Mary Ellen Spero, and from previous foster kids of the family. The gist of the case was that after Tristan had been bailed out of juvie (by Mrs. Spero) and when Mr. Spero had told him about Meaghan's suicide attempt—but not where she was or how she was doing—Tristan had gone ballistic.

The cops were called, Tristan was arrested on new charges, and the judge threw the book at him to teach him a lesson.

"I think I might have gone apeshit, too," Preston said. "It doesn't seem like anyone took into account the kids' feelings for each other."

I completely agreed with Preston—for a change. A first love was imprinted in a heart forever because of its power. It seemed cruel and unusual to keep Tristan in the dark regarding Meaghan's condition or whereabouts.

As Preston started humming Bruce Springsteen's "Fire," Sean typed in the Web address for the Federal Bureau of Prisons. He searched the inmate locator for Tristan Rourke.

I tapped the screen. "He was let out three years ago. Time served."

"He's twenty-five years old now. Plenty of time to build an identity," Sean said.

I followed his reasoning. If Tristan had been released from prison recently, then he wouldn't own property or have credit cards or even a permanent address. Finding him would be incredibly difficult. But since he'd been out for a while, there would be a trail.

"This story is more Romeo and Juliet than Meaghan let on," Preston said, taking notes.

Sean said to me, "Someone I know would wax poetic about true love knowing no bounds. Not distance, or money, or time. That reuniting these two is what love is all about."

"But you?" I asked, amused by his tone. He wasn't quite mocking me, but there had been a teasing lilt.

"I say we need to be careful with this case."

The pinch of foreboding turned to a nudge. This case wasn't what I'd imagined when Lost Loves was created. But I still wanted to help. My Love Conquers All syndrome was hard at work. "Maybe Tristan is now an upstanding citizen. We shouldn't judge so soon."

"Right, right," Preston intoned. "Because zebras often change their stripes."

I noticed that Sean's shoulders stiffened and his superhero jaw jutted, but he didn't say anything. After a second, he relaxed and it was as though he'd never tensed at all. Preston apparently hadn't even noticed, since she was so busy fussing with her heel. Sean caught me watching him and looked away.

"What's with you and the sayings?" I asked her, wondering at his reaction.

"I don't know! Maybe I'm spending too much time with your grandmother."

Hear, hear! I'd second that. "Maybe you should take some time off?" That way she might not pursue her line of questioning about the curse.

Her eyebrows snapped downward. "No."

It had been worth a try.

"Tristan Rourke shouldn't be too hard to find," Sean said. "I'll do a search this afternoon."

"Well, I'm free tonight to go see him when you get

an address," Preston said, standing. She tested her weight on her broken heel.

I glanced at Sean. We had plans for the night that involved watching *The Princess Bride* with a big bowl of popcorn. By the look in his eye, I predicted we wouldn't see much of the movie.

"I think tomorrow is soon enough," I suggested.

"Besides," Sean said, "I told Dovie I'd get started on the Gladstone case."

Preston tipped sideways, grabbed onto a chair back for balance. "I don't suppose you'd let me come along?"

Sean shook his head.

"I didn't think so." She frowned at her boot. "Do you think Suz has any glue?"

"Suz has everything," I said.

As soon as Preston wobbled out, Sean pulled me down into his lap and kissed me. His fingers threaded into my hair, and I could feel the steady thump of his heart against my chest. He drew back, whispered, "I saw you eyeing my thigh."

I smiled. "You think you know me so well."

His hands slid down my shoulders, my arms, stopped just short of my hands. Even still, I felt the electricity jumping along my palms. I still hadn't figured out why I saw images of us together in the future when we touched hands. Pictures of our future. Those were the images I loved best, but I often avoided holding hands for fear that one day I might see something I didn't like. Or that I might see nothing at all.

"Did you find an apartment?" I asked, holding my breath as I waited for the answer.

"Nothing's quite right."

I felt the relief down to my toes. "You can—"

I almost did it. Almost said he could move in with me.

What had come over me? It had to be Dovie's (bad) influence. Mum's. Why else would I take such a risk?

You love him.

Right. But wasn't that exactly why he *shouldn't* move in?

"What?" he asked.

"Nothing."

"You sure it's nothing, Lucy?"

My insides melted like chocolate on a hot day. It was the way he said my name. Filled with love and tenderness, heat and passion. He looked into my eyes. I was lost in his pearly gray gaze.

I realized just how much I wanted him to move in. "No. Yes. No." Panic warred with euphoria.

He smiled. "That's clear."

A warning buzzed at the back of my head. "No."

"No, it's not clear?"

I nudged him with my shoulder. "No. I'm sure it's nothing. What's that look?"

"Sometimes I wonder what's going on in that pretty head of yours."

"You don't want to know."

He tightened his hold on me. "I think I do."

"Trust me, you don't. It's chaos in here."

He laughed and kissed me. I threw myself into the heat of his lips, the lazy sweep of his tongue, as if he had all day to sample me and was looking forward to every minute.

"Well, well, well," a voice interrupted.

We pulled apart and I was giddy when Sean whispered in my ear, "Later."

My mother stood beaming in the doorway. "I hate to interrupt, but could I have a moment, LucyD?"

Sean said, "I'll go."

"No, no," Mum said, pulling a chair up next to us. "Stay. It's okay."

"What's wrong?" I asked. She was acting strangely.

"I need a favor."

"What kind of favor?"

She cleared her throat. "There was a time I wasn't so happy with your father."

"Most of my childhood?"

She ignored my jibe. "As you know, I stopped wearing my wedding band and engagement ring a long time ago. Here's the thing. I can find my wedding band but not the engagement ring. I thought they were together in my jewelry chest, but there was only the band."

In my mind's eye, I could picture her engagement ring with its glittering princess-cut diamond set into a band of glowing rubies. I'd loved that ring, the color, the sentiment—my father had chosen rubies because they matched my mother's aura.

"I've looked everywhere, LucyD. Can you help me find it?"

"Defin— Wait. Why?"

Her hand flew to her throat, where a blush was rising. "What do you mean why?"

"Why *now*?"

"I don't kn—"

I jumped up. "No, no, no."

"Now, Lucy . . ."

Sean said, "What's going on?"

"She's dating my *father*!"

Sean's gaze whipped to my mother. "True?"

Mum stood. "You make it sound like a bad thing."

Although they'd been separated just shy of forever, they remained close friends. Sometimes lovers. But I'd never seen Mum this gaga over him. I didn't know how I felt about it. My parents had been happily separated for over twenty-five years, content to lead their own lives. Without each other.

Often with other people.

Hence, Cutter's existence.

"I thought Dad was seeing Sabrina?" Mum's news had tipped my world a little, sending emotional baggage tumbling. Sean was wisely keeping quiet.

Fussing with the cowl of her sweater, she said, "That ended almost as soon as it began."

Sabrina McCutchan and Dad had rekindled an old flame right around the time Cutter's true paternity had been revealed.

"But thank you for bringing her up, Debbie Downer." Mum pursed her lips.

I immediately thought of Preston. She'd be using the phrase in no time. "I'm sorry, but you know how Dad is."

For decades Dad's playboy status had been kept quiet—until the day he had a heart attack during a rendezvous with a paramour. The *Herald* caught wind of the affair, and the gossip was just now settling. But the fact that my father was—is—a playboy remained.

"How long have you two been dating?" I recognized how silly the question sounded. My parents were still legally married. "It must be really serious if you're asking about your engagement ring."

She rubbed the toe of her shoe against the area rug. "A while now."

"And I'm just finding out?"

"We wanted to keep it to ourselves for a bit. I thought you'd be happy. Doesn't every child want their parents back together?"

"I . . . am happy." Maybe. "Does Dovie know?"

"Yes."

"The subterfuge."

"We asked her not to tell you."

"The deception."

"Dramatics don't become you, LucyD."

"Raphael?" I asked, my lungs squeezing.

"Doesn't Raphael know everything?"

Raphael was my father's valet, his right-hand man, his closest friend for nearly twenty-five years. And a second father to me. He and his girlfriend, Maggie Constantine, were planning a monthlong getaway to put their relationship to the test. Both were having a hard time believing true love had been under their noses all along. Although Raphael was still working full-time with my father and still living at my dad's penthouse, he spent a good part of his day helping Maggie as a chef downstairs at the Porcupine, the restaurant she leased on the first floor of the building.

Unlike Raphael, I didn't have a colorful guarantee Sean and I were destined to be together. All I had was blind trust. And I was having a hard time with it.

I couldn't help but wonder if Raphael's romance had played a role in my parents' rekindling. It was only a matter of time before Raphael and Maggie married and Raphael moved out. My father wasn't a man who liked to be alone.

It was cause for concern. And to know all these people had been keeping secrets smarted. "I'm a big girl."

Over Mum's shoulder, Sean was looking as if he wanted to escape. But then he winked at me and set my heart aflutter.

"But still my baby," Mum said, coming over to me and pressing her cheek against mine. She was all curves, soft and enveloping. As she looped her arms around me, the sweet Chanel scent she always wore wrapped around my heart. She was . . . my home.

It was so cheesy, I wanted to laugh. But more than that, I wanted to hang on. The last thing I wanted was for her to be hurt. "You and Dad—"

She interrupted. "I can see you're concerned, but there's no reason to be. We're adults. We know what we're doing."

I pulled back, my eyes wide in shock as I realized something. "That's what this diet is all about!" Dad was a health nut, obsessed with eating right and fitness. His heart attack months ago had been quite a surprise. "I should have figured that out."

"Hush now," Mum said. "It's time I took care of myself."

"As long as you're doing it for yourself and not for Dad."

"I am." She tucked my hair behind my ear. "We're happy, Lucy."

Grudgingly I had to admit she was right. My father had been in a great mood lately. And all it took was one look to see Mum was practically floating.

"Okay," I said. "I'll be happy for you."

"That's my girl. Now about the ring. I want to surprise your father by wearing the set again."

A guilty flush crept up my neck. When I was younger, I used to love dressing up in Mum's jewelry. I especially coveted her engagement ring and had declared, as only a child could, that there was not a more beautiful piece of jewelry ever made. I had a sickening feeling that I had misplaced the ring, but I couldn't for the life of me remember where I might have stashed it.

"Lucy?" Mum held out her hand. "Please?"

Crisscrossing lines sank into her soft fleshy skin. Which was the love line? If I could read palms, would I be able to tell at a glance if this current fling with my father would work out?

No point in going there. I couldn't read palms. But I could find her ring.

Reaching out my hand, I settled it on top of hers. My ability to find lost objects came straight from the energy released from the palm—contact must be made. Images came in a dizzying blur.

I pulled my hand away and opened my eyes, trying to chase away the lingering vertigo.

"Did you see it?" Mum asked.

I crinkled my nose. "Yes."

"What's with the nose?"

"It's in my old room. In the little music box next to my bed, mixed in with a bunch of old trinkets."

"What, LucyD, is it doing there?"

I shrugged and gave my best "mea culpa" smile while I explained my love of the ring. "I must have forgotten to return it. Sorry."

"No, no, I'm glad you used it. It is too nice be stuck

away in a drawer, but honestly? I always thought it too much."

I gasped.

"I know, but I'm a simple girl."

So was I, but I loved that ring.

"You won't tell your dad I said so, will you?"

"My lips are sealed."

"Good. You know how he is; everything has to be over-the-top. He wouldn't understand."

True. Very true.

She eyed her bare fingers. "I don't know why I even care. It's not as though your father is going to put on his ring."

"He has one?"

Mum laughed. "He never wore it even when we were first married. I should have known then what I was in for."

"Yet now all that's changed?"

"Absolutely."

"Positively?"

"As certain as I can be."

She sounded so sure, she almost convinced me. I felt the need to offer support. "Em rarely wore her engagement ring. She wanted something small, but Joseph didn't listen."

It was also in kindergarten that I fell in love for the second time. With my best friends, Marisol Valerius and Emerson Baumbach.

Mum put her hands on her hips. "Are you trying to say my relationship won't work out, either?"

Em had recently broken off her engagement and was currently living with Dovie. "Not at all!" Okay, maybe subliminally.

Mum kissed my cheeks, squeezed Sean's hand. "It will be fine; don't worry." She sashayed out of the room.

I drew in a deep breath.

Sean came up behind me, circled me in his arms. "You're going to worry, aren't you?"

Between my parents dating, Preston on the trail of uncovering my family's biggest secrets, Meaghan Archibald's love life, and the disappearance of Mac Gladstone . . .

I could practically feel the ulcer starting. "Not at all."

5

I was packing up for the day, skipping out early so Sean and I could go to Mac Gladstone's house, when there was a knock on my office door.

"Hey," I said. "What are you doing here?"

Oliver "Cutter" McCutchan kissed my cheek. "Just came to say good-bye. I'm on the way to the airport. My flight leaves in two hours."

"Good-bye?" Every time I saw him I was taken aback by how much he resembled my father. His height, his smile, his chiseled cheeks, his strong chin. Even his mannerisms.

"I'm hitting the road for a while. I have a showing in New York, and then one in Miami at the end of the week. I should be back this weekend."

"Busy."

"You say that like it's a bad thing."

I zipped my tote bag closed. "It just feels like you're on the go a lot these days."

"That's the nature of my job."

He was a gifted artist. His work was amazing, especially his portraits. He used his abilities to see auras and worked them into his pieces. They were breathtaking and were taking the art world by storm. "I know. You'll send postcards?"

"No."

"You'll call?"

"Maybe."

"E-mail?"

"Definitely." He gave me a hug. "I should go before Oscar spots me."

"Something wrong there?"

"Nothing at all if I want to take over the family business."

My heart sank. "And if you don't?"

"Then there's something wrong."

"Do you think you'll ever want to match?" He had been through so much in the last couple of months. He learned he had a father he never knew, a sister, a grandmother, and oh yeah, that he's the last in the line of Valentines to be able to read auras, the end of a legacy.

Reunions should be all about warm and fuzzies, not bottom lines, but on the flip side, I could also see my father's point of view.

"The company should go to you," Cutter said.

"It wouldn't survive. I can't see the auras anymore, remember? Only you and Dad."

"That's a lot of pressure, and I love my art."

I didn't want to push but couldn't help myself. "You could do both."

"Not you, too, Lucy."

"Sorry." I gave him another hug.

"I forgive you." He smiled. "I might even send you a postcard."

"Dinner when you get back, you jet-setter?"

"Saturday night. It's a date." He checked his watch. "I have to go."

"Don't even think about standing me up, because there's something I want to talk to you about. Rather, someone."

"Sounds interesting. Are you trying to match me?"

"Hardly." I had to warn him about Preston. "And maybe it's time you found out about the curse."

"The curse?"

"Cupid's Curse."

"Why do I feel like I don't want to know?"

"Because you don't."

"But you're going to tell me."

"It's my sisterly duty. Now go. It takes forever to get through security."

With a wave he was gone. And I was left wondering how I was going to get him and my father to compromise where Valentine, Inc., was concerned. Luckily I had a week to figure it out.

Cohasset was one of those gorgeous New England towns used in the movies—literally. Several feature films had been shot here. There's a lot to love. Stunning ocean views, a quaint village with charming shops, harbor, and town green.

Not the kind of place where one disappears without a trace.

Snowflakes fell lazily as Sean turned onto Atlantic Avenue, one of the most picturesque streets in Massachusetts, known for its magnificent oceanfront mansions. In the summer, sightseers clogged the tree-lined road for glimpses of fame and fortune. This area used to be the vacation spot of Boston's rich and famous, but over the years more people came, stayed, lived. My grandparents settled here in the forties. My mother lived a couple miles away, on Jerusalem Road, another tourist hot spot.

Even though I'd lived here all my life, I never took it for granted. This area was special. Magical. It pained to think something horrible could have happened to Mac here.

I checked my cell phone again. I was expecting a return call from Aiden Holliday. Although Cohasset wasn't in his jurisdiction, as my connection with the Massachusetts State Police he would be allowed access to the case because of my involvement. I hoped the Cohasset PD or the state police had information that hadn't been released to the public. Information that might help Sean and me find Mac.

Sean drove past the driveway to Aerie, Dovie's manor house, and turned into a sleek paved driveway a mile down the road. A wrought-iron gate in a geometric pattern blocked the drive even though Mac's daughter, Jemima Hayes, was expecting us.

Sean lowered his window, pressed the intercom for the main house, which couldn't be seen from the road.

A bored voice female said, "Yes?"

"Sean Donahue and Lucy Valentine. We have an appointment."

The gate slowly swung open.

"Friendly," Sean said, sliding me a glance and a wry smile.

The driveway snaked uphill through dense woods, filled with evergreens, low-lying shrubs and roots, and bare branches of deciduous trees. The lane was lined on each side with a low granite wall inset with small, round lights. The woods gave way to an expanse of lawn, where the brown tips of dormant grass were sticking through the pristine white of accumulating snow.

The driveway widened, and the granite gradually tapered into a decorative garden border, lining the length of extensive beds, snowy now but probably glorious in summertime.

The house sat proudly, nakedly, at the edge of the bluff. The home stood out as a modern masterpiece with its glass walls, straight lines, and boxy design. It was a rarity among the classic New England architecture of its neighbors. The whole place had been remodeled five years ago after the original manor had burned down—an electrical fire that had killed Mac's wife, Betty.

The Gladstones had come from money, old money, but Mac had also made a fortune as a children's book illustrator and print artist. Some of his work had been shown in the *New Yorker* and *Life*. Dozens of museums proudly displayed original pieces from early in his career.

Gusts laced with February chill blew off the water. I drew up the collar of my coat, but snowflakes stung my cheeks like little pinpricks. Sean rang the bell and a loud *dong* went off inside the house.

Through the tinted glass front door, I saw a blurry blob slide across the floor, right itself, then charge toward us. Barking echoed. I held my breath, afraid the dog was going to launch at us straight through the glass, but he slowed and bounced like a giant hyperactive rabbit, waiting impatiently for someone to let us in.

"Rufus, I presume," I said through chattering teeth.

A silhouette appeared in the distance. "Rufus! Down! Down!"

The va-va-va-voom figure edged the dog aside with the swing of a curvaceous hip as she opened the door. Rufus surged forward. She grabbed hold of his collar, yanked him back. "Damn it, down!"

A colorful pink and black skull bandanna came loose from Rufus's neck and fluttered to the ground. The dog barked happily.

"Esme! Esme! Come get the dog." After a second, she muttered something about good help, then dragged the dog toward the stairs. "Christa, honey!"

"Jemima Hayes?" I asked.

"Unfortunately."

Okay, then.

She was tiny, maybe five feet tall, and built like a mini Mae West, with curves in all the right places. Thick red hair cascaded past her bare shoulders. Enormous breasts bulged from a skintight tube top. The bare skin of her tiny waist showed above the Chanel belt holding up a pair of flared designer jeans that sat snug on her waist. Barbed-wire tattoos circled muscled biceps. Her feet were bare, her toenails painted a vibrant pink and dotted with tiny rhinestones.

On one hand, she looked like a groupie from a bad eighties hair band, yet on the other, culture in her voice hinted at a prep-school upbringing. Her makeup was extremely well done. No over-the-top black eyeliner and fake lashes, but a subtle violet smudge of eyeliner that picked up purple flecking in her brown eyes.

Jemima turned toward the marble steps leading to the second floor and shouted, "Christa!"

Maybe Mac *had* run away.

If so, I wouldn't blame him a bit, not if this kind of yelling was common around here.

Rufus was nuzzling Sean's hand. The retriever's eyes were bright, happy, his golden coat healthy and shiny. Someone was obviously taking care of him.

A thin, pale teen appeared at the top of the steps, an iPod in one hand, a cell phone in the other. Shiny straight auburn hair hung down, covering her face like a shield.

Jemima's tone softened, and I immediately liked her a little better. Not much, but a little. "Christa, honey, please, please, please come get this dog. Bring him downstairs." Christa slowly came down the steps and Rufus rushed over to her.

Jemima stooped and picked up the bandanna. She waved it at the girl, then set it on the newel post with a smile. "Pink again? You're going to give the mutt a complex." To Sean and me, Jemima said, "Come on back to the kitchen."

I glanced over my shoulder in time to see the girl retie the bandanna around Rufus's neck.

Jemima looked over her shoulder. "That dog is such a nuisance. All jumpy and slobbery and needy. I'm not a dog person. Never was, never will be. Sit, sit," she insisted, pointing to two counter stools at the kitchen island. Sleek stainless-steel counters gleamed in the waning sunlight. Floor-to-ceiling windows were dotted with salty sea mist, but the view of the ocean beyond was still breathtaking. The water was choppy today, angry and wild. "Dad wanted a dog after Mom died and who could argue with that? But I can't take much more."

A roux simmered on the gas stove top on the other side of the island. Jemima stuck a finger into the sauce, pulled it out, and licked it clean. She added a pinch of salt, a dash of pepper, and a bit of thyme. Picking up a small paring knife, she began expertly dicing cloves of garlic into tiny, perfect bits.

"Much more of what?" Sean asked, holding out my stool for me. It looked like a giant stainless-steel Frito on a stick. It was probably designer, had probably cost a fortune, and was probably the ugliest piece of furniture I'd ever laid eyes on.

"That dog," she said, waving the knife. "He has to go. I hate to say it, I really do, but he has to go."

"You can't get rid of him. What if Mac comes home?"

She moved on from the garlic and started taking mushrooms out of a plastic grocer's bag. Gingerly she placed each on the counter.

In the silence, I picked up on the soft strains of classical music coming from a speaker nearly hidden in the ceiling. Something staccato, feisty, and rebellious.

Jemima Hayes looked me straight in the eyes. The dying sunlight softened the angles of her face. I was surprised to notice how pretty she was. She dampened a cloth, set about wiping down the mushrooms. "*If* he comes back."

"About that," Sean said. "You know Dovie Valentine has hired me to look into Mac's disappearance."

"Good luck to you. If he was coming back, he'd be back by now. He'd never leave the mutt behind. Or Christa, either. They were close, those two."

Nothing in Jemima's voice hinted at any pain in relation to what she had silently implied. That Mac hadn't been close to her. But I could sense it like an electric undercurrent, ready to shock when least expected.

Pulling a small notebook out of his leather coat, Sean said, "When did you realize Mac was missing?"

She heaved a sigh that sent her breasts near to spilling out of her spandex top. "You're really going to make me do this again?"

"It might help find Mac," I said.

"Mom?"

I jumped as Christa came into the kitchen—I hadn't heard her.

"Are they looking for Granddad?"

Rufus barked from somewhere downstairs. Jemima's lips pressed together. "I swear to God. That dog is going to be the death of me. Please go quiet him down, take him for a walk. Something," Jemima begged.

"But—"

"Christa," Jemima said with more patience than I had given her credit for. "We've been through this."

"But . . ."

I spotted moisture in Jemima's eyes before she looked away. "Please go take care of Rufus. Dinner's almost ready. We'll talk about it then."

The teen turned and walked out.

"That girl could sneak up on a flea." Jemima turned off the flame beneath the roux. "Mac took Rufus for a walk on January third. The stupid dog came back; Mac didn't. Knew something was wrong right off the bat. Esme and I drove around and around. Searched culverts, drop-offs, beaches, everything. There was no trace of him. He was just," she drew in a breath, "gone."

It was mid-February now, and there hadn't been any sign of him since.

"What was he wearing?" Sean asked.

"Jeans, sneakers, white gym socks, hideous knit sweater, corduroy coat, gloves."

"Were any of those items gifts?" I asked.

Jemima popped the top off a mushroom. "Not that I know of. Most of it was replacement clothes." She bit her bottom lip.

"After the fire?" I asked.

Drawing her shoulders back, she ripped the head off another mushroom. "That's right." Her breath hitched. "We moved in with Mac right after the house was rebuilt. Dad needed someone to look after him in those early days. The dog was actually my idea, if you can believe it." She ruthlessly tore off another mushroom cap. "I have to admit Mac was a lot happier after Rufus." She shook her head, sending a shock wave through her red hair. "That's why I know he's not coming back. That dog . . . he was Mac's world."

A housekeeper came in carrying a small stack of dish towels.

"Thank you, Esme," Jemima said, taking one from the top.

"Did he have anything else with him?" I asked. "Like glasses or an iPod or a cell phone?"

"No. Mac's vision is just fine, and he doesn't believe in modern technology."

I raised an eyebrow, looked around at the state-of-the-art kitchen with its luxury appliances, wine cooler, and high-tech toys.

Jemima smiled. "Mac gave me carte blanche when we rebuilt. Said I might as well design the new place since it would be mine one day. It's glorious, isn't it? My dream house."

"It's something," I said. Grudgingly I had to admit the place was a showpiece. It didn't fit the neighborhood, but that didn't mean it wasn't amazing.

Sean tapped on his notebook with the tip of his pen. "Did Mac have any enemies?"

"Mac only had a handful of close friends. Liked to be by himself most of the time. Can't imagine anyone would want to do him any harm."

"Any chance he just walked away?" I asked.

"I just can't see that happening."

I said, "What about suicide?"

Her eyes filled with such sadness it tugged at my heart. She shrugged. "Are we almost done?"

"Any chance we can look around?" Sean asked. "Does Mac have a den or an office?"

Her gaze narrowed. "Mac's space is downstairs. No one has touched anything down there since he's been gone. You have five minutes. Then you need to leave."

6

Opening the door to the lower level was like falling down Alice's rabbit hole.

This was Mac's domain and it showed the minute we took the first step down. There was nothing contemporary down here; instead there were sturdy, gleaming oak steps, lined with a carpet runner.

The stairs curved, leading down into a cozy masculine one-bedroom apartment, scented with pipe tobacco that had me immediately thinking of my Grandpa Henry. Instantly I was a little girl again, curled up with him in his favorite chair while he puffed on his pipe and read me storybooks of faraway lands and handsome princes. A feeling of warmth and love washed over me, and the moisture in my eyes took me by surprise.

Rufus charged toward us, jumping. He dropped a squeaky rubber chicken at Sean's feet.

"Chicken toss is his favorite game," Christa said. She was tucked into a hunter green leather armchair. She pulled an iPod bud from her ear and stretched out her long legs. I guessed her to be sixteen or seventeen—more woman than little girl.

Sean picked up the chicken and tossed it across the room. Rufus thundered after it, tail slashing.

It was quite spacious down here. Wooden bookcases lined chocolate walls that were bare of any artwork, but there were family photos on the mantel. I was drawn to them. All looked recent and most were of Christa and Rufus.

"All the older pictures were lost in the fire." Christa stood behind me.

Sean threw the chicken again and headed toward an L-shaped desk built into the corner of the room.

"It must have been a horrible time."

"Did you know my grandma?"

"Not really. Just to say hello. My grandmother was good friends with her."

"Would she have any pictures?"

Why hadn't I thought of that? "I'm sure she would. Do you want me to get you some copies?"

She nodded.

I glanced around. There was a small kitchen, a bathroom, and a bedroom. Near double doors leading outside, an easel sat empty. Open-faced cabinets held hundreds of tubes of color, dozens of paintbrushes, and canvases of every size imaginable. "Your granddad was still working?"

"He'd just finished a project when he went missing."

"Had anything else been going on around that time?" I asked, hoping I wasn't pressing too hard. She was old enough to know what was going on, but that didn't make it any easier to understand.

Sean went through files, pausing every few moments to throw the rubber chicken.

"Not really," she said.

"Did Mac have many friends?" Two dog bowls had been placed at the end of the kitchen peninsula. One bowl was filled to the brim with water; the other had kibble spilling over its edges, chunky brown blobs littering the floor as if Rufus played with his food more than he ate it. On hooks near the double doors hung a small silver dog whistle and two leashes—a plain blue one and a red retractable leash imprinted with rubber chickens.

"To hang out with?" she asked. "He had his weekly poker game at Mr. Ross's house. Every Wednesday night. He never missed it."

Fred Ross lived right across the street and had been a friend of Dovie's for close to three decades. I made a mental note to talk to him.

Sean walked over, holding a sheet of paper. "Christa, how was your grandfather's health?"

She shrugged. "Good. He was hardly ever sick."

Sean tucked the paper into his coat pocket and gave me a look that said he might have found something.

"What do you think happened to Mac?" I asked her.

She bit her lip. Her eyebrows dipped. "I don't know, but the night before he went missing, I heard him on the phone. He was angry."

I glanced at Sean. He said, "Do you know who he was talking to?"

"No." Her cheeks turned pink. "Granddad didn't know I was listening."

That girl could sneak up on a flea.

I had a feeling Christa knew everything that went on in this house.

"Do you remember what he said?" Sean asked.

"Something like, 'My life is my concern. My decisions are my own. Mind your own business.'"

"This was right before he disappeared?" I asked.

"The night before," she said. "I told the police."

"That's good," I said. Maybe they had checked phone records and knew who he'd been talking to.

"Do you know if anything he was wearing the day he went missing was a gift from someone else? Your mom mentioned an ugly sweater—had someone knitted that for him?"

"Granddad bought it to drive Mom crazy. She was always trying to get him to change his look. She buys him leather pants for Christmas every year. She told him he dresses like a geezer. He told me that he'd show her geezer. He bought it at a consignment shop in Hingham. Said it was the ugliest sweater they had."

I bit back a smile. "It must have been truly ugly."

"It was bright orange with colored shapes all over it that looked like confetti."

"Yep, that sounds hideous."

I wanted to ask about Jemima and Mac's relationship but couldn't bring myself to do it.

"Do you think you'll be able to find him?" Christa seemed more curious than desperate.

Sean picked up the chicken, tossed it. Rufus scaled the leather sofa, slid across the wooden floor, and collided with an end table. A lamp teetered, then fell over with a crash.

"Not again," Christa mumbled, rushing to pick up the pieces. I went to help.

Rufus grabbed the chicken and brought it back to Sean.

Jemima ran downstairs. "What happened now?"

"It was my fault," Sean said, holding up the chicken. Rufus took it out of Sean's hand, brought it over to Jemima, and dropped it on her bare feet.

She shuddered.

"I'll gladly replace the lamp," Sean said.

"I thought we threw this thing away?" Jemima held the chicken by one rubber leg. "After the last lamp incident?"

Christa had found a paper bag and was putting chunks of broken porcelain into it. I opened a closet, looking for a broom. Next to the broom was a recycling bin no one had emptied in the last month. Mixed in with empty water bottles, a mayonnaise container, and a plastic strawberry container was a brown prescription bottle. I picked it up. The label had been torn to remove the patient's name, but the medication and strength remained. I quickly pocketed it.

"I can't take it anymore," Jemima said, shaking the chicken. Rufus jumped around, following each jerk of the chicken with an eager eye.

I quickly swept little shards into a pile.

"It won't happen again," Christa said. "I promise."

"You promised the last time, too," Jemima said. She sighed. "It's time Rufus found a new home."

Christa slowly stood up. I paused mid-sweep.

"It was my fault," Sean said again. "Not Rufus's."

Jemima's eyes flashed. "It's time you left, too. Your five minutes are long up."

"Where will Rufus go?" Christa asked in an even tone, as though she'd been preparing for this day a long time now.

"The shelter for now." Jemima finally dropped the

chicken and Rufus pounced on it. "Someone will adopt him."

I didn't think twice. "I'll take him."

A slow smile spread across Sean's face.

Christa looked at me, her eyes watery.

Jemima shrugged. "Suit yourself." She turned toward the stairs. "You can see yourselves out. Be sure to take the rubber chicken. Christa, dinner is ready."

"But I should get Rufus's things together. His food . . ."

"Now," Jemima said softly.

"You can come visit him," I whispered. "Whenever you want."

Christa nodded once, sharply. "His leash is by the door. The chicken one is his favorite—Granddad special-ordered it. His dog bed is in the bedroom, and his brush and comb are in a basket by his bed." She gave Rufus a big hug and ran upstairs.

Rufus dropped the chicken at Sean's feet. He picked it up, tossed it, and looked at me. "Grendel's going to be pissed."

I cringed at the thought of my cat having a hissy fit. "Don't worry. I have a plan."

My plan included my grandmother.

"No. No way," she said, tossing the rubber chicken.

She didn't mean it. I could tell. "But just look at those eyes."

"What do you think this is? A halfway house?"

"Hey!" Em cried. She was searching Dovie's fridge for something to eat.

"No offense," Dovie said to her. She made kissing noises in Em's direction.

Emerson Baumbach, one of my two best friends, had been living here since breaking off her engagement and moving out of the condo she shared with her ex shortly before Christmas. She would have moved home to her parents' house, just down the road, but there had been a big fight about the wedding and the ex and there was a lot of puffed-up pride stuff still going on.

Em kissed back.

"You two are making me queasy," I said.

Sean had headed back to Sam's place to pick up Thoreau and a change of clothes, then was coming back here. It *was* like Sean already lived with me, but making it permanent seemed to be tempting the fates a little too much for my liking.

Em, apple in hand, laughed as she sat next to me in Dovie's morning room, which was my favorite room in the house. It was dark now, but in the morning, sunlight flooded this room, filling it with happiness and life as it bounced off the blue walls, the overstuffed furniture, the knickknacks Dovie had collected over the years. This was the room where Dovie spent most of her time, and it showed in everything—the indent in the seat of her favorite chair, the teacup on the table, and the crossword puzzle folded, unfinished, on the floor near the fireplace.

Rufus trotted over, sat in front of Em, then dropped his chicken on the floor and his head in her lap. She rubbed the underside of his chin.

"He likes Em," Dovie said. "Give him to her."

"Okay," I said. "Congrats! It's a boy!"

Em, wild-eyed, looked between us. "Dovie, you do realize I live here, right? Don't you remember the halfway-house comment?"

Dovie snapped her fingers. "Marisol."

Marisol Valerius was my other best friend. She and Em had been part of my life since we were little things, running amok on the beach as topless toddlers. The topless thing hadn't lasted (except in Marisol's case), but the friendship, after a rocky start, had.

Marisol was a veterinarian who often left her unadoptable charges at my place, which explained my three-legged cat, Grendel, and my one-eyed hamster, Odysseus. Turnabout would be fair play. "I'll call her."

"He is sweet," Em said. Rufus looked up at her with adoration. "And when I find a place of my own, it would be good to have some company."

"I was kidding about the halfway house!" Dovie quickly said. "Don't go thinking about moving out because of that."

Em bit into her apple, chewed. "It's about time I start looking, don't you think?"

The conversation brought me back to Sean and his apartment hunt. He was due at my place in less than an hour. How easy it would be if he just stayed . . . forever.

"No," Dovie said. "Tea, anyone?"

My nerves were jumping. "I'll have some."

Em's red hair had been pulled into a sloppy bun atop her head. Her full cheeks glowed with happiness. She'd put on some weight since the breakup, but she was happier than I'd seen her in a long, long time. "How's school?" She'd recently quit her job as a pediatric intern to go back to school for a degree in elementary education.

Em smiled. "Really good. Spring break starts in a couple of days."

"Are you going anywhere?"

"I'm a little old for spring break, don't you think? I'm going to rest, relax, and catch up on my reading."

"Exciting."

She bit into her apple, ignoring me.

"You should go somewhere, not mope around here."

"I'm not moping."

She was totally moping.

"Besides, where would I go?"

"Anywhere you want."

"Not Paris." Rufus lifted his eyebrow as she took another bite of apple. She broke off a chunk and gave it to him.

"Definitely not," I agreed. She was supposed to go to Paris on her honeymoon—which would have been this week if the wedding hadn't been canceled. No wonder she was moping. "But anywhere else."

"By myself?"

I hated the thought of her going alone, but it was better than the alternative—moping here alone. "Why not?"

"I don't know," she said. "I have a lot of reading to catch up on."

In the kitchen, Dovie made a snoring noise.

"Hey!" Em said.

"Live a little," Dovie said. "You're only young once."

"Why do I feel ganged up on?"

My phone rang, the *Hawaii Five-O* theme song I'd programmed to let me know when Aiden was calling. "Hi, Aiden," I answered.

Em's face lit before she caught herself and focused on Rufus's ear. Her aura and Aiden's were a perfect match. They were destined to be together. Soul mates. True love. It had all the makings of a happily ever after. If only one of them would make a move. It was like watching paint dry, seeing the two of them dance around a relationship. Even though my father had told Em about the perfect match, she claimed she didn't want to rush into anything, and Aiden claimed he was waiting for Em to heal.

It was enough to drive me crazy.

"I got your message about Mac Gladstone," Aiden said. "And I made some calls. I'm meeting with the lead investigator first thing in the morning. He made it sound like there might be something we'd be interested in but didn't want to get into it over the phone. I'll call after."

I ran through my morning to-do list. Near the top was finding Tristan Rourke. "Anytime."

I hung up. Dovie held out my tea as I walked by the kitchen island. "Anything?" she asked.

I filled her in as Rufus snored from his spot at Em's feet. "Sean also found a notice from an insurance company in Mac's desk." I fished it out of my tote bag and showed it to Em.

The sheet of paper had "This Is Not a Bill" stamped across the top and itemized all Mac's claims for the last six months. In the past three months he'd seen three different doctors, visited the hospital twice, and made monthly stops at the local pharmacy.

Em tapped the paper. "This doctor, Gregory Mc-Donald, is a big-time oncologist."

"Mac had cancer?" Dovie said.

"Maybe." Em stood and stepped around Rufus's prone body. "These hospital visits are probably for scans."

I rummaged around my tote bag for the prescription bottle. "And this?"

"It's a strong painkiller often used for cancer patients, so yeah, I'd say Mac had cancer. Aiden can probably get his medical records."

"But his granddaughter said he was healthy." I was trying to wrap my brain around this turn of events.

"Maybe she didn't know," Dovie said. "I certainly had no idea he was having any health problems, and news like that would spread around here."

I also told them about the phone call Mac's granddaughter had overheard. Dovie let out a long sigh and leveled a knowing look at me. "Sounds as though someone was trying to stop him from doing something drastic."

"Something drastic like suicide?" Em said.

It was certainly beginning to look that way.

7

Coffee. Nectar of the Gods first thing in the morning.

I sipped gratefully as Thoreau slept on my lap and Sean drove down Roxbury side streets. To my surprise, he hadn't had any luck finding Tristan Rourke online. Tristan was completely off the grid. No credit cards, no license, no state ID, no work history, no tax filings— ever. He didn't own any property and had no death certificate.

For all intents and purposes didn't exist.

Except we knew he did.

The tires of Sean's Mustang crunched over roads sanded for better traction. Almost eight inches of snow had fallen overnight. Preston had to beg off coming with us as her editor had called with an unexpected assignment, but she made us promise to take notes.

So far, there wasn't much to be noted.

I had to confess I wasn't thrilled to be looking for an ex-con. I reminded myself I wasn't in business to judge Meaghan. Or Tristan. Just to reunite them and let destiny take its course. But now I had some serious reservations. "I had high hopes he'd turned his life around, left crime behind."

"There's still hope, Pollyanna."

I arched an eyebrow.

"Living underground is a bit suspicious," Sean conceded.

"Very suspicious. I don't know what to tell Meaghan."

The voice of reason, Sean said, "Nothing to tell yet."

He was right. We didn't know anything for sure. All we had was an address for Rourke's grandmother, who had been listed as his next of kin through the prison, and a picture of Rourke faxed from a contact of Sean's at Cedar Junction.

I plucked the photo out of a folder. Shorn blond hair, striking pale blue eyes, a scar crossing his nose. He didn't look like a stereotypical bad guy. If I stared long enough, I could almost see the boy he once was, the boy Meaghan Archibald had loved.

Still loved.

I had to keep that in mind with this case. Had to keep an open mind, period.

The houses on Maureen Rourke's street were surprisingly well maintained for the rough-and-tumble neighborhood. The triple-deckers sat nearly side by side with freshly painted clapboards, newer-looking porches, and bright, clean windows. Tiny strips of snow-covered lawns bled into the street, no sidewalk boundary protecting home sweet home from the big bad world beyond. Cars sat along the blurred line separating yards from traffic, most plowed into their spot until a good thaw or someone with the wherewithal to dig out the car came along.

Roxbury, in general, was one of Boston's transitional areas. High crime, drug houses, and drive-by shootings were mixed in with hardworking residents just trying to make their way in life.

By all accounts, Maureen Rourke was one of the latter. According to tax records, she'd worked two or three jobs at a time since she was fifteen years old. Everything from chambermaid, to washwoman, to entrepreneur.

I remembered what Meaghan had said—that Tristan's grandmother had been too poor to take him in when his mother died. I couldn't imagine how hard that must have been—for both of them—and wondered if she had worked so hard to raise the money to get him back from the state, only to see him arrested and taken away for good.

Three years ago, right after Tristan had been released from prison, she opened her own business, a Laundromat we'd driven past on our way here, A Clean Start.

Someone had a sense of humor.

Thoreau lay snuggled on my lap. We'd opted to bring him along instead of leaving him at my place. Dovie would have her hands full with Rufus as he adapted to his new surroundings. She had decided to keep him— I'd never had a doubt.

Someone at Maureen Rourke's house had been quite industrious. Not only had a car, a newer-model Camry, been shoveled free of snow, but the walkway and front steps had been cleared as well.

We idled in front of the three-decker. Sean said, "The deed is in Maureen's name. And apparently the house was bought with cash two years ago. There was never any mortgage on record."

I heard the undertone in his voice. I had a dozen reasons why Maureen would suddenly have so much cash on hand, but reality was hard to overlook. Tristan probably helped buy the house. His release from prison and the timing of the business opening and the purchase of the house were too coincidental. Where he found the money was anyone's guess at this point, but I had a sinking feeling that whatever he was doing wasn't on the up-and-up.

Sean hopped out, removed the plastic chair saving the empty parking spot in front of the house, and parked. I bundled Thoreau in a blanket and left him in the front seat.

The wooden door had been painted a beautiful colonial red. An arched window at the top of the door didn't have a speck on it. I knocked. A moment later, an older woman answered the door. Reddish hair streaked with white was pulled back into a bun at the nape of her neck. Beautiful creamy skin was dotted with freckles, and wrinkles creased the corners of her eyes and lips. Ice blue eyes twinkled at us as she wiped her hands on a dish towel. "What you be needing, darlin's?" Her voice was rich with an Irish brogue. She had to have been a stunning beauty in her younger years.

"Are you Maureen Rourke?" I asked.

Behind her, dark wooden floors gleamed in the morning light. The scent of coffee and something baking lingered in the air. She tipped her head, and some of the cheer left her eyes. "Who be asking?"

Sean stuck out his hand. "I'm Sean Donahue. And this is Lucy Valentine."

"Donahue, eh? A good Irish lad you be?"

"Depends who you ask."

She chuckled and turned her blue eyes my way. "Valentine? Certainly not Irish."

I loved the roll of her *Rs*. "I'm not certain what it is."

She tsked as though this were a grave sin and addressed Sean. "What brings you here?"

"We're looking for Tristan Rourke," Sean said, handing her a business card. The Lost Love logo took up half the card: two hearts, one fading into the background. "Sean Donahue, Private Investigator" was on the other half, along with his contact information.

"You're a detective?" she asked.

"A private investigator," I answered. "We've been hired to find Tristan."

She stared at the card for a long second before looking up at us. "I'm sorry, but I haven't seen Tristan in years. He doesn't keep in touch."

Irish bluster if I ever heard it. Her Irish eyes were lying.

"Are you certain?" Sean asked.

"Quite, young man. I haven't gone dotty in my old age."

She was hardly old. Early sixties if a day.

"I'm afraid the two of you are wasting your time. Tristan is long gone from these parts. I don't get so much as a phone call from the lad. 'Tis very sad."

"Yes," I said dryly. " 'Tis."

The twinkle was back in her eye as she looked at me. "Valentine, you say?"

I nodded.

"There may be a bit of Irish in you after all. The pair of you have a good day now."

She winked as she closed the door.

Sean looked at me. "That went better than I thought."

I started down the steps. "That's only because she liked you, the good Irish lad that you are," I said, testing a brogue.

He laughed. "Jealous?"

"Terribly."

Sean whispered, "We have company."

Two men leaned against Sean's Mustang. Thoreau had his little black nose pressed to the window as if he could sniff through the glass. He hadn't barked at all. A watchdog he wasn't.

The men were dressed in dark suits and dark trenches and wore dark sunglasses. They flipped open thin black wallets, revealing golden shields inside. "FBI," the man on the left said. He was cute in a nerdy, grumpy kind of way. The kind of guy a woman loved to fall for in hopes she could change him into something wonderful. The kind of guy who would never change. The ultimate Mr. Wrong. "I'm Special Agent Thomas."

"Agent St. John," the other added. He was bald and a head shorter than his partner.

"It's Donahue, right?" Agent Thomas asked, then nodded to me and added, "And you're Lucy Valentine? What's your business with Maureen Rourke?"

I shouldn't have been surprised the agents knew who we were. If they'd been watching Maureen Rourke's house when we pulled up, they could have easily called in Sean's license plate. It wouldn't have taken much more investigation to tie my name with Sean's.

But . . . I glanced at Maureen's house. There was also a very real possibility the house had been bugged, that they'd heard our whole conversation with Tristan's grandmother.

Sean said, "We're looking for Tristan Rourke."

This news hadn't surprised them. The house was definitely bugged. This pretty much sealed the deal that Tristan was living a life of crime. Law-abiding citizens didn't often have the FBI looking for them.

"And having no luck finding him," I added, passing them a business card. "We were hired to reunite him with a lost love."

"Lost loves?" St. John smiled. Spirals of steam rose off his bald head. His skin was so tight against his bumpy skull it looked more like a topographical map.

I kept that observation to myself as I struggled not to be offended. "We all have our callings."

Agent Thomas pinned me with a warning glare. "I suggest you stop looking for Rourke."

"Why?" I asked.

"He's the prime suspect in an ongoing federal case."

Sean squared his shoulders. "Has there been a warrant issued?"

Baldy said, "Not yet."

"What did he do?" I asked.

"That's need-to-know information."

"We'll keep that in mind," Sean said, unlocking the car.

"Do us a favor, Ms. Valentine," Agent Thomas added. "Go back to playing with the Staties. We'll be watching to make sure you do."

They turned away, walked toward a black SUV parked two houses down.

The Staties—slang for the state police. The parting comment stung, but their dismissal hit a nerve. I didn't like being told what to do. "Charming," I said to Sean as he held open my door.

He stared after the men. "I'm getting a bad feeling about this case."

That made two of us. Instinct. Intuition. They weren't feelings I pushed away easily. It was only the look on Meaghan Archibald's face that fueled my desire to find Rourke.

Well, that and the fact that the FBI had told me to stay out of it.

As I nudged Thoreau aside to sit, my eye caught movement in the upstairs window in the house next door. A lacy white curtain swayed.

The FBI weren't the only ones who'd been watching us.

8

The Porcupine was packed. I sidled up to the lunch counter, waited until someone left, and snagged a stool on the end. Raphael bustled back and forth, setting down orders, taking others, clearing plates.

I checked my phone for messages. I was still waiting to hear from Aiden. He was supposed to have met with the investigator on Mac's case first thing this morning, then gotten in touch with me. Curiosity was killing me. I wasn't known for my patience.

I had a voice mail—from Mum. "Oh, happy day, LucyD! My ring was right where you said it was. Thank you, thank you! Smooches!"

Smiling, I rolled my eyes and dropped my phone back into my tote.

"Good news?" Raphael asked. He gave me a quick kiss on my cheek. He motioned for another server to cover his station.

"Mum. She found her engagement ring."

His dark eyes turned serious. "So she told you."

"About her and Dad? Not so much told as I figured it out."

How long would they have waited?

"Are you staying for lunch, Uva?"

"Not today. I just need some coffee and two turkey spinach wraps to go."

"Something for the pooch?" he asked, nodding to Thoreau, who was nestled in the crook of my arm. Sean was looking for a parking spot.

I supposed Thoreau could have a little treat. "A plain turkey wrap."

"To go? You sure?" Raphael punched the order into a computer.

"Definitely. This place is a nuthouse." All the tables were full, and there was a line forming at the take-out counter.

"It's the Lone Ranger."

I whipped my head around to look out the glass storefront. "Where?"

Raphael laughed. "Not literally, Uva. He's caused the upswing in business. People are using the Porcupine as home base while they hope to get a look at him."

"More like take his money."

"More like use our restrooms."

I smiled, but my heart wasn't in it. Too much going on in my mind.

Raphael took a long look at me. "Is there something wrong?"

He had been part of my life since I was three years old. If I were being completely honest, I'd admit he'd been more a father to me over the years than my own.

But being completely honest made me feel slightly traitorous.

He'd nicknamed me Uva, Spanish for "grape," when I was a tiny thing, throwing a temper tantrum of such proportions I'd turned myself as purple as a grape. Not long after, I'd begun calling him Pasa, "raisin," because one day I hoped to turn into someone as good, as nurturing, as wise, as him. Well, that and he'd looked like a raisin, his whole face squished, wrinkled, when he scolded me over the hissy fit.

It didn't surprise me he'd seen trouble in my eyes. I doubted there was anyone who knew me better, who could look straight through my many masks.

"Too many things to go into." Like Mac, like Tristan Rourke, like the FBI watching me, like wanting Sean to move in with me.

"Hmmm," Raphael murmured.

Maggie Constantine hurried over, carrying a plate of salad. She set it in front of the man next to me with a smile. "Lucy! Are you staying for lunch?" She looked around. "I can clear your favorite table."

I wasn't sure how the couple currently sitting at my favorite table would feel about that.

"I'm actually not staying," I said.

I saw how very happy Maggie and Raphael were with each other, even though on paper it wouldn't seem as though they'd make a good match. She was a Yankee fan; he was a die-hard member of Red Sox Nation. She liked classical music; it made Raphael's ears bleed. She was younger by a good decade. Yet . . . they worked. Perfectly.

Something crashed in the kitchen. Maggie winced.

"I should check on that." She leaned across the counter, kissed my cheek. "We'll have dinner soon, okay?"

"Okay."

Raphael watched her leave, his eyes glowing.

"When are you going to marry her?" I asked.

"There's time enough."

"Is there?" I asked.

He rubbed an imaginary spot on the countertop. "I have a feeling you're not talking about me."

A server appeared and dropped off a to-go bag. I grabbed it and hopped off the stool. "Look at that. Gotta run. Sean's probably already waiting upstairs and—"

"Uva."

"Pasa, do you think it will last?"

He immediately knew what I was talking about.

My parents.

He tipped his head back and forth as if weighing options, then narrowed his gaze on me. Softly he said, "Does it matter?"

I knew what he was saying. They were happy now. In this moment. Wasn't that what mattered most? Honesty hurt. "To me I guess it does."

"Then it's not so much about them as it is you, no?"

He was right, of course. He was always right.

"This is about Sean?" he asked.

Thoreau licked my chin. I rubbed his head, scratched under his chin. "I'm trying. Really trying to not to fear the future."

"The curse," he tapped his temple, "is here."

"How can you say that? Without the auras . . ."

"Uva, even with auras love isn't easy. There are still

compromises, concessions. Still the need to understand, truly, the person you love. Their hopes, their fears."

"But in the end the auras don't lie. If you know for certain you're a perfect match it's easier to work through any problems. You know, without a doubt, that love will conquer all. With Sean, I don't know. I don't have that guarantee."

Raphael tapped his temple again. "You do, Lucy. You just need to choose to believe."

I closed my eyes in frustration.

"You'll see," he said.

Opening my eyes, I found him smiling. "Will I?"

Smugly he said, "Of course. When have I ever been wrong?"

I shifted Thoreau to my other arm, readjusted my tote bag, and made sure there were three sandwiches in the to-go bag. "There was that time you insisted a tomato was a vegetable."

He snapped his hand towel at me. "Get out of here, you."

As I pushed open the door, I heard his voice over the crowd: "Just believe."

If it were only that easy.

9

Suz stood at the window, binoculars in hand. "Preston," she said by way of an explanation as I opened the door to the office.

I set Thoreau down. He ran over to Suz, sniffed her boots.

"She's recruited you as a Lone Ranger lookout?"

Suz sheepishly said, "She didn't need much arm-twisting. I have my eye on a new camera, a fancy-pants Nikon, for Teddy's birthday. I could use some extra cash."

I looked down over the snow-covered Common. "Is she down there?"

"Yep. Has been for the last hour. The Lone Ranger usually shows up around lunchtime."

"But he was just there yesterday. He won't be back for another few days."

"You don't know that."

I smiled. "Not this again."

She laughed but didn't budge from the window. "By the way, Sean and Aiden are in your office."

Aiden must have learned something juicy if he came in person. I tapped my leg for Thoreau to follow me. "Is Dad in?" I asked Suz. I wanted his take on the Meaghan situation.

"Nope. Took the afternoon off. I think he had plans with Judie." She made smoochy noises and winked at me.

"I think I'm going to be sick."

Laughing, she lifted the binoculars and continued her watch.

Sean and Aiden were both leaning on the conference table when I walked in. Thoreau pranced over for love and attention.

Aiden said to me, "Well, if it isn't the FBI's newest best friend. I got a call from Special Agent Thomas himself. He'd very much appreciate it if you would keep your, and I quote, 'cute little nose' out of his case."

"The nerve!" I said.

"It *is* pretty cute," Sean agreed.

"Gag, gag," Aiden said, dropping into a chair.

I opened Thoreau's wrap, pulled out chunks of turkey that he ate from my fingers. The Dog Whisperer would have a fit.

Detective Lieutenant Aiden Holliday of the Massachusetts State Police had come into my life when a little boy had disappeared in Hingham's Wompatuck State Park. Because of the outcome of that case Aiden, acting as a liaison for the state police, had offered me a position as a special consultant. Using my psychic abilities, I helped with missing-person cases, cold and new.

Some with happy endings.

Most without.

Over the course of the last few months Aiden had

become more than my link to the state police—he'd become a friend.

"You could be just as gag worthy if you'd ever ask Em on a date," I prodded.

"How'd this get turned around on me?" he asked Sean.

"I think it was the gag comment."

Aiden looked between the two of us. "As I was saying, the good Agent Thomas phoned. Told me all about your visit to Maureen Rourke's house."

Thoreau bounced up and down on all fours, waiting for his next bite of lunch. I didn't mention the change of subject, but I wasn't giving up on getting Em and Aiden together sooner rather than later. Apparently Cupid needed a little nudging. "Does he have the power to keep us from investigating?"

Aiden popped a Tic Tac in his mouth. "Not formally."

"But," Sean said, "he can make our lives fairly miserable if we don't comply."

Aiden swiped a hand through his hair, a high and tight blond crew cut. He wore a pair of navy blue pants, a white button-down with a dark blue tie, and a corduroy blazer. His police credentials were clipped to his waist. "You two have apparently stepped on some big toes."

"Why? Who *is* Tristan Rourke? What's he done?"

"Something's going on with Tristan?" Preston stood in the doorway. By the hangdog look on her face I had the feeling the Lone Ranger hadn't made an appearance.

Sean waved her in. Since she was writing Meaghan's story, Preston had every right to hear the news.

Aiden said, "Tristan Rourke is the suspected mastermind of the biggest art theft ring in the United States.

Private homes, museums—doesn't matter. The Heinz theft—Tristan Rourke. The Mayhew? Tristan Rourke."

Preston's eyes had widened as big as saucers as she sat down. "The Mayhew?" she whispered.

The Mayhew was a small, privately owned museum here in Boston, with some of the greatest masterpieces in the world under its roof. Three years ago it had been robbed, millions of dollars' worth of paintings stolen. There had been no clues, no leads, no arrests. It was the biggest heist in U.S. history.

"How do they know Tristan is the mastermind?" Sean asked.

"And why haven't they arrested him?" Preston added.

"I'm just the messenger," Aiden said. "I don't know anything about the case at all."

"But you can find out?" I asked hopefully.

"I can poke around."

I glanced at Sean. "We have to tell Meaghan."

Preston said, "Of course we have to tell Meaghan!"

I eyed her. "This isn't about her reaction and the quote you're going to get."

"Killjoy," she said, tugging her blazer to smooth out a wrinkle.

Aiden smirked. I had the feeling Preston amused him. Much like a sideshow act.

I crumbled the empty sandwich wrapper. Ignoring Preston was sometimes best.

"Whatever you do, be careful. You're playing with fire." Aiden rose, headed for the door.

"You're leaving already? But what did you find out about Mac?"

"I didn't learn much more than you did about Mac

Gladstone, though I'm still waiting to hear on his medical records. There is one thing that stands out."

"What?" I asked.

"He's been withdrawing nine thousand dollars a month from his bank account for the last six months. Some of it has been going to his daughter and her husband—a monthly allowance of sorts—but the rest, about five grand a month, is unaccounted for."

Sean whistled low. "Why?"

"No one knows for certain. But we've seen this pattern before."

My stomach was in knots. I pushed my sandwich away. "How so?"

"In blackmail cases. My best guess is Mac Gladstone has been paying someone off."

10

Aiden's revelation had knocked some wind out of our suicide theory. If Mac was being extorted, then he might have disappeared on purpose. Maybe even staged his own death.

He might even have been desperate enough to leave his beloved granddaughter behind to worry. Not to mention Rufus.

But it all begged the question of who Mac was paying off. According to his family and friends, he had no enemies.

Sean, Preston, and I were speculating.

"Tax fraud?" I suggested.

Preston rolled her eyes. "That's not a big deal. According to my sources, Mac's worth upward of fifty million. He'd easily be able to pay off a tax bill."

Sean sat at my desk, his back to us as he used the computer to look up the Mayhew heist. He'd been quiet since Aiden's visit. Too quiet.

I dialed Meaghan Archibald. Her phone rang and

rang. It finally clicked over to voice mail. I left a message asking her to call me back.

"Maybe Jemima is the result of an illicit relationship," Preston suggested. "Oh, wait. This isn't your family we're talking about." She smirked.

"Low blow," I said. Funny but low.

"How is Cutter these days?" she asked.

"He's fine."

"How long will he be out of town?"

She stared at her fingernails as if not caring about the answer, but there had been something in her tone that had me watching her carefully. Even Sean swiveled in the desk chair for a closer look.

A rosy blush stained her cheeks as she picked at a hangnail.

"Why are you so interested?" I asked.

"Who says I'm interested?"

Thoreau stirred from his doggy bed in the corner as I picked up my tote bag, put Meaghan's file inside. "I do."

"I do, too," Sean said.

She stood, running her palms over her pants, then bending to straighten the cuff. "Well, you're both wrong. Find anything?" she asked Sean, ditching the conversation.

Sean tapped the screen. "None of the pieces from the Mayhew robbery were ever recovered. There were classics like van Gogh and Monet stolen along with more modern pieces from Andy Warhol. Several items of vintage jewelry were also taken from the precious-gems exhibit, including a pink diamond ring worth upward of two million. There were also several Norman Rockwell pieces taken and—" He stopped abruptly.

"What?" I asked.

"Two of the prints stolen were Mac Gladstone's."

"Mac?" I repeated. "It has to be a coincidence. That robbery was three years ago."

Preston leaned in to read over Sean's shoulder. "Reporters don't believe in coincidence."

"Okay, Ms. Reporter-Pants," I said. "What's your theory?"

She frowned. "I don't really have one. I just don't believe in coincidences. Besides, I can only do so much. You two are the investigators. You figure it out. Then let me know, so I can write an article about it." She headed for the door. "I'm going back to the Common to see if the Lone Ranger has made another appearance. You'll let me know if Meaghan calls, right?"

"Right," I said.

As Preston left, Thoreau raised his nose, sniffed, and went back to sleep.

Sean turned off the computer and leaned against the table. I cozied up, rubbed the deep lines between his eyebrows. "Why the concern?"

His hands spanned my rib cage, pulled me close. "This case. I have a bad feeling about it."

"We do have escape clauses. Or we can just return her retainer. If it's bothering you that much we can walk away."

"No," he said, kissing my neck. "Not yet. Not until we have more information on Tristan."

Sean's shoulders stiffened when he said the name. It reminded me of when he did the same thing yesterday. I drew back, looked him in the eye. "What upset you yesterday when Preston was talking about zebras changing stripes?"

He kissed my lips, edged away. "I wasn't upset."

As I watched him put his files in a messenger bag and gather up Thoreau, I had to wonder why Sean was lying to me.

Looking for more information on Tristan had us headed to Squantum, a small peninsula that jutted like a baby toe into the waters between Boston Harbor and Quincy Bay.

The Speros, the foster parents who had taken in Rourke and Meaghan as teenagers, were living in a blue-collar, family-friendly neighborhood with sidewalks and tree-lined streets. Sean pulled up to a three-foot-tall snowbank that acted as a curb.

The sun was sinking on the horizon as I dug into Meaghan's growing file to brush up on what we knew. From what Sean and I had been able to gather so far, Anthony Spero had worked most of his life as a steel-worker but was now on disability after an accident at the Quincy shipyard. His wife, Mary Ellen (née Murphy), currently held a full-time job as a librarian at the Thomas Crane library in Quincy. No kids. There was one auto loan outstanding for a Chevy pickup. The house, however, belonged to Mary Ellen's sister, Catherine Murphy. The Speros had been living here for the past nine months. Their former house in Jamaica Plain had been foreclosed on when Anthony could no longer work.

I tucked the paperwork back into the file and dropped it into my tote bag. I rubbed Thoreau's ears and he yawned, his little pink tongue sticking out.

We were hoping Mary Ellen and Anthony Spero would tell us their side of what happened eight years ago. Would it match what Meaghan had told us and what was in the newspapers?

"Ready?" Sean asked.

Thoreau jumped up, wagged his tiny tail so fast there was a draft.

"Not you," I said to him. I lowered the window a crack, tucked a blanket around him. I grabbed my tote bag as I opened the door.

Lights glowed in the house, a small split-level ranch probably built in the forties or fifties. It was painted dark beige with black and cream trim. Cracks split the shoveled concrete walkway as we headed to the front door.

In answer to Sean's knock, a man filled the doorway, his potbelly jiggling under a white T-shirt. Sweatpants sagged as if he'd recently lost weight.

"What?" he asked.

"Anthony Spero?" Sean asked.

"Yeah? What?"

I pegged him as the kind who hit the bars every weekend, who talked too loudly (mostly about himself) and only worked hard enough not to get fired.

I immediately felt bad for his wife.

"We'd like to speak to you and your wife," I said, pasting on a bright smile. "About Tristan Rourke and Meaghan Ar—" I caught myself. He might not know her adopted name. "Chaney."

"Who're you?"

Sean handed him an SD Investigations card. "We're looking for Rourke."

With a jerk of his head, Spero motioned for us to come in. He didn't hold the door. In the tiny kitchen, he opened the fridge. "Only one beer left." A top popped, fizzed. "You two want some water?"

I bit back a smile at his attempt to be a good host. "No thanks."

I could tell by the set of Sean's jaw that he didn't like Spero at first glance.

"Why are you looking for that punk Rourke?" Spero shuffled into the living room, plopped down on a slip-covered armchair, set his beer can on his belly. "What kind of house doesn't have a recliner? This ain't my place, if you can't tell. It's my old lady's sister's place.

"We've been here a couple months. It's not permanent. Just till we find a place of our own. Damn economy. Meaghan tell you we were here?"

Delicate pink paint covered the walls, casting a girlish glow over the room decorated with antique furniture—a gorgeous Georgian side table, a pair of mahogany armchairs. Not pieces a man like Spero would ever appreciate.

"License bureau." Sean sat on a settee, taking up a little more than half of it. "Mary Ellen listed a change of address."

Spero's face screwed up as he processed the information. He scratched his stomach. White-tinted stubble covered his jowly chin. He reminded me a bit too much of Dennis Farina's mug shot.

I really needed to stop reading the gossip mags at the Shaw's checkout. "Is Mary Ellen around?"

"Nah. Working late all this week, overtime. We need the money."

"Do you see Meaghan a lot?" Sean asked, redirecting the conversation.

"Me? Nah. Mary Ellen still talks to the girl, time to time. She don't think I know, but I let it slide."

"Slide?" Sean asked.

"Those kids were all messed up," Spero said, tapping his head to indicate mental problems. "We don't need them interfering with our lives. Did she listen? No. It's why women shouldn't make no decisions. I had my choice, those kids never would've left the hellholes they crawled out of."

Sean tensed, coiled, as if he were about to spring. I set my hand on his leg and could practically feel the anger coming off him in heated waves. What was with him lately?

"Whiny bunch of bloodsuckers, kids are. Only good thing about those kids Mare brought in?"

"What?" Sean asked through clenched teeth.

"The dough. Made some good money back then. Could use some now."

"Why aren't you still fostering?" I asked, probing.

His eyes went wide. " 'Cause I like breathing, thank you very much. I put my foot down after Rourke tried to do me in. Happiest goddamned day of my life." I could picture him on the bar stool, telling this same story, guffawing with his buddies.

I couldn't help myself. "The day he tried to strangle you?"

He tipped his head to the side, sized me up. "No, Goldilocks. The day I kicked all those kids out."

"And Mary Ellen?" Sean asked.

"She got over it."

Obviously not if she still kept in touch with Meaghan. "Do you know if Mary Ellen also keeps in touch with Rourke?"

Anger weaved into his eyes. "If she knows what's good for her, she best not be talking to Rourke."

I wanted to ask, "Or else what?" but held my tongue. I was afraid of the answer.

I nudged Sean. We both stood to go. It was Mary Ellen we needed to talk to if we wanted to know what had happened eight years ago.

Anthony Spero was nothing but a dead end.

11

I watched my footing as I came down the front steps, careful of icy patches. "Do you want to swing by the library on the way home?"

Home.

Such a simple little word that held so much meaning.

It wasn't as though Sean didn't spend all his free time there. He had space in the closet, a toothbrush next to mine, two bureau drawers. He knew to run the hot water for a few minutes before getting into the shower in the morning to kick-start the water heater. He knew how to operate the stackable washer and dryer and that the oven temperature ran hotter than what the knob indicated.

My home *was* his home.

Why not make it official?

Right. The curse.

The damn curse.

I hated that thing.

Still angry, he said, "It's on the way."

I faced him. "Are you going to tell me what's going on?"

"What do you mean?"

"You. The anger."

"The guy was a jerk, Lucy."

"It's not just him. You've been off ever since we took this case."

"It's getting late. We should go."

In the muted glow of the streetlights, I could see the pain etched in his eyes. I wanted to know where it came from and how to get rid of it. But now wasn't the time or place to push him. My heart aching, I spun and lost my footing. Sean grabbed my elbow. Warmth flowed from his fingers through my coat, down my forearms, and tingled in the tips of my fingers.

"Whoa," he said.

"Whoa" was right. "Look!" I gasped, pointing at the car. Both doors were wide open. Thoreau was nowhere in sight.

We stood frozen for the briefest of seconds as we took it all in. The scene, the repercussions.

Sean let go of me and rushed forward. He stuck his head in the car and pulled it out a second later. "He's gone." Pained, he said, "I locked it, didn't I? I remember locking it."

I nodded. I recalled hearing the beeps. "What else did they take?"

"Nothing. Nothing else is missing that I can tell." He went to the trunk, opened it. Pulling out two flashlights, he handed one to me.

Thankfully, I'd brought my tote bag in with me.

I heard him mumble, "Son of a bitch," under his

breath before he said, "Let's split up. Look for prints in the snow, in case he's running loose and not stolen."

My heart sank to my toes. Stolen. Thoreau was a purebred Yorkshire terrier. He'd get good money on the black market.

73 minus 5 is 69. Shit. 68.

So much for math calming me down.

I started off down the block, calling Thoreau's name. Street lamps offered little extra light as the beams from the flashlight swept back and forth across front lawns, searching for any sign Thoreau had been here. There was no sign of him—or of paw prints, either.

Twenty minutes later, I was still looking. I walked up and down four streets before heading back to Sean's Mustang. I fought a wave of nausea as I looked inside the car. Thoreau's leash was gone. He hadn't been hooked to it when we left him in the car—someone had come along, broken in, and stolen Thoreau.

Deflated, I leaned against the door. Tears welled in my eyes. The little dog had become a part of my family. I couldn't believe he was just gone. And that I couldn't use my abilities to find him.

The tears overflowed.

I quickly swiped them away when I spotted Sean jogging down the street, slipping and sliding on the black ice.

"Any luck?" he asked as he neared.

I shook my head, unable to stop more tears.

He pulled me into his arms, held me close. Kissing my temple, he said, "We'll find him."

"His leash is gone, too. Someone had to have taken him."

Sean pulled a hand through his hair, raising dark

tufts. A smile spread across his face, stretching until both dimples popped. Using the pad of his thumb, he whisked away my tears.

I couldn't think of one thing that was amusing. "Why are you smiling?"

"You can find him."

Sean knew how my abilities worked—I could only get readings from inanimate objects. Nothing living, breathing. Confused, I said, "No, I can't."

His hands curved around my shoulders. "The leash, Ms. Valentine."

The leash! I could get a reading from Sean since he technically owned the leash.

My heart was suddenly pounding. I'd never held Sean's hand for more than a few seconds. And then I only saw visions of us. Could I even do a normal reading with him?

"Is it possible?" he asked, obviously thinking along the same lines.

I'd broken out in a cold sweat. I unbuttoned my coat, unwound my scarf. "I don't know, but we have nothing left to lose at this point."

"Are you okay? You've gone pale. We don't have to do this," he said. "I'll contact the police, we can put up flyers—"

I put my finger on his lips, quieting him. "Stop. We have to do this. It's Thoreau. Grendel would never forgive me." My cat was in love with Sean's dog. There would be hell to pay if we didn't bring Thoreau home.

Home. There was that damn word again.

"Never mind *me*. It's all about the cat."

"Sorry. Priorities."

Smiling, he held out his hand, palm up. I took a

deep breath and said, "Think about that leash, okay? And try just to think about the leash. Don't let any other thoughts creep in."

"Like what? You and me, later tonight in front of the fire?"

I hit him in the arm. "Yeah. Like that."

Somberly he said, "I'll try my best, but now the image is kind of stuck there."

I closed my eyes. I tried to clear my thoughts. "Ready?"

"Yeah."

"Okay." My arm quivered as my hand hovered over his. Slowly, I lowered it, skin against skin.

The air was sucked from my lungs. Images came slowly, lazily, as they always did when our hands touched.

Pictures of Thoreau came first, mixing with images of Sean and me at my cottage. The two scenes slammed into each other, breaking apart into pieces left for me to sort through. A black car. Me in my robe. A street sign. Sean lying in the snow. Thoreau bouncing. Me bent over Sean's lifeless body. Blue eyes watching intently. Heartbreak.

I pulled my hand away, gasped for breath.

"Lucy?" Sean cupped my face. "What is it? What did you see?"

I bent forward, drawing my hands to my chest protectively, then to his to feel his heartbeat. It pulsed under my palm. Tears filled my eyes, slowly leaked out. The pain I'd felt was so overwhelming, consuming.

Sean pulled me forward, toward him. When I gathered myself together, I looked up at Sean. "He's watching us," I whispered.

Sean's shoulders stiffened. "Who? Spero?"

"Tristan Rourke. And he has Thoreau."

"Where?"

"Across the street, two houses down. Parked in a black Mazda. He's probably been watching us the whole time."

We both turned, stared at the car. It had slightly tinted windows. Sean started forward. I was right behind him.

Much to my surprise, the driver's door opened. Tristan Rourke held Thoreau under one arm as he clapped.

"Bravo," he said, setting Thoreau down.

Sean called to him, and the dog bounced over. Sean scooped him up and Thoreau commenced licking his chin.

Rourke casually walked over to us. "That was impressive. Sorry about taking the pooch, but I've been reading about your capabilities, Ms. Valentine, and decided to do a little test. No harm, no foul."

He had a charming way about him, an easy confidence. Longish dark blond hair gave a boyish air, and his blue eyes were open and friendly. I wouldn't be the least surprised to hear a "gosh, gee" from him any time now. He hardly seemed the criminal-mastermind sort. In fact, he didn't even look capable of so much as nipping a grape in the produce aisle.

I reached over, let Thoreau lick my hand. I was so relieved to have him back, it was hard to summon any anger.

"I heard you wanted to speak with me," Rourke said, sitting on the hood of his car. It didn't have front plates. "Call me curious, but I wanted to know why someone who locates lost loves for a living was looking for me."

I was starting to shiver. "Maybe we could go somewhere a little warmer?"

Rourke said, "Sorry. My time is limited." He smiled. White teeth gleamed under the soft yellow glow of the street lamp. "Speak now or forever hold your peace."

I didn't quite know what to say. Meaghan hadn't yet returned my call, so I didn't know if she wanted to pursue any kind of meeting with Tristan. I trod carefully. "We were hired by Meaghan to find you. Meaghan Ar—Chaney." He wouldn't recognize her adoptive name.

His eyes grew wide as the color drained from his face. His voice rasped as he said, "What kind of sick joke are you playing?"

"No joke," Sean said, watching him carefully.

He gazed at us, his eyes filled with unspeakable anguish. "Meaghan's dead."

I gasped in surprise. "What?"

"She killed herself eight years ago."

"No," I said, "she lived."

"You're lying."

"Why would we lie?" Sean asked.

My heart twisted painfully. "She was taken to a local hospital, treated, and eventually adopted by a doctor who cared for her. She's alive and well, Tristan."

Rourke dropped into a crouch, his head down. He was taking deep gulping breaths, dragging in cold air, letting it out in big whooshes. "He told me she died, that it was all my fault."

Sean glanced at me, his eyes troubled, as he said, "Who told you?"

"Spero."

"When?"

"When I came back that day." He glanced up at us. "I was only seventeen. I believed him." He stood and let out a roar of pain and anguish. "Why did I believe him? Everything would have been different."

The pieces fell into place. Tristan had arrived back at the Spero house after being bailed out of jail for stealing the prom dress. He'd heard about what had happened with Meaghan, and Spero, the sick bastard, had told Tristan she'd died. Grieving, Tristan had lashed out at his foster father, nearly killing him.

"Why would he do that?" Tristan paced.

I cleared my throat. "I don't know."

"And she hired you to find me?" he asked, still sounding skeptical.

I noticed his hands were shaking as I briefly explained the purpose of Lost Loves.

"She's really alive?" Tristan asked.

I hooked my hand around Sean's arm. "She really is."

Tristan took another deep breath. "How do I get in touch with her? My God, I'll call her right now. Just give me her phone number."

I shivered. "We can't do that."

Rourke's eyes narrowed. In that instant, I saw beneath the boy next door to exactly how dangerous he could be. "I'm sorry," he said. "I was of the belief that a reunion was in order."

"If you want to give us your information we can pass it on to Meaghan. It will be up to her to make contact."

"But she's the one trying to find me?"

"She doesn't know about your," I searched for the right phrase, "career choice yet. We just found out about it this afternoon, but like I said, you could give us your number."

White puffs of air burst from his lips, dissipated in the cold night. "I'm sorry, but as you now probably realize, my personal information is highly classified." Rourke walked to his car door. "I'll get Meaghan's information one way or another."

I didn't like the sound of that.

Sean said, "Do you know anything about Mac Gladstone, Rourke?"

His eyes flashed in surprise. "I know his work."

I bet he did.

"He's been missing for a month. You wouldn't know anything about that, would you?" Sean asked.

Tristan smiled again, wide and warm. He held up his hands in surrender. "Not my line of work, buddy."

The genuine surprise in his eyes had me believing him. But it was easy to get caught up in his aw-shucks personality and not see the criminal mastermind under the surface.

Rourke suddenly shifted, his gaze intent on the little split-level ranch.

I glanced over my shoulder. Anthony Spero was watching us through the front window.

There was murder in Rourke's eyes as he ducked into his car. He backed up, made a quick U-turn, and drove off.

Sean pulled a hand over his face as he looked at me. "Think we should warn Spero?"

Though Tristan claimed that wasn't his "line of work," he'd also just found out he'd been lied to all those years ago, that the girl he loved wasn't dead after all. His whole life might have turned out differently, if only Anthony Spero had a decent bone in his body. "Nah. But I think we should warn his wife."

Truthfully, I really just wanted to go home, forget about everyone else for a while.

Home.

The word didn't come with warm and fuzzies this time. As we walked to the car, I couldn't help the knot of worry in my stomach. I hadn't told Sean everything I'd seen in my vision.

Some things were just too upsetting to talk about.

12

The Thomas Crane library wasn't far from Quincy Center. We pulled up to the historic library, stunning with its stone and stained glass. Sean fed a meter while I bundled Thoreau in a blanket. "Now, no letting people steal you, okay?"

He licked my nose.

I took that as an agreement.

Sean made sure the car was locked tight, put his arm around my shoulder, and said, "Not quite what I had planned for tonight."

"And what did you have planned, Mr. Donahue?"

He leaned in, kissed the sensitive spot between my jawbone and my ear. "A little of this." His lips dropped to my neck. "And a little of that."

"Only a little?"

"We can negotiate." He pulled open the door to the library. "And I'm not above bribery."

I let the joy chase away the long shadows cast by the vision. I smiled. "It's good to have strong morals."

Inside, I asked a very stern older woman at the information desk if she could tell us where to find Mary Ellen.

Her pursed lips flattened into a grim line. A lanyard hanging from her neck held a badge that said her name was Abigail A. "Is this personal or business?"

It was definitely personal for Mary Ellen but business for us. I fudged the truth a little and said, "Business," with as much confidence as I could muster. The situation seemed to call for a little deception. Abigail had a look about her; her severe brown bun, squinty eyes, and pointy chin had me thinking she had flying monkeys at her beck and call. She wouldn't tolerate anything the least bit personal.

She leveled me with a look that blatantly declared she didn't believe me.

Maybe I wasn't so good a liar after all.

I kept quiet, mostly to suppress my sudden need to confess my every transgression, from the time I added red food coloring to vases of Dovie's prized white peonies to see if they'd turn color (they did) to when I'd "borrowed" my father's Mercedes as a senior in high school so Marisol, Em, and I could drive to Providence to see a Pearl Jam concert.

Sean turned on the charm, flashed his dimples. "It's quite important we speak with her."

Abigail softened, dropping her shoulders, dipping her chin. It was the power of his dimples. Did it every time. Smiling shyly, she said, "Upstairs. Children's."

As we headed for the steps, I said, "It's not fair you have that kind of influence."

"You have your gifts, Ms. Valentine, and I have mine."

A little of this. And a little of that. I could definitely attest to his gifts.

"Humble, too," I said, passing him on the steps. "I'll race ya." At the top, I looked back and my heart nearly dropped out of my chest.

Sean was six steps down, bent at the waist, his hands to his chest. He was huffing and puffing.

"Sean!" I ran down the stairs. "What's wrong? Are you all right?" Oh my God. Oh my God. I knew this day would come. Hadn't I taken CPR as a precaution for just this sort of thing? Shit. And I couldn't remember a damn bit of it. Mouth-to-mouth, compressions. Gone. Poof.

He looked up at me, winked, and took the stairs two at a time. "I win."

I stomped upward. "That wasn't funny! You scared me half to death."

My heart was still pounding, quaking so hard it would cause the Richter scale to malfunction. In my mind, I saw him in my vision, deathly pale. Lifeless. But my vision had taken place at my cottage—not here—so I knew it was still in the future. . . .

"Only half? I thought I'd rate a little higher than that."

I punched his arm. My hands were still shaking. "Right now you're not rating at all."

He cupped my face, kissed me gently. "Now?"

"I'm thinking about it."

His kiss deepened a bit. "Now?"

My knees went rubbery. "A blip."

"I'm sorry. I won't do it again."

"Promise?"

"I promise," he said solemnly.

If I believed him—and I did—that meant in my vision he wasn't faking. I fought against sudden tears and said, "Okay, you rate again. But only this much." I held two fingers close together, a pinch.

Almost two years ago, Sean had been working with the Boston Fire Department. He'd been on a call to a car accident and was pulling hose toward the crash when his world went dark.

He'd died.

Miraculously, he'd been brought back to life and an implanted defibrillator kept him that way. He'd had to quit his job, start his life over.

But knowing his defibrillator could malfunction, that his damaged heart could give out at any moment, was never far from my thoughts. Especially now, after that vision.

"What's this?" Sean asked, wiping the tears. "Oh, Lucy. I'm sorry. Really."

"I love you," I whispered.

"I love you, Lucy Valentine." He pulled me to him, brought his lips hard against mine, and kissed me.

I'd waited my whole life for a kiss like that. One so full of love, of promise. Of babies and houses and happily ever afters.

I felt a twinge, a twist of pain deep in my soul, but I wouldn't let it surface. Not now, not today. I was just going to enjoy.

"Excuse me." I felt a tug on my sleeve. Someone cleared a throat. "Pardon."

Sean and I pulled apart.

A pair of close-set blue eyes peered up at us. I placed the woman around my mother's age, early fifties, with soft reddish blond hair. She was tiny, with delicate features and a birdlike frame, but that didn't stop her from wearing multiple strands of vintage beads and numerous rings on her fingers. A smile stretched the remaining collagen in her cheeks to its limits, and her eyes sparkled almost as much as the large sunburst earrings she wore. "The romance section is downstairs," she admonished with a wink.

"Sorry," Sean mumbled.

She fanned her face. "I'm surprised the two of you didn't set off the fire alarm."

"Really sorry," I echoed.

Waving a hand in dismissal, she said, "Not a worry. But perhaps this isn't the place for such," she paused, searching for the right word, "affection."

I looked around. The library was all dark woods and muted light. Several people sitting at nearby tables were openly staring, and one man in the corner was giving Sean a thumbs-up.

My cheeks flamed. "We were just looking for the children's section."

One of her thin, penciled-in eyebrows shot up. "Really now?"

"Well, you know, we were a little sidetracked, with the stairs and his heart and—" I snapped my lips closed. There was no need to get into *that*.

There was laughter in Sean's voice as he said, "What I think Lucy is trying to say is we're looking for Mary Ellen Spero."

As he spoke, I noticed her lanyard. "Catherine M."

Wrinkles formed in a deep V on her forehead, reminding me, oddly, of a flock of geese flying south for the winter.

"Are you Catherine Murphy?" I asked. "Mary Ellen's sister?"

With a wave of her hand, she beckoned us to follow

her. I felt a bit like Gulliver in the children's area, towering over bookcases and tiny tables and chairs. Little faces peered up at us curiously, and in the quiet a soothing, rhythmic voice could be heard reading.

In a colorful nook filled with floor pillows, children sat rapt, listening to the woman read from *The Velveteen Rabbit*. Mary Ellen was heavyset, with a kind face and sad eyes. I liked her instantly, maybe because of knowing what she had endured the last twenty years.

"Story time will be over in ten minutes," Catherine said. "Who are you two?"

Sean handed her a card and related the story of Tristan Rourke.

Her fist closed over the card and her eyes clouded over. She motioned with her head to a corner where two desks had been pushed together, creating a separate work space. Sitting down, she said, "I had a feeling I'd hear his name again, but I had expected it three years ago when he was released from prison."

"You thought he'd come after Anthony again?" I asked, sitting in a chair in front of the desk. Sean took the other one.

"Absolutely. And I can't say I would have blamed him. I heard what Anthony had said to that boy. . . . It was unforgivable."

"By all accounts," Sean said, "Tristan isn't violent."

I glanced at her desk. It was piled with everything from Dr. Seuss to William Sachar. There was a stack of adult titles in the corner. Jane Austen's *Mansfield Park* was on top, but a bright yellow spine beneath that caught my attention. I pulled the book loose. *The Worst-Case Scenario Survival Handbook*. I smiled as I paged through it. It had everything from how to land a plane to how to run atop a speeding train. Handy, that one. I especially liked the chapter on how to wrestle an alligator.

I set the book down, picked up *Mansfield Park*. It was the only Jane Austen book I wasn't crazy about.

"Don't you think, Mr. Donahue, that every person has their limits? That there is only so much pain a person can endure without striking back? I assume you do, since you're here."

For a moment there it seemed as though she wasn't talking about Tristan.

Sean conceded with a nod.

"We felt it only right to warn you that Tristan now knows the truth," I said. "He also knows Meaghan is looking for him, trying to reunite."

"You say he knows where I live?"

Sean shifted uneasily in his seat. "He must have followed us there."

"I see. I'll need to make reservations at a hotel. I won't feel safe going home tonight. Imagine how easy it would be for him to set the house on fire while we slept? Or to break in? My house is old. The locks are old. The windows could easily be jimmied. I don't have an alarm system, not even a dog." She blinked rapidly. "I never felt the need before. It's a safe neighborhood. It *was* a safe neighborhood."

"Ms. Murphy," Sean began, but she held up a hand to stop him.

"No, no. I'm all right. It's simply a little jarring." She pulled in a deep breath. "I'll call a hotel. We'll have Anthony meet us there." Her brow crinkled again. "Do you think Tristan will follow him?"

I wanted to talk her out of it, to assure her Tristan would do no harm. Deep down, however, I felt his anger, his need to lash out over everything that had been taken away from him. Catherine, I feared, had reason to worry.

"It's probably best if he's careful," Sean said, "and takes precautions. Watches his rearview mirror, doubles back, takes side streets. Makes it easier to tell if someone is following you."

"Right," she said, shuffling papers nervously. "We'll do the same. He was a smart boy, and I could see him following us instead of Anthony, leading him right to his target. No need to take chances."

A knot of dread puckered in my stomach. Maybe we ought to talk to the FBI after all. It felt like we were in over our heads.

"Did you know Tristan well?" I asked.

"Of course. I knew all the kids. Tristan was bad news from the start, but Mary Ellen had a soft spot for the tougher cases, and especially Tristan. She felt as though he was only wearing a veneer to protect himself from more pain. We had a rough childhood ourselves. She felt she could make a difference in his life. And I have to say, it seemed like she was making a difference with him. He was making good grades, smiling more. Meaghan may have had something to do with that, too."

"How about Anthony?" Sean asked. "How'd he feel about the foster children?"

She rolled her eyes. "He was rarely home, which was mostly a blessing to those kids. If there was a male counterpart to Cinderella's evil stepmother, it would be Anthony Spero."

"Catherine!"

We turned and found Mary Ellen Spero staring at her sister, her mouth open in shock. "To say such a thing."

Catherine squared her shoulders, fiddled with her necklaces. "I speak the truth."

I certainly believed her.

Catherine introduced us and related why we were there.

Mary Ellen paled. Her hand fluttered at her throat, then went to her earlobe, where she tugged on a pearl earring. But all she said was, "The library is closing soon. You two better be on your way."

13

Dovie must have been waiting for us to get home. No sooner had Sean shut off the car than Rufus was dragging her across the lawn toward us.

I unlocked the door to my cottage while Sean let Thoreau and Rufus get to know each other. Rufus looked as though he could eat the Yorkie in one bite.

I turned off the alarm system and detached Grendel from my slacks. I lifted him up, murmured sweet nothings until he purred his contentment.

My Maine coon had a bit of separation anxiety, but he was easily appeased. He'd be even happier now that Thoreau was here. The two had an *interesting* relationship.

"I'm afraid to take Rufus off the leash outside," Dovie was saying as she came in. "He might go racing and fall off the bluff."

As soon as Grendel spotted Rufus, he clawed his way up my chest and onto my shoulder. His back arched; his fur stood up. Hissing, he dug his claws in deeper.

"Ow, ow, ow!"

Sean helped pull him off and set him on the floor. Grendel took off on his three legs toward my bedroom. Rufus chased him, obviously thinking he was a furry rubber chicken.

"Huh," Dovie said.

"Either he's jealous that Thoreau has a new friend or he doesn't like dogs bigger than him," I said, rubbing my shoulder. I checked for blood. Only a few drops.

Grendel dove under my bed. Hissing ensued.

I was pretty sure he'd stay under there until mollified that the big scary dog was gone. Cheese would go a long way in earning Grendel's forgiveness. He loved cheese.

Sean turned on the gas fireplace, caught my eye, and waggled his eyebrows.

My blood pressure ratcheted up a notch. I hadn't forgotten what he'd said earlier about him and me, me and him, in front of the flames.

Feeling myself flush, I said, "Tea, anyone?" Anything to distract from the lust in my eyes. No need to scandalize Dovie.

Who was I kidding? Dovie could probably teach me a thing or two, though I'd certainly never ask. Some things a granddaughter should never know.

"Lovely," Dovie said, settling in a leather chair. "I'm worried about the pup. He's not eating. I've tried everything."

"Did you call Marisol?" Sean asked.

"She's coming by tomorrow to take a look at him. Poor thing. He probably misses home."

I glanced at Sean. Unfortunately for us, Dovie looked like she was staying for the long haul. Damn it. I had plans that included Sean being naked and me having my way with him.

"You want tea?" I asked him, trying to keep the disappointment out of my voice.

He gave me a look, half regret, half promise. "No." He went to the fridge, pulled out a Sam Adams, and popped the top.

I put the kettle on, then checked on Grendel. He'd stopped hissing but was refusing to look at me. Rufus sat on his haunches, his tail wagging as he waited for Grendel to come out and play. Fat chance.

Thoreau paid no attention. He'd curled up in front of the fireplace. Apparently he'd had enough excitement tonight, being dognapped and all, and had worn his little doggy self out.

"Anything on Mac?" Dovie asked.

Sean sat on the sofa, dragged a hand over his face. He looked tired. "Not yet. We were trying to figure out if the theft of some of his prints a few years ago had anything to do with his disappearance now."

Dovie's eyes widened. If I tried hard enough, I could picture her aura. A golden glow that pulsed with energy. A pang of remorse hit me hard. Sometimes I really missed my ability to see the colors of the people I loved.

She said, "There's a connection?"

The kettle started a slow whistle. I pulled it from the flame. "It's not looking like it."

While I poured, Sean explained about Meaghan Archibald and Tristan Rourke.

"How gothic," Dovie enthused. "A wanted man, the woman who loves him."

I poured hot water into the mugs. "Sounds more like a Lifetime movie."

Sean smiled. "Or a disaster waiting to happen. Now that the FBI is involved."

Dovie gasped. "How do I miss all the good stuff?"

By the time we explained, my tea was cool enough to drink. I settled on the couch next to Sean, my legs curled under me, my thigh pressed against his. He glanced at me out of the corner of his eye. I pressed against him a little harder.

Dovie set her mug on the table. "So we're back to square one with Mac?"

"Essentially," Sean said.

She stood up. "Then you've got a lot of work ahead of you, young man."

Sean looked at me. "Did she just 'young man' me?"

" 'Fraid so."

"Should I be worried?" he asked.

"I'm standing right here!" She stomped her foot in case we weren't paying attention.

"Definitely," I answered him.

Wagging a finger at us, she said, "This other case can surely wait, LucyD?"

It was as much of an order as she was going to issue. "We can do both."

She arched an elegant eyebrow. "You think so?"

Fighting a yawn, I said, "I know."

"And just how can you be so sure?"

"I'm psychic?" I said, lifting a shoulder in a shrug.

A smile split her face. "Rub it in, why don't you?"

Dovie was forever moaning about marrying into a psychic family instead of being psychic herself. But I wasn't so sure. Dovie seemed to have some pretty special powers.

"Rufus, come! Come on. Let's go."

Case in point. Rufus bounded over, sat at Dovie's heel, and gazed up at her adoringly. Animals loved her.

Dovie clipped his leash, straightened the pink bandanna still tied around his neck. It reminded me to check on Christa to see if she wanted to visit the dog. I stood, kissed Dovie's cheeks. "I'll check in with you tomorrow. Promise."

She clucked my chin, motioned for me to follow her to the door. Outside, she said, "Have you asked him yet?"

I wrapped my arms around myself for warmth. "Asked him what?"

"To move in, of course!"

For a second there, I thought she was going to stamp her foot again, but she only leveled me with a stare I couldn't look away from.

"It's too soon." How many times was I going to have to say it?

"What are you waiting for?" she asked.

"I don't know, Dovie."

Her green gaze softened and filled with compassion that twisted my heart. "I may not be psychic," she said, "but I know love when I see it, LucyD. And I know you're no fool. So do what needs to be done. I'm too old to be worrying about your love life."

"Em's is up for grabs."

Dovie swatted me. "Sass! I'm leaving. See me leaving?"

"I see."

"Don't beg me to stay. I won't."

I laughed as Rufus pulled her down the walkway. "Rufus wouldn't let you anyway."

"And don't think I've forgiven you for dumping him on me!" she called, her voice rising above the crashing waves.

She wasn't fooling me for a second. She already adored that dog. I went back inside, my teeth chattering.

I walked over to the hearth, held my hands out to the flames. My palms warmed. Sean came up behind me, wrapped his arms around me, and pulled my hair aside so he could have free access to my neck. He kissed and nuzzled.

In between he said, "Did that conversation outside have anything to do with what you saw earlier when you held my hand?"

I stiffened, pulled away. "No."

"What did you see, Lucy?"

I fluffed a pillow and decided now might be a good time to check for loose change in between the cushions. "I saw Thoreau with Rourke."

"What else did you see?"

Shit. Only one quarter and lots of crumbs. "I don't know what you mean."

"You're a lousy liar."

Huh. Twice I'd heard that today. I gave up looking for loose change—and made a mental note to vacuum in between those cushions more. "Lying? Me? Ha!"

He dared to smile. As if that dimple of his could distract me enough to tell him the truth.

He knew me too well.

"All right," I said, about to spill my guts. "It was you

and me and we were . . . and well—" Damn, this was harder than I thought.

"And?"

My cell phone rang.

"Let it go," he said.

I jumped for it. "It may be important! Really important. Life-or-death important."

He rolled his eyes as I answered.

"Talk me off the ledge," Mum said.

"What ledge?" To Sean I whispered, "See? Life or death."

"The cheesecake ledge."

Or maybe not. "Is this about the diet?"

Sean went into the bedroom, lay flat on the floor, and lifted the bed skirt. A loud hiss filled the air.

"Try cheese," I told Sean.

"Are you talking about cheese to me?" Mum said. "I'm dying!"

"Not of the cake variety. The cheese is for Grendel."

"Oh. Okay. Like that makes it all right."

"You're cranky."

"I'm starving."

"You don't need to diet. You're perfect the way you are."

"Yes, I do. You've seen those girls your father usually goes for. All size minus zeros, jutting cheek- and hip bones. I couldn't find my hip bone if I had a map with a big X on it and a shovel."

"Mum." I dropped into my favorite chair.

"Lucy."

"Eat the cheesecake."

"What kind of help are you?"

"Dad obviously likes you as is."

"As is? Like I'm a used car without a warranty?"

My call-waiting beeped. Thank God. "Gotta go, Mum."

"Wait! What about the cheesecake?"

"One little tiny bite won't hurt. Just do some extra cardio tomorrow."

"Extra cardio? Brilliant! Smooches."

I clicked over to the other call. "Lucy Valentine."

"It's Meaghan," she said. "I just got your message. I can't believe Tristan is wanted by the FBI! What do they think he did?"

Interesting wording. She wasn't ready to believe the worst of him. Yet. "Technically not wanted. Just a person of interest at this point." I explained about the theft ring.

"Wow."

"What I need to know from you is how you want us to proceed. Or if you want us to at all."

The fridge opened, closed. I heard the crinkle of a cellophane wrapper. There was a long stretch of silence over the phone line. I didn't want to tell Meaghan we had met with Tristan, spoken with him. Not yet. Not until she knew whether she wanted to continue with the case. "Meaghan?"

"It's a lot to take in."

"I know. Why don't you sleep on it? It's a big decision."

"I'll call you in the morning," she said softly.

I hung up. Sean was rinsing his hand. "Grendel took the cheese, and gave me a nice thank-you." A long scratch stretched across his wrist.

I grabbed a paper towel, wadded it up, and dampened

it. Carefully I lifted Sean's wrist and dabbed at the wound.

"And he still won't come out from under the bed. Was that Meaghan?"

"She's going to call with a decision in the morning."

I lifted his arm to my mouth, kissed it. "Better?"

His eyes sparkled. "I'm not sure. Try again."

I gently kissed his forearm again, working my way up to the tender spot on the underside of his elbow. "Now?"

"My arm's okay, but I have this other ache. . . ."

"Oh? I'm feeling a bit achy myself."

"We'll just have to see what we can do about that." He pulled in, kissed me hungrily as his hands slipped under my shirt, skimmed my skin. The heat from his palms seeped in, infusing my blood with a heat so blistering I wanted to strip off my clothes.

Sean must have read my mind. He unbuttoned my blazer, let it slide to the floor. His fingers grabbed the hem of my sweater, pulled it over my head.

My hands threaded through his hair as I kissed him with blind passion. It was always like this with us—a desperate desire, as though we were never going to let each other go. As though we knew that at any moment what we had could be gone.

His hands went to the buttons of my shirt. "Just how many layers do you have on, Ms. Valentine?"

"Only two more. Well, three if you count the bra."

He groaned. "You're killing me."

I smiled against his lips. "It's winter. It's cold. I need layers."

The buttons were finally free and he slid my shirt down my arms. "Funny," he said as he lifted my cami-sole. "You don't feel cold."

I tugged his shirt over his head, ran my hands down his chest until they stopped on the button of his jeans. With a twist, I had it undone. "Imagine that."

He was reaching for the hook on my bra when my phone rang my tinny version of the *Hawaii Five-O* theme song.

Sean's hand stilled. "It's late."

I glanced at the ringing phone. "Only bad news comes this late."

I thought of all the cases I'd helped Aiden with. The late-night calls usually meant a fresh case, someone recently reported missing. Time was of the essence. There was a three-hour window crucial to an abduction.

"Go on," Sean said, handing me the phone.

I let out a breath, stared longingly at my hand, still on the zipper of his pants. I reached for the phone.

"Sorry, Lucy," Aiden said when I answered. "I know it's late."

"A new case?" I was suddenly chilled, though it had nothing to do with my lack of clothing.

"In a way. I just got a call from Agent Thomas."

An icy finger of dread slid down my spine. I shivered. "And?"

"He wanted to let us know . . . I'm sorry to tell you this, but Anthony Spero is dead. . . . And there's a massive manhunt on for Tristan Rourke."

14

For the three hours I was actually in bed, I hadn't been able to sleep. I just lay there, wide awake, staring at the shadows shifting along the ceiling. I was afraid to move, to jar Sean. I was afraid of what the day would bring. How was I going to break the news to Meaghan that Tristan was wanted for murder? I was just . . . afraid.

I didn't like it. Not a single bit. Yet I hadn't figured out how to change it.

For years I had busied myself with dead-end jobs, numbly going about my days, feeling I couldn't use my psychic abilities for anything other than finding the odd lost object. A book, a cell phone, car keys. Nothing *important*. I'd spent almost ten years flitting from one job to another as a paralegal, a dog walker, a day-care worker. As hard as I tried, nothing made me feel like I was making any difference with my life.

But when I found that lost boy in Wompatuck, utilizing my abilities in an altogether new way, I realized I'd held the key to my happiness all along. Using my ESP, I had the power to help other people, to locate loved ones, to find closure. It was a calling, truly a gift. One I treasured.

Why, then, did I suddenly feel like going back to work as a telemarketer? Back to the days when missing-person cases were news bites, when evil was something on the fringe of someone else's life, never smack-dab in the middle of mine.

On days like today, I had to remember the sheer joy I received from reuniting long-lost loves, from finding a missing child. Even the simple pleasure of locating a lost ring for my mum.

And I would do well to remember I'd hated telemarketing. That job had lasted less than three hours.

By seven, I was up and dressed. I fed some Cheerios to Odysseus, who immediately stuffed them in his cheeks and went back to his burrow.

I glanced at Sean, who was sleeping on his side, a fistful of blankets twisted under his arm. He was a restless sleeper, often tossing and turning fitfully in the night, his dreams taking him places I suspected I'd never been.

What startled me most was that before now it hadn't mattered. Whatever he'd been through had shaped him into the man he was today. But now I longed to know more of him. I wanted to know all those little secrets, his dreams, even his nightmares. It only seemed fair since he knew mine.

I tapped my leg to get Thoreau's attention. He bounded to the floor. Not to be outdone, Grendel raced him to the kitchen. I fed them both, setting their bowls a good two feet apart (Grendel had been known to distract Thoreau to steal his food), and poured myself a cup of coffee. It was endlessly amusing to watch them eat, with Grendel's method of dragging his kibble from his bowl to pounce on it and Thoreau inhaling rather than eating so Grendel didn't steal his breakfast.

A soft knock sounded from the front door. Thoreau yipped and bounced on all four paws as if he were on a trampoline.

"You're ferocious," I said to him as I peeked out the window before opening the door.

"I saw your light on while I was walking the beast," Dovie said. Rufus sat peacefully at her heel.

"Vicious." If Rufus and Thoreau tag-teamed, they might be able to take down a Slim Jim.

"I have a huge breakfast cooking up at the house. Come up. Marisol's here."

I brightened. "She is?"

"Came to see the pup."

Rufus was hardly a pup, though sometimes he still acted like one. "Sean's still sleeping."

"Leave him a note."

"I haven't showered yet."

"We're scandalized," Dovie drawled. Slyly she added, "The waffles are already on the table."

My stomach ached and I wasn't very hungry, but waffles were my favorite and Dovie had made the effort to come down here. "You make a tempting offer."

She winked and strode off the porch. "See you in a couple of minutes."

I let Thoreau out to do his thing, rinsed my mug, and left a note for Sean on the counter next to the coffeepot.

The sun was barely breaking the horizon as I trudged through the snow and carefully navigated Dovie's back steps. I could smell bacon from the deck. I stamped the snow from my boots and looked down toward my cottage, nestled at the bottom of the lane, the bluffs and a fifty-foot drop on one side, a small garden and woods on the other. It was an idyllic little house, postcard perfect. I felt such strong affection that it was *my* home.

I turned to go into Dovie's, and from the corner of my eye I caught a flash of movement in the trees. Startled, I squinted. I couldn't see anything, anyone, yet there was a feeling deep in my stomach.

The back door swung open. "Lucy!"

I nearly fell over the railing. Pressing my hand to my pounding heart, I asked Preston, "Why not scare me to death?"

"It would be a great story. What are you looking at?"

"Do you see anything in the woods?"

The woods were still rimmed in dusky darkness, the pines a deep dark green, the scruff along the forest floor a dense, dark ominous cloak.

Preston squinted. "Trees?"

"You're funny." I eyed the woods. All was still. "What are you doing here anyway?"

"Dovie invited me for breakfast. There's waffles." Her nose wrinkled. "You haven't showered yet?"

I brushed past her, leaving my paranoia behind. I was being overly sensitive was all. A perfectly normal response after what had happened last night. Anthony Spero had been walking from the parking lot of the hotel where Catherine had booked rooms to the front door when he'd been run over by a speeding car. He'd died on the way to the hospital from massive brain trauma. Boston PD had confiscated the hotel's security footage and was looking for the car, but there was only one suspect.

And there was still no sign of Tristan Rourke.

In the kitchen, Dovie had the *South Shore Beacon* spread across the island. Marisol and Em were sitting at the breakfast table. Preston and I joined them. Em had brochures spread out in front of her.

Eye to eye with Rufus, Marisol engaged him in conversation. "I know you miss him," she said, "but you need to eat."

Rufus tipped his head.

"Even if you're not very hungry," she added.

He pawed his rubber chicken, which was lying at Marisol's feet. She sighed and threw the chicken. Rufus galloped through the kitchen and down the hallway.

"I don't know, Dovie. I think he may need to come into the clinic for some tests."

Dovie took off her reading glasses. "You really think so? He seems fine other than the food."

I eyed Em's brochures. Palm trees and lots of beaches. "Are you going somewhere?"

"Hawaii," Em said. "You were right, Lucy."

"I was?"

"She was?" Preston echoed.

Em's hair was pulled up and twisted into a sloppy bun. The look showed off her high cheekbones, long graceful neck. "I shouldn't spend my whole break just sitting around, moping. I'm trading in my plane tickets to Paris and going somewhere warm and sunny. I think I'll spend whole afternoons on a beach just . . . being."

"Paris?" Preston asked. "You're trading in Paris for Hawaii? Are you crazy?"

I shoved the plate of waffles toward her and glared. "Aren't you hungry?"

"It's okay, Lucy," Em said. To Preston, she clarified,

"Joseph and I were supposed to go to Paris for our honeymoon."

"Oh." Preston stared at her plate. She forked a huge piece of waffle and made a show of shoving it in her mouth. Her cheeks puffed out, reminding me of Odysseus. "Sorry," she mumbled.

"It's okay," Em said. "I think the more I talk about the breakup the better I'll be. I mean, thanks to Oscar, I know Joseph and I weren't meant to last—"

My stomach free-fell.

Marisol started coughing, hacking really.

Dovie rushed over, started slapping Marisol on the back, and shoved a piece of bacon in Em's mouth. "Tasty, isn't it? Now, Marisol, what were you saying about Rufus?"

At his name, Rufus barked and brought his chicken over and set it in Preston's lap. She threw it down the hall. "Wait. Back up. How would Oscar know—"

"Rufus could really be sick," Marisol said loudly. "We should get him checked out immediately." She jumped up. "The sooner, the better."

Em mouthed, *Sorry,* to me. She'd forgotten Preston didn't know about the auras. Easy enough to do— Preston was around a lot these days, so much so that it was hard to remember she wasn't another branch of our dysfunctional, piecemeal family tree, but a reporter who'd love nothing better than a big scoop.

"Right now?" Dovie asked.

"Right now. You can pick him up this afternoon."

"I can get him on my way home from work," I volunteered.

"No!" Marisol shouted.

We all stared at her.

"I mean, there will be paperwork. It has to be Dovie."

"I'll get his leash," Dovie said.

Marisol grabbed my arm. "Can I talk to you for a minute?"

As she pulled me into the front hall, I heard Preston say to Em, "How much do you know about Cutter?"

I should have stayed in bed.

Marisol's shoes tapped along the slate floor in the entranceway. A wide stairway split the large front hall, and I leaned against the oak newel post. "What's going on, Marisol?"

"Shh, shh. Okay, so you know how you're looking for a boyfriend for Dovie?" Marisol's dark eyes gleamed. "I was thinking she'd be a great match with Dr. Kearney." She took her quilted coat from the rack near the door and did a fancy looping thing with her scarf.

"Your boss, Dr. Kearney?"

Indirect sunlight was starting to spill through the transom window and sidelights, illuminating just how cozy Dovie had made her home over the years. The warm woods, the natural elements like the stone floor, and the rich colors all worked so well together. Throw in the little bits of glitz and glam, like the tiny crystals on the curtains, and the place fairly radiated Dovie's personality—the interesting mix between an elegant woman and the showgirl she used to be. "Didn't you sleep with him?"

"No, he's twenty years older than me!" Her tone tried for offended but couldn't quite pull it off.

I tapped my chin. "Didn't you *want* to sleep with him?"

Sheepishly she tucked her hands in her coat pockets and rocked on her heels. "Briefly, during my Professor Higgins phase."

Marisol had gone through many phases. "But didn't you two date?"

"We had coffee. Once. Lucy!" She clapped her hands. "You're getting sidetracked."

"But he's twenty years younger than Dovie."

Marisol grinned. "I know. Isn't it great? Dovie as a cougar?"

"What cougar?" Dovie asked, coming down the hall with Rufus, his toenails clacking on the stone. "Don't tell me you have one at the clinic."

Marisol's dark eyes sparkled. "I will this afternoon."

Dovie glanced my way with an I-didn't-serve-mimosas-this-morning-I-swear kind of look, but before she could say anything, Marisol grabbed the leash, the rubber chicken, and kissed my cheek, then Dovie's. "Thanks for breakfast. Bye!" she yelled down the hall, and slipped out the front door, Rufus leading the way down the curving walkway.

Dovie stared after them with a long-lost look in her eye.

I sidled up, slid my arm around her shoulders. "You're going to miss him, aren't you?"

"Ha! He's such a nuisance. Always begging me to throw that damn rubber chicken." She craned her neck to watch as Marisol opened the back door of her SUV and urged Rufus inside. Dovie might not have realized it, but her hands were shooing him into the car from afar. "I'm going to get carpal tunnel from that mutt."

"Uh-huh," I said. I closed the door and Dovie moved to peek through the sidelight as Marisol drove down the lane, disappeared down the slope leading to the street.

"Well, back to the real world. I need to get ready for Zumba, and stop at the bakery, and my nails are in desperate need of a manicure. Oh, and a massage would be heavenly." She stopped, grabbed my arm. "He'll be okay, right?"

I smiled. "He's in the best of hands."

She nodded, but I knew she wouldn't be convinced until Rufus was home.

In the kitchen, Em was alone at the breakfast table. "Where's Preston?" I asked.

"Powder room. What do you think? Kauai or Maui?" She held two brochures, one in each hand, as if weighing them.

"Can't go wrong with either." Dovie patted Em's head as she walked by.

I noticed the newspaper on the counter. I skimmed the article. "Preston wrote a story about Rufus getting a new home?"

Dovie rinsed a mug, set it in the dishwasher. "I may have mentioned it would be a good way to keep Mac's name in the news. Someone has to know something. People just don't disappear without a trace."

I worried my lip. I didn't want to burst Dovie's bubble, but many people often disappeared just that way. Poof, gone, as Preston would say.

"I'm going to go back to Mac's house today. Mac's granddaughter, Christa, mentioned something about Rufus's food. I wonder if he eats a special blend. That might explain why he's not eating now. While I'm there I can press Jemima Hayes for more information. Have you met her husband?"

"Rick? No."

"Rick Hayes?" Em said, dropping her brochures. "My God," Em sputtered. "I had a poster of him on my wall as a teenager."

"Who?" Preston said, coming into the room.

"Rick Hayes," I said.

"Jemima's husband? Why?"

"He was hot," Em said.

"He's *old,*" Preston said, wrinkling her nose.

Dovie shot her a look. Rick had to be at least twenty-five years younger than my grandmother. And if there was one thing Dovie didn't like being labeled, it was old.

Em explained how Rick had been a contemporary of Bryan Adams and George Michael (a name Preston actually recognized but for all the wrong reasons), but he had never really had a hit until the late nineties, when one of his songs was chosen as the theme for a popular sitcom. It stayed at the top of the charts for months and even won a Grammy. Rick toured for a while, the arenas getting smaller and smaller. Now he took jobs wherever he could.

"I saw him sing at the Marshfield Fair last year," Em said, heading for the coffeepot. "He wasn't very good, but he still has a certain appeal."

"He's broke," Dovie said, "and trying to sell a reality show based on him making a comeback."

Shaking her head, Em said, "That's just sad."

There was nothing worse than a fallen idol.

I glanced at the plate of waffles, but sadly I had no appetite. I poured a cup of juice.

Preston said, "I have to go— Algebra calls. Have you talked to Meaghan Archibald yet, Lucy?"

I'd called Preston right after I hung up with Aiden last night. "Not yet. I'll call you as soon as I do."

As Dovie walked Preston to the front door, Em looked at me. "Am I crazy?"

I smiled. "Why do you ask?"

"For this?" She held up the brochures. "For wanting sunshine, warm sand, and lots of fruity drinks with umbrellas? I wouldn't be opposed to a muscled, gorgeous cabana boy, either, but I don't want to be greedy."

"Crazy like a fox! It's a great idea, and with spring break it's the perfect time to go. I just hate seeing you go alone."

She lifted her shoulder in a shrug. "It won't be so bad. It'll give me some time to sort through my life." Jumping up, she launched into a hula dance. "Just think, this time tomorrow I'll be on a beach in Kauai."

She hulaed around the breakfast table. "Did you know I wanted to go to Kauai in the first place for the honeymoon, but no. Kauai wasn't good enough for Joseph. You know what?" she asked, swaying her arms. "I gave in a lot with him. Now I don't have to. It's freeing. I'm free. To do what I want. See who I want."

I hulaed with her and said softly, "Like Aiden?"

A smile spread across her face. "Maybe."

They'd been tiptoeing around each other, fighting their feelings for months. But now . . . Now Em was free.

I swayed my hips. "How long will you be gone? A week?"

I couldn't help a tiny stab of envy. A vacation sounded wonderful. An escape from life. Just for a little while. I could easily see Sean and me taking a long walk on a beach, watching the sun set in the Pacific. No missing persons, no one wanted by the FBI. Heaven.

Except . . . that vision.

I winced as pain shot through my stomach. I had to stop thinking about it.

Em's arms jerked up and down. She really needed hula lessons. "I'm going to skip classes tomorrow and Friday. That gives me ten days."

"I'm jealous."

"It is a bit decadent, isn't it?" She stopped dancing. "There's a flight at two. I'll take a train into town."

When Em set her mind to something there was no stopping her. "Take my car. You can leave it with Raphael and take the water taxi to Logan. You don't want to lug your suitcases on the train."

She threw her arms around me. "What would I do without you?"

I hummed a Hawaiian song that came out sounding more like a Swiss yodel. We danced side by side, giggling like we were five years old again and making up dances in my mother's music room.

The back door opened and Thoreau bounded in, barking and shaking snow from his fur. Sean stood in the doorway with a dazzling smile, taking in the scene. Em and I kept on hulaing.

"Em's going to Hawaii," I said.

"I'm jealous," he said. He looked handsomely rumpled with his bed head. He must have seen the note I left and come straight up to the house.

"You two should go," Em said. "You know, when this case is over. You two deserve a vacation. Sun, sand, romance," she added, batting her eyelashes.

Oooh, oooh, and oooh la la.

"What? Who's going where?" Dovie asked, joining in the hula. Her moves put Em's and mine to shame.

"Lucy and Sean. To Hawaii," Em said.

"No, no. Just dreaming," I said.

Dovie jabbed my rib cage playfully and winked. "Sometimes, LucyD, dreams really come true."

I glanced at Sean.

I love you, Lucy Valentine.

"I know," I said to Dovie. "I know."

15

Sean had stolen Dovie's newspaper and had it spread out on my couch. He leaned back, stretched his arms over his head. His gray eyes looked nearly opaque in the morning light. Stubble covered his superhero jaw, and the slightest hint of darkness caressed the skin under his eyes. He hadn't slept well, and it showed.

I'd taken a quick shower and was letting my hair air-dry today, using extra antifrizz cream to control the waviness. Sean had already put away the dishes in the dishwasher and cleaned the coffeepot.

"Do you feel okay?" he asked.

I didn't want to lie. "So-so."

He came into the kitchen. "You haven't been sleeping well."

"Neither have you."

"This isn't about me." With the pad of his thumb, he traced my jawline. I pressed my cheek into his palm, let my eyes close.

He leaned in, rested his forehead against mine. His hands slid down my arms, stopping just above my hands. I turned my palms over so they hovered just under his touch.

My fingers tingled with the electricity.

I couldn't explain the how or the why. I could just feel. The electricity. The magic.

He kissed me. A soul-searching, heart-pounding, all-out curl-a-girl's-toes kind of kiss.

By the time we pulled apart, a small drumbeat of happiness was pulsing through me. I took a deep breath. It was now or never, a complete leap of faith. "Move in with me."

There! I'd said it. And it hadn't been all that hard, either. Maybe Mum and Dovie, Suz and Preston were right. It was meant to be.

Only . . . Only Sean wasn't looking as happy as I thought he should.

"I don't know if that's a good idea," he finally said.

I quickly grabbed a sponge and began wiping down the counters, scrubbing at invisible spots. Throwing the sponge in the sink, I turned on him. "Why isn't it a good idea? You practically live here anyway. You have clothes here, a toothbrush, deodorant, your own shampoo, your favorite beer in the fridge, your own side of the bed, and books on the nightstand. Thoreau has food in the pantry, his own food bowls, and a doggy bed. Hell, you *already* live here—there's no 'practically' about it."

At the sound of his name, Thoreau lifted his head from his sunny spot on the floor and stared at us as if annoyed for waking him from his nap.

Sean smiled at me.

"Don't you dare smile at me right now." I jabbed him with a fingertip.

Trying to be serious, he pressed his lips together.

I folded my arms. "I don't think this is funny."

A strangled I-can't-hold-it-in-any-longer laugh escaped him.

I picked up the sponge, eyed him, and squeezed it over his head.

Water dripped down his face. "Is that how it's going to be?"

"Yes. Yes, it is. Smile at me, will you."

He turned the water on in the sink. Picked up the sprayer.

"You wouldn't," I dared.

He tipped his soggy head to the side, his black hair curling at the tips, and sprayed me, a quick, freezing-cold blast. Water dripped down my nose, off my chin. My shirt was immediately soaked through.

Grendel watched us from the top of the fridge, his tail swishing back and forth as if we were great entertainment.

I grabbed for the sprayer, using hips and elbows to my advantage, and all the while water rained down on us as though we were caught in a spring shower.

Amused no longer, Grendel *rreowed* and made a run for it.

Sean held on tight, his laughter mixing with mine.

I lost my footing on the slippery floor and made a grab for his shirt. He caught my wrist, but I still fell onto my backside, my legs splaying out, taking his out from under him. He grabbed onto the counter to help break his fall, but the wood floor was too slippery and he fell backward, landing next to me.

With goofy smiles, we lay there, staring at each other a long time, our chests heaving with exertion, the water running in the sink a backdrop to our heavy breathing.

Finally, I said, "You pissed off my cat."

Sean rolled slightly and kissed me. My body sizzled at his touch, the water droplets evaporating. He rose up on his elbows, cupped my face, kissed my cheeks, my nose. "I can't move in yet because you're not ready."

"How can you say that? I wouldn't have asked if I wasn't ready."

"You were caught up in the moment."

"Was not."

He smiled, that damn dimple popping. "Were, too. You're ready here," he said, pressing his hand to my heart. "But not here." He tapped the top of my head. "Because you haven't quite realized it yet."

"Realized what?" A drop of water dripped off his chin onto my neck. I felt it sliding downward, tickling its way to my nape.

"That I'd never willingly leave you." He levered off the ground. Reaching out, he grabbed my wrist and helped me to my feet. "When you realize that, I'll gladly move in."

I stared at him. "It's like you're talking in riddles."

We did have something special between us. Something that went beyond simple attraction. Something no other Valentine ever had. But was it enough?

He pulled out a roll of paper towels. "You forget. I can *feel* it, Lucy. And I still feel the fear. Until it's gone . . ."

I grabbed a dish towel, soaked up some water. I had forgotten. Forgotten he could feel my emotions when he touched my palm. Only he didn't realize the fear I was currently feeling wasn't from commitment—it came from seeing him lifeless. And I had no idea how I'd ever get rid of the fear that his life would be cut short due to his bad heart.

"You're lucky I'm a patient guy."

"You're lucky I don't kick you and your tooth-brush out."

He smirked. "You'd never."

My cell phone rang the *Hawaii Five-O* theme. I was smiling as I answered—it didn't last.

"Mac Gladstone has liver cancer," Aiden said. "The doctor gave him three to five years to live if he started treatment right away."

Limply I leaned against the counter. "When did Mac find out?"

"End of summer."

"He didn't start treatment, did he?"

"No," Aiden said. "He has maybe a year, tops."

Sean continued to wipe down the kitchen, but he was watching me carefully.

"What does this mean for the investigation?" I asked.

I heard the fatigue in Aiden's voice: "The hell if I know."

"We're going back to Jemima's today. I'll let you know what we find out."

Sean and I often worked together on cases for the state police—especially when my visions were involved. This was the first time Aiden was working with us on one of Sean's cases and it felt a little awkward. "Thanks for checking with the doctor."

Sean and I never would have been able to get that kind of information. The state police had a lot more pull—including the ability to get warrants—than we did.

"By the way, the car that hit Spero was found around the corner from the hotel last night. It had been stolen from a nearby neighboorhood. It's being processed."

"Any word on Tristan Rourke's whereabouts?"

"No."

"How sure are the police that Tristan is the one who ran down Spero?" I was holding out hope it had all been a mistake, some sort of coincidence.

"One hundred percent, Lucy."

"The surveillance tapes were conclusive?"

"Not at all. They were too grainy to see anything. Completely useless. But they don't matter when there's an eyewitness."

"A witness?"

"Yeah. Saw the whole thing go down and made a positive ID."

A positive ID? On Tristan Rourke? That could only mean one thing. It had to have been someone who knew him. "Who was it?" I asked. "The witness?"

I heard some rustling of papers. "The guy's wife. Mary Ellen Spero."

16

A half hour later, Grendel was still mad about getting wet. He liked a bath almost as much as he liked Rufus—and Grendel's impromptu shower in the kitchen had him skulking around the cottage in search of things to destroy. I already twice had to stop him from climbing the drapes. I brought out my best kitty placater—a can of tuna.

As soon as Grendel heard the pop top, all was forgiven as he rushed over and twined his body around my legs, doing feline figure eights as I spooned the tuna into his bowl.

The pipes knocked in the wall as Sean finished up his shower. I was trying to work through what he'd said, but I simply didn't understand. Yes, I was scared—who wouldn't be in my situation? But I was willing to take a leap of faith and didn't understand why Sean wasn't yet. It was giving me a headache, trying to sort it out.

My cell rang as I was reaching for the Advil bottle. "This is Lucy," I answered, the phone pressed to my ear as I shook two tablets into my palm. My stomach was also still hurting, but I was trying to ignore the pain.

"Hi, Lucy, it's Christa Hayes."

I checked the clock. It was a little after nine. "Are you feeling all right? Shouldn't you be in school?"

"Late start today. I was wondering if I could come by and see Rufus after school today. I saw the article in the paper this morning. I miss him."

"I'm really sorry, Christa, but he's at the vet's."

Her voice rose. "He is? Why?"

"Just for a checkup. He's not eating very well. Is there a special kind of food he likes?"

"I told my mom he needed his food. . . . I can bring it over after school today."

"Actually, Sean and I were coming over to see your parents this morning. I can pick it up then."

"You're coming soon?"

"About half an hour. Is that all right?"

She coughed. "I mean, yeah. That's fine. Just, ah . . ."

"What?"

"Nothing. It's fine. Thanks. I won't be there—classes are starting soon—but I'll have Esme leave it out for you."

"Esme?"

"The housekeeper."

"Okay. Rufus should be back tonight if you want to stop by then."

"I have play practice tonight, but maybe tomorrow?"

"Sure," I said, imagining that it was hard for her to lose not only her grandfather but her dog as well.

I'd just hung up with her when my phone rang while still in my hand. I glanced at the readout, cringed.

"It's Meaghan," she said as I answered.

Her tone had lost some of its joy. She must have heard the news about Tristan. "I'm glad you called." I downed the Advil with a gulp of water.

"Did you hear the news about Tristan?" she asked.

Grendel was hissing at Thoreau, a warning to stay away from his tuna, as I walked into the bedroom. I wanted to get some laundry started before Sean and I left to meet with Jemima. I stripped the sheets from the bed, dropped them onto the floor.

"Unfortunately, yes." I tossed a fitted sheet over the mattress as the water turned off in the bathroom.

"The police think it was Tristan who ran him over," she said. "It's just not possible. Tristan isn't the violent type, Lucy; he just isn't."

"Meaghan, did you know Anthony Spero told Tristan you were dead and that it was Tristan's fault you took your own life? It's what led to the attack eight years ago."

"He didn't!" she cried in a quivery voice. "He wouldn't. That's so . . . so cruel. Beyond cruel."

I couldn't agree more, but it didn't change the fact that Tristan now had a very big motive for killing Anthony. I gave up on getting the corners of the fitted sheet to cooperate one-handed. Sitting on the edge of the bed, I said, "Tristan just found out last night you were alive. That kind of shock might have led to what happened to Spero."

"He thought I was dead all these years? How do you know all this?"

I figured it couldn't hurt at this point to let her know. "Sean and I spoke with Tristan last night."

"You did? When? How's he seem? How does he look? Did he say anything about me?"

And just like that, I could picture Meaghan in high school. "He was angry, Meaghan. Anthony had lied to him. Not a little white lie, either."

"Did he want to meet me?"

I sighed. This was what I was afraid of. "On his own terms."

"What's that mean?"

"He wanted to us to hand over your information to him so he could contact you on his own."

"Did you?" There was an edge of panic in her voice, and I realized it had nothing to do with Tristan being a criminal and everything to do with her thinking she might never see him again.

"No, I needed to check with you first. You're forgetting he's a wanted man, Meaghan."

"I don't believe it. I just don't. It's not in Tristan's nature."

Mary Ellen Spero might disagree. "I hate to be blunt, Meaghan, but denial can be dangerous."

Sean stepped out of the bathroom, wrapped in a towel. I lost my train of thought for a moment as my gaze skimmed his muscled shoulders, chest, stomach. His scar, a thin red line, marred the skin near his left shoulder. If only it was as easy as kissing and making it better. . . . He'd be the healthiest guy around.

Sean raised a questioning eyebrow at the phone.

Meaghan, I mouthed.

"What if he's not involved?" she was saying. "What if this was some colossal coincidence?"

"There's an eyewitness."

"Eyewitnesses can be wrong."

She was sounding desperate, and as I knew her history, it worried me. This news might send her over the edge again. "Nevertheless, as my client, I'm worried about *you*."

"You have no reason to be. I'm fine. And I want you to give Tristan my information."

Sean pressed a kiss to my neck as he crossed the room. He slipped on a pair of black trousers and took the floppy corner of the fitted sheet, pulling it over the edge. "I'll do this," he whispered, grabbing the top sheet.

"It's not that easy anymore, Meaghan." I scooted off the bed.

"Why not?"

Grabbing the pile of bedding from the floor, I headed to the door. "There's no way to contact him. He said he'd be in touch with us, which isn't likely to happen now that he's a wanted man. Besides, that sort of thing might be considered aiding and abetting."

"Are you dropping my case?" she asked.

In light of the new charges against Tristan, I really had no other choice. "I'm sorry," I said. "I wish it had turned out differently."

I tried not to dwell on the guilt. That it was because of Lost Loves—of me—that Tristan had any current contact with the Speros at all.

I brought the load of laundry into the kitchen, where a stackable washer and dryer hid behind a pair of bifold doors.

"You can't be serious."

I felt the hurt in her tone. "Look, Meaghan, I'm a little out of my comfort zone here. What's going on now is beyond any service I can provide for you through Lost Loves."

There was a long pause. "You work closely with SD Investigations, right? With Sean?"

I blushed at how closely I'd worked with Sean last night. I started the wash. "I do. Lost Loves is part of their agency, too."

"I want to hire Sean, then."

"Technically, you already have." The bed was made and Sean was fully dressed by the time I went back into my bedroom. "And I'm afraid he can't help you, either. He has to follow the same rules."

"No, not to find Tristan, we can put that on the back burner for now, but to prove he had nothing to do with that accident. I don't care what it costs. This isn't fair to Tristan. I have to fight for him, Lucy."

I worried my lip. On one level, fighting for Tristan would make any romantic swoon, the good girl saving the bad boy. But on a more realistic level, Tristan was a dangerous man and seeking him out was akin to playing with fire.

"It's not illegal for a private investigator to look into what happened, is it?"

"No. . . ." Though the police probably wouldn't be too happy about it.

"Could you run it by Sean? See what he thinks?"

"Hold on a second, okay?"

"Yeah, okay."

I covered the phone with my hand.

"What's going on?" Sean asked.

"I had to drop the case."

He nodded. We had already talked about it.

"But she wants to hire you through SDI. To clear

Tristan's name. She refuses to believe he had anything to do with it. I told her I'd run it past you, but I really think it's not a good idea for us to stay involved in this case."

"I'll do it," he said without hesitation.

Slack-jawed, I stared at him.

"Here," he said, motioning to the phone. I handed it over. "Meaghan? This is Sean Donahue."

His back was to me as he spoke and I could see his broad shoulders tighten with tension again. Muscles bunched along his spine. Damp dark hair curled along the nape of his neck.

I blatantly eavesdropped as he made plans to meet with Meaghan this afternoon to get the paperwork out of the way.

When he hung up, he slowly turned around.

I lifted an eyebrow, waiting for an explanation.

"Trust me on this?" he asked.

Trust me. I'd asked him to trust me not so long ago, when I had no one else to turn to. He hadn't hesitated. It was all about leaps with Sean, no baby steps. No easing into a relationship. It was headfirst or nothing at all.

I softened. Nodded.

He handed me the phone and walked out of the bedroom without another word.

The front gate at Jemima Hayes's house was open wide. We pulled into the drive, the tires of Sean's Mustang splashing over rivulets of melting snow. Sunbeams reflected off Mac's glass house, making it sparkle like the glistening water beyond the bluff.

I'd called ahead to make sure Jemima would be home, and Rick Hayes had answered the phone. Em would have been beside herself with glee to be speaking with a rock icon. To me, he sounded like a normal middle-aged man who wasn't entirely happy to be talking with me. Especially after I explained why I was calling. To his credit, he relented to a visit.

Tension hung uneasily between Sean and me. There was obviously something he wasn't telling me about the Rourke case, and I couldn't help feeling a twinge of hurt at being left out.

I said I'd trust him. And I would. But I couldn't help wondering.

Wondering about the secrets he was keeping. Wondering when he'd let me fully into his life. Wondering what our future held.

It always came back to that last one. Dovie had once implied that Cupid's Curse might have skipped my generation or the electrical shock that had scrambled my psychic abilities might have reversed the curse as well. . . .

I didn't know. And yes, I lived with the fear. I didn't know how to get rid of it. I could live with it, yes. Deal with it, yes. Deny it, yes. But get rid of it? How?

Until I figured that out, it would always be one step forward, two back, with Sean.

"Ready?" he asked.

My stomach ached. "Yeah."

A cool breeze blew in off the ocean, a hint of spring in the spray, as I rang the bell. With no barking from Rufus to drown it out, the gong pealed through the glass door. An elegant woman dressed in a black housedress, white apron, and thick-soled black shoes opened the door. I recognized her from when we were last here.

"Follow me," Esme said crisply in a British accent.

"And I'll see to it that Rufus's food is brought to your car."

"Thank you."

She tipped her head. "You're welcome."

Sean's hand rested at the small of my back as we walked down the hallway, past the kitchen, and into a large formal family room. Rick Hayes rose to greet us, but Jemima remained on the streamlined couch, her legs tucked under her, a book on her lap. I strained to see the title. *Tao: Feeling the Flow.* She set it on the glass-topped coffee table as we came in.

Sean shook Rick's hand, and reluctantly I did, too, wishing I'd worn gloves. With gloves, it was the only time I was able to hold a hand without seeing any visions at all.

In an instant, I was in another state, in a decrepit hotel room with water-marked ceilings, a threadbare coverlet covering the lumpy mattress, and a dark-stained and cigarette-burned carpet. I thanked Cupid for not having a sense of smell along with my visions as I pulled my hand away, having seen a pink guitar pick behind a chipped nightstand.

Rick watched me intently, but I wasn't in the mood to play "test the psychic." He was tall, extremely so, at least six foot four, and rail thin, but he looked healthy enough, with good skin tone and a sparkle in his brown eyes. He had an allure about him, a pull. A Hollywood director would call it the "It" factor. Coupled with his musical talents, it was easy to see why Rick had been popular enough for Em to have his poster on her wall but not why he'd never truly reached superstardom. All the elements were certainly there.

Jemima barely looked at us as Sean and I sat in

matching Italian leather armchairs. Today she wore a sleek designer pantsuit with a ruffled silk blouse peeking out from the lapel. Her feet were bare, her toes painted a lush red. Her hair was curled and flowed over slumped shoulders. She wore no jewelry except a plain platinum wedding band. Makeup couldn't hide the dark circles under her eyes.

Rick sat next to Jemima, his long legs stretching out beneath the coffee table. "I must apologize for missing your visit the other day. I had fittings. How's Rufus?"

I glanced around, looking for any indication Christa also lived in this house, but didn't see so much as a precocious baby picture. Everything was cold, sleek, sterile. I itched to leave. "He's settling in. My grandmother is adopting him."

Jemima slanted me a look. "Christa mentioned your offer to let her visit the dog. I don't think it's a good idea. It's best to cut ties permanently, don't you think."

A statement rather than a question, but I didn't let it go. "No, not really. It might make the transition a lot smoother for the both of them if they're allowed to see one another."

"I don't think so," Jemima said coolly.

So much for a Taoist attitude. She needed to keep reading that book of hers.

Rick put his hand on her knee. "Perhaps we could keep the visits to a minimum?"

Jemima brushed his hand aside and abruptly stood. She strode toward the windows overlooking the ocean, her arms crossed over her chest. Red hair free-fell down her back. Framed the way she was, with the glass and ocean just beyond the pane, the sunlight reflecting just so, she was beautiful.

Rick said, "It's been stressful around here, as you can imagine. We want only what's in Christa's best interests. On the surface she seems to be handling this situation remarkably well, but she *is* a teenager, and teenagers are quite adept at hiding their true emotions until all hell breaks loose." He gave us a charming smile.

Jemima turned on him. "*I* want what's best for Christa. *You* want a quick fix. The sooner Christa can grieve for that dog, the better for her in the long run. She doesn't need constant reminders of the pain. And that dog represents pain."

I bit my lip. Suddenly it was crystal clear why Jemima had wanted Rufus to leave. I looked at her in a whole new light and could see the softness under the steel.

"Nonsense," Rick said. "You're being irrational."

Uh-oh. Not the *i* word.

Jemima's hands fisted.

I cleared my throat to remind them that there were witnesses. "Did Christa know Mac was dying?" Might as well get it out in the open.

Christa was at school, so there was no chance she might be eavesdropping.

"No. Mac asked us not to tell her." Rick clasped his hands together and looked down at his feet. "The police know of Mac's illness, then?"

"Yes, but why didn't you tell them?" I asked. "It may have helped in the investigation."

Anger colored Jemima's cheeks crimson. "It wasn't my decision."

Rick said, "I simply don't see how it would have helped the situation."

Sean said, "It supports the theory that Mac may

have taken his own life, rather than disappeared against his will."

"And exactly how does that help us?" Rick asked. "Mac is still dead."

Jemima's breath hitched.

"Did Mac have life insurance?" Sean asked.

"Of course," Rick said.

"Did his policy have a suicide clause?" Sean looked between the two of them.

Rick leaned back, draped his arm across the back of the sofa. "I wouldn't know."

"What's a suicide clause?" Jemima asked.

"Certain insurance companies won't pay if the policyholder commits suicide. The policy becomes null and void."

Her eyes flashed to Rick. His head bopped as if he was singing to himself. "That explains a lot," she said.

"Who's the beneficiary?" Sean asked.

"I am," Jemima said. Without a word, she stormed from the room.

Rick gave us a weak smile. "Oftentimes Jemima's anger is misplaced. This isn't about the money."

"Isn't it?" I asked. "I heard you were looking for financial backing for a new reality show."

"I am," Rick said easily. Faint lines creased his eyes, his mouth, his forehead. He was holding up well for an aging rocker. "But only because I'd rather not take the financial risk alone. Why should I? There are plenty of people out there willing to back a great project."

"Are there?" Sean asked.

I heard skepticism in his voice and wondered which comment had sparked it. That there were plenty of people with money to throw around? Or that the show was a great project? Or both?

"Definitely. I received notice that filming starts next month."

Sean leaned in. "Have you seen Mac's will?"

"Yes. We're starting proceedings to declare Mac dead."

He said "we," but I had a feeling it was all his idea.

"And?" I asked.

"I don't suppose it can hurt to tell you. Mac left a good portion of his estate to charity. The rest goes to Christa upon her eighteenth birthday. The life insurance is a separate entity and goes to Jemima."

"The house?" Sean asked.

"Sold off, with the proceeds going into his estate," Rick said smoothly, evenly. "It's just as well. The new project will be filmed in Los Angeles. It doesn't make sense to keep two homes."

Sean and I followed Rick's lead and stood up. I couldn't help thinking of Mac's granddaughter. "You're moving? What about Christa? Next year will be her senior year of high school."

He led us out of the room. "It will make for great TV, don't you think?"

I stumbled. Sean grabbed my hand to steady me.

Sean and I were sharing a hammock tied between two palm trees, overlooking ocean so beautifully blue it stole my breath. Vibrant green islands dotted the horizon. A sailboat swayed, anchored just offshore. Sean turned his head, looked at me, a smile in those pearlescent eyes of his. Our bodies were nestled, skin on skin, my hand on his chest, my bare leg draped over his, his arm around my shoulders pulling me closer, tighter.

He leaned in, his gaze on my lips, his intent crystal clear. . . .

Sean pulled his hand away. The images faded into a distant blur, but the emotions remained. Joy. Pure, raw joy filled my every pore, every bit of oxygen I breathed in. I glanced at Sean. He reached up, brushed my cheek with his knuckles. In his eyes, I could see he felt it, too.

The magic.

"The network believes documenting Christa's readjustment will be a big draw to younger viewers."

Rick hadn't noticed my little stumble. Did he ever notice what was going on around him if it didn't directly affect him? Or care? I suddenly doubted it. His tone made it clear he didn't mind that Christa would be taken away from the school and friends she'd known all her life. He actually approved of the disruption and its effects being documented for all the world to see? It was disturbing. "Rick?"

"Yes?" he said, pulling open the front door.

"When does Christa turn eighteen?"

He smiled that charming smile again. "Two months from now, in April. I can hardly believe it. Kids grow up so fast, don't they?"

17

An hour and a half later I was behind my desk, my feet up, my head back. I couldn't shake my bad feelings about Rick Hayes. Yeah, he was pretty on the outside, but he was slimy on the inside. Karma, maybe, that his star had never truly risen.

Unfortunately, if Mac was dead Rick would be set for life. Between the life insurance policy Jemima would inherit and Christa's trust fund, he had covered all his bases. . . . If either one fell through he had a backup. I figured it wouldn't take long before he had a hand in those money pots.

Sean and I had dropped off Rufus's food at Dovie's, picked up Thoreau, and brought him to Sam's house, where Lizzie, Sam's wife, offered to dog-sit for the day. Very generous of her, considering the state in which Thoreau had left her carpets.

The ceiling creaked above my head—Sean was in his office upstairs getting ready for his meeting. I was trying to understand why he'd taken the case.

I dropped my feet to the floor when I heard someone coming down the hallway. Preston burst in, a manic look widening her eyes.

"He's back," she said breathlessly. "Help me catch him. I have a plan."

She didn't need to clarify the "he." By the crazed expression, I could tell the Lone Ranger had made another appearance. Digging in her bag, she pulled out a two-way radio and tossed it to me.

"Watch from the front window, okay? Tell me which way he goes. I need eyes in the skies."

"Couldn't afford a helicopter?"

"No."

She zipped out of the room before I could stand up. I never realized how fast she was before. Out front, Suz's desk chair was empty, and I had a pretty good idea of where *she* was. I picked up the binoculars on the window ledge and focused on the center of the commotion. Sure enough, I spotted Suz in the crowd on the Common, jumping around, snatching money out of thin air.

The walkie-talkie crackled. "Lucy, can you see him?"

The crowd had gathered around a man in a cowboy hat, but the focus of the group was solely on the twenty-dollar bills swirling in the breeze. Abruptly the masked man ducked out of sight. I squinted. "He's heading toward Charles."

"Got it."

"He's wearing a black shirt, black jeans." My pulse kicked up a notch. "He has a duffel bag strapped across his shoulders. He's taking off his mask!"

The mask went into the bag. Unfortunately, his back was to me and I couldn't get a good look at his face.

"I see him!" Preston said.

I pulled the binoculars away for a wider, panoramic

view and saw Preston closing in on the man. They were but two specks in the distance. Looking over his shoulder, the Lone Ranger spotted Preston and broke into a slow run. His hat flipped off his head and somersaulted along the ground behind him. He glanced back at it but kept on moving. He disappeared behind a stand of trees and dropped out of sight.

My heart thudded.

Preston hauled ass chasing him, her arms pumping like an Olympic sprinter with the finish line in sight. Suddenly she wobbled, then pitched forward and landed face-first in the grass.

"Preston!" I cried into the walkie-talkie. I trained the binoculars on her prone form. "Are you okay?"

Nothing.

"Preston!"

Slowly, she lifted her head. I saw her bangs puff upward on an exhale. She rose to her elbows and drew the walkie-talkie to her mouth. "Damn heel! I swear I'm going to start wearing flats. Just see if I don't."

I had the feeling she was talking to her boots more than to me.

"Are you okay? Did you hurt your ankle?" I asked.

"Only my pride. I was so close."

She crawled over to the cowboy hat and picked it up. Clutching it to her chest, she asked, "Did you see which way he went?"

"Lost him behind some trees. It looked like he might be headed to the Garden gates."

A slew of curses came through the radio. Then she said, "I'll be back at the office in a sec." Slowly, she stood up, dusted off her pants, and started hobbling across the park, bypassing the frenzied crowd.

Five minutes later, she dragged herself through the door. Plopping onto the couch, she kicked her legs out and stared at the ceiling. "I can't believe I was so close."

I handed her a bottle of water. "You gave a good chase."

Twisting off the cap, she frowned at me. "I would have caught him if not for my heel coming loose again."

"I know." I felt it best to placate her. "You should have seen the look of fear on his face."

She perked up. "Really?"

"Scared to death."

"You're humoring me, but I don't care. Next time, I'll be wearing sneakers. He won't have a chance."

She was tenacious; I'd give her that.

Beaming, she shook the hat at me. "This will get me a front-page story at least."

"Absolutely. The Lone Ranger is the hottest story in town. You have something no one else does."

Running a finger along the brim of the hat, she said woefully, "Why can't you get readings from the lost object itself?"

I lifted an eyebrow. "Sorry to disappoint."

"Maybe you *do* have that power and just don't know it yet."

It was true there was a lot I didn't know about my abilities, but I knew for sure I couldn't get a reading from object. I'd tried. Multiple times. Hundreds. It wasn't happening. "I don't work that—"

She tossed the hat at me. "Focus. Try really hard."

I caught it. She wasn't going to let this go, so I closed my eyes and said, "Ohhhhm," for a good twenty seconds.

My eyes popped open. "It came from The Medford Millinery!"

"Oh my God! You did it!" She jumped up and down—on one leg. The heel had broken off clean from her other boot. "This is amazing. Think of all the possibilities, Lucy!"

I hated to burst her bubble. Flipping the hat over, I said, "Don't get so excited. It's on the label."

She snatched it away from me and growled. "You're not funny. I don't even know why I like you. Why do I like you?"

"You don't. You use me for stories."

A grin tugged at her lips. "Right. I forgot."

"And I'm sorry, I couldn't help myself. But hey, it's a lead. That's a custom-made hat. Custom-made hats leave a trail. Someone had to order it."

Her eyes lit. "You're right. Are you up for a field trip?"

I didn't know how long Sean's meeting with Meaghan would be, and the paperwork on my desk could surely wait. Besides, I was just as curious about the Lone Ranger as everyone else. "Okay. But we have to swing by my father's penthouse. I need to pick up my car."

"Only if I can come in for a tour."

"No."

"But, Lucy, I heard he has a Vermeer. Is that true?"

It hung over his fireplace. "Still no."

"Lucy!" She huffed, then smiled deviously. "I'll tell you about the tip I got about Tristan Rourke."

I said, "You should be sharing tips anyway!"

"Why? You're not on the case anymore."

Oh. Right. But still, Sean might be interested. And the sooner he was off this case, the better I would feel.

Something about it had affected Sean on a deep, dark level, dredging up the pain that haunted his eyes.

"Sean might want to know. . . . Suz mentioned he had taken Meaghan on as a client."

Preston knew my weaknesses. The urge to throttle her was slowly coming back.

Wide-eyed, she said, "The Vermeer?"

I slipped on my coat and gave Preston a once-over. She was super-gluing her broken heel, trying to appear innocent. I wasn't buying it—I knew her too well. She was up to something. "What did you learn about Tristan Rourke?"

Testing her heel, she repeated doggedly, "The Vermeer?"

For Sean's sake. "Okay."

"I've been calling in favors from some of my more, shall we say, shady sources. Word on the street is that Tristan Rourke has underground headquarters in Roxbury. For two hundred dollars, one informant gave me the address, but I haven't checked it out yet. That payment will be on my expense report."

"You don't have expense reports."

"I do now."

My father was going to love that. But I had to admit, two hundred dollars was nothing if it truly led her to Tristan. Now that he was the subject of a massive manhunt, he was a huge story—bigger than reuniting him with a lost love. "Is your contact reliable?"

Offended, her face scrunched. "Of course. What kind of reporter do you think I am?"

"A good one." I had to give credit where credit was due.

She glowed under the compliment, and I almost forgot how devious she could be.

"Will you come with me? To Tristan's secret hideout?" she asked.

"I'm not on the case anymore, Preston, remember?"

Her lips twisted. "Well, I am."

"Have fun," I said, grabbing my satchel, several files, and my coat. "But I'd like that address for Sean."

She widened her eyes, blinked at me like a wounded puppy. "It's in Roxbury. One of the worst neighborhoods. I don't want to go alone. I mean, I will if I have to. If I disappear, you will tell the police my last known location, right?"

I sighed. "Fine. I'll go with you."

"I knew I could count on you."

Okay, she'd completely manipulated me, but she was right. She could count on me. I was loyal to a fault, even to people who hadn't quite earned it yet.

In the hallway, my father's office door was closed tight, he must have been with a client. I ran upstairs to see Sean, give him Preston's information, but his office door was closed and I could hear Meaghan's voice inside.

Sam wasn't around, and Andrew, SDI's office assistant, must have been at lunch. I left a note on Andrew's desk to give to Sean and headed out.

Preston and I passed Suz (she'd scored eighty dollars) on the stairs. I told her where we were off to in case Sean came looking for me—or if the police needed a last known location.

18

I used my key on my father's penthouse door, let myself in. Preston was right behind me, eager to get a glimpse at my father's home. Or, more likely, hoping to find anything that might give her a clue into my family's background. She wasn't fooling me with her sudden desire to see my father's art collection.

There was a big clue on the console table to the right of the door—a bronze of Cupid. Preston looked right past it, her eyes sweeping in all she could in one big glance.

Yes, so far she had kept her word about not sharing with the world that Cutter McCutchan was a Valentine, and she'd also kept the secret about my parents' topsy-turvy relationship. . . . But could she keep quiet about Dad's and Cutter's ability to see auras? Was her loyalty to my family bigger than her desire for a national—an international—scoop?

I really wanted to trust her, but I didn't, so I had to do everything I could to protect the secret. Now if I could only figure out how.

"Raphael?" I called out, setting my purse next to Cupid. "I need to pick up my car keys."

"Where's the Vermeer?" Preston asked, looking around, her eyes wide.

I gestured toward the fireplace. Dad's waterfront penthouse had stunning views of Boston Harbor. Sunlight cascaded through floor-to-ceiling windows, setting the living room aglow. Right off I noticed three of my father's designer suitcases stacked by the door. If he was going out of town, he hadn't mentioned it.

Preston started toward the painting and stopped suddenly when a tiny giggle came from the other side of the broad couch.

She took a step backward, bumping into me. I steadied her and said, "Hello?"

A head popped up, peering at me over the back of the couch.

I grabbed my chest, willed my heart to beat normally. "Dad, hi."

Preston gave a little wave. "Hello, Oscar. I came to see the Vermeer."

His hair was rumpled, his eyes shiny. "Hello, girls."

I said, "What're you doing home? Shouldn't you be at work?" His office door had been closed when Preston and I left, and I'd assumed he was with a client.

"Just, uh . . ."

My mother's head suddenly popped up next to his. Her short blond hair stood on end. "LucyD, this is a surprise."

Preston let out a little gasp, then clamped a hand over her lips.

In addition to the unkempt hair, my parents had rosy cheeks and guilty smiles. My gaze dropped to the area rug and I noticed my father's trousers balled up near the end table as if they'd been thrown there. . . .

Realization hit hard, and I threw my hands over my eyes. I let out a squeal.

My father said, "Just came home for some . . . lunch."

Mum giggled.

"Is that what they're calling it now?" Preston asked with a straight face, but humor danced in her eyes.

Grabbing her sleeve, I dragged her through the kitchen. Raphael's quarters were off the back hallway. "I'm traumatized," I declared loudly. "I'm scarred for life. I'm going to need therapy."

"I have a good one if you want his number!" Mum called out.

"Scarred!" I yelled back. "Is Raphael even home?"

"In his room," my father answered.

Once I reached the safety of the hallway, I let my hands drop. Would I ever get used to seeing them . . . like that?

Preston sagged against the wall. "You have the most interesting family."

"Interesting" was a good word. "Dysfunctional" also worked. "You don't know the half of it."

Her eyes sparkled. "What else is there?"

I really had to watch what I said around her. I knocked on Raphael's door.

"It's open!" he yelled.

Raphael stood in the middle of his one-bedroom apartment surrounded by boxes.

Preston closed the door behind her, leaned against it. "It's safe in here, right? Maggie's not going to pop out of one of the boxes, is she?"

Crisp, creased black pants were specked with

cardboard dust, and his white button-down had been rolled to his elbows. His dark salt-and-pepper hair had been gelled, slicked back in a style straight from the fifties. His olive skin glowed with the faint sheen of working hard. "It's safe."

I looked around. "What's all this?"

His brown eyes warmed. "I'm packing."

"This is an awful lot to be taking on vacation, even if it is a month long."

The room was filled with cardboard boxes, taped and neatly labeled. Walls were bare, small nail holes the only hint there had been artwork and photos.

Raphael watched me take everything in. "I'm moving out."

There was a sudden pain in my chest, like a thorn wedged in my heart. "Where?"

Preston picked up some Bubble Wrap.

"I'm moving in with Maggie," he said. "Her house. In Cambridge."

Pop. Pop.

Of course. It had been a stupid question but the only one my brain could form at that moment.

"It seems so sudden." There was a catch in my throat. He hadn't mentioned a thing about it yesterday.

His eyes locked on mine. "I woke up this morning, rolled over, and looked at the empty space next to me, and I realized I don't want to spend a single night away from her, and that I didn't have to."

"Awww," Preston said. *Pop. Pop.*

"It is rather sappy." His fingers flexed as though he was itching to steal the Bubble Wrap from her.

She added, "Another Oscar Valentine success story. His success rate is quite remarkable, isn't it?"

Raphael didn't take her bait. "He isn't the King of Love for nothing."

I couldn't worry about Preston's suspicions right now. My mind was too wrapped up in the moving boxes. I sat on the arm of the sofa. Selfishly, I was going to miss Raphael always being around whenever I needed him. At the same time, nothing made me happier than seeing him so happy. Loved. I wouldn't want it any other way. He and Maggie were meant to be together. It was destiny. And I wasn't about to stand in the way of it.

I stood, hugged him tight. "What is Dad going to do without you here full-time?"

He smiled. "I believe he has plans of his own."

"Oh?" I said. "Like what?"

"Not for me to say."

There was a tap at the door. My father stuck his head in. He was freshly showered. If he'd been fazed by the interruption from Preston and me, he didn't show it. He was as cool and calm as ever. "Preston, I thought you'd like to see the Vermeer. And I've just obtained a Gandolfi. You must see it. Come."

She snapped to attention, but as she glanced at me her eyes were wide and blank.

Apparently, her studies of the masters were limited. Luckily, she was a quick learner and my father a good teacher. She was about to endure a crash course of Art 101.

"Enjoy," I said, waving as she followed him out of the room.

Raphael said, "What is that about?"

"Preston has a newfound appreciation of the arts."

Wisely he said, "Cutter?"

"Yes, I believe so."

"Have you warned him?"

"Not yet."

"You'd better soon."

"He's due back in town this weekend. We're having dinner. I can bring it up then."

Raphael picked up the Bubble Wrap Preston had left behind. "So annoying, this."

Yet I yearned to pop a few of the bubbles myself.

"Is Cutter staying in town for good?"

"I'm not sure. He's been traveling a lot with his art. A different gallery, a different city, every other week, it seems."

"Mmm," Raphael said.

"Hmm," I agreed.

He lifted an eyebrow, amusement in his eyes. "Running from your father?"

"As fast as he can. I'm hoping they will come to a compromise; otherwise I'm scared Dad may push Cutter away for good."

"Oscar must learn patience."

"And Cutter has yet to learn the value of his gift." A lesson I had learned the hard way.

"Did Em leave my car keys with you?" Preston and I still had to go to the millinery and then check out the tip she had received on Tristan Rourke.

Raphael pulled a key ring from his pocket. Folding his arms across his chest, he said, "Do you want to take the back way out?"

"My purse is on the console table. Besides, I need to rescue Preston."

"Ah."

I kissed him good-bye and as soon as I reached the

hallway I heard a *pop, pop*. I stuck my head back in the door.

Raphael smiled. "Irresistible."

I left him to his packing and popping and found Mum in the kitchen, shredding a carrot.

"Do you have time for a salad?" she asked.

"Sorry. We can't." I eyed the sofa. I'd never be able to sit on it again. "When did you start liking salads?"

"People change," she said, biting into the carrot with gusto.

"Do they?" I asked, ripping the bandage off emotional wounds. "Truly?"

She waved the carrot at me. "I hear what you're saying, Lucy. And the truth is, I don't know. But right now, this minute, it doesn't matter. And if I'm okay with it, then you should be, too."

I didn't think it was that easy.

She added, "This may last one week, two. One year, two. Who knows? Life is about living, not about constant worrying."

Ha! She didn't know my life very well. I sat on a stool. "But how, when you know there may be pain in the end?"

"Life is not without pain. You ache and you move on. And you do it all again."

And again and again in my parents' case.

"This go-round happens to come with the added benefit of a lifestyle change. Your father's so fit that he's inspired me. I've also joined a gym."

A diet, Zumba, and now a gym as well. This current fling was pretty serious. "You're perfect as is."

She smiled broadly. "Thank you, LucyD. I knew you were my favorite child."

"I'm your only child, unless you have something you want to tell me."

"Such sass. I need to do this." She swept her hands over the salad. "I'm not getting any younger. I need to start thinking about my health."

"You know Dad has a gym downstairs."

"You've clearly lost your mind if you think I'm going to exercise where he might see me."

I laughed. "Those who exercise together stay together?"

She threw a cherry tomato at me. The rubies on her finger glistened.

I took hold of her hand, felt my heart tug. "The ring looks great."

Holding it up, she admired it. "It needs a good cleaning, but it's really quite beautiful. I'm not sure why I ever thought it was a hunk of junk."

"I think it had something to do with your feelings for Dad at the time."

"Hmm. You may be right."

Murmured voices came from the hallway. As Dad and Preston appeared, her gaze pleaded with me.

I took mercy on her—I had experience with my father's tutorials. "We should be going, Preston."

"Right." She hurried over to me. "Going."

As I gathered up my purse, I spotted the suitcases. "Are you going out of town?" I asked my father.

He stood behind my mother, his arm around her waist. "In a way."

She smiled. "Dad is moving in with me."

Preston slid a look my way as she said, "That's wonderful."

"Absolutely." I meant it, but my stomach ached nonetheless.

"We want to have a big dinner to celebrate. This Saturday. Everyone's invited."

"Me?" Preston asked as though she were the gawky, unathletic kid who'd just been picked first for a game of dodgeball.

"Of course!"

"But I'm supposed to have dinner with Cutter on Saturday," I protested weakly.

"Bring him! It wouldn't be a party without him."

Cutter and Preston in the same room. Great.

As I rung for the elevator Preston said, "So just *when* is Cutter getting back?"

19

Medford Millinery was appropriately located in Medford. Medford Square to be exact, about fifteen minutes north of the city.

Preston said, "Next time I'm driving. You drive like a granny."

"Are you insulting Dovie?" I clicked my key fob and my car beeped twice, locking the doors. I slipped on my gloves and looked around, immediately drawn to the coffee shop across the street. Feeling the pull, I started toward it, only to be suddenly jerked backward.

Preston held firm to the strap of my purse. "The hat shop is this way." She started down the sidewalk.

"Can't I meet you?"

"You're not going to be able to focus until you get a latte, are you?"

"Nope."

"Let's hurry up then."

Ten minutes later, we stood inside the millinery shop, surrounded by some of the fanciest hats I'd ever seen.

The man behind the counter didn't look too pleased to see us.

Preston marched up to the counter (she really needed to work on her finesse) and placed the Lone Ranger's hat next to the cash register. "Hello. We found this hat, and were hoping you could help us reunite it with its proper owner." She tried batting her eyelashes, but her direct manner of speaking overruled any kind of flirtatiousness.

Thank goodness, because that would have been too much for me to handle. The shopkeeper looked to already have one foot in the grave. He was small and skeletal, his paper-thin skin stretched across his drooping features. Dark splotches covered his neck and face, rising onto his forehead and creeping across his shiny bald spot until disappearing into his receding dull gray hairline. Tufts of white hair shot from his ears, reveling in freedom by twisting and curling along the veiny skin covering protruding cartilage.

He had to be ninety if a day.

"Did you not see the sign?" he asked in a heavy Italian accent.

"What sign?" Preston asked. "No returns? This isn't a return; it's—"

He slammed his hand on the countertop. "No food or drink!" he bellowed, his voice shaking the windows.

"Cripes!" Preston jumped back, splashing her coffee onto her winter white wool coat.

The man placed both hands on the glass countertop, leaned forward, and huffed, much like a bull before he charged.

I backed slowly toward the door.

"Do you happen to have a paper towel?" Preston asked the man in a dulcet tone.

He let out a hearty, "Arrrrgh!" that had those windowpanes shivering in fear.

I confess to a shudder as well.

"No need to be surly," Preston growled in return, only mildly fazed by the outburst. I, on the other hand, was ready to run away. Far, far away.

Preston spun, removed my coffee from my hand, and set both our cups outside the door. When she passed by, she said, "You just had to have your coffee first, didn't you?"

"We should go," I whispered.

"The Lone Ranger," she forced through clenched teeth. She turned back to the shopkeeper, a broad smile stretching the limits of her face. "Better?"

He smiled, a closed-lip affair sure to give me nightmares. He hooked his thumbs on his vest and drummed his bony fingers on his hollow chest. "I am Dominic Pagano. How may I help you lovely ladies?"

"The hat?" Preston said, pushing it his way.

"Ah yes." He picked it up, ran a hand lovingly along the edges. He handed it back to her. "I can't help you."

Her shoulders stiffened. "What do you mean?"

"My clientele is confidential. I absolutely cannot divulge who purchased the hat."

"But you do know *who* purchased the hat?" Preston asked, digging for information. Her fists were clenched at her sides.

I stepped up beside her, just in case I had to hold her back from leaping the counter and strangling the old man.

"My memory is limitless." Dominic tapped his

temple. "I never forget a hat, a face, or a name. I made this hat in 1989. July. An unusually hot summer, as I recall." He ran a hand over the hat as though it were a pet.

I rummaged around my satchel, pushing aside the files I'd shoved in there, a bottle of water, a hair pick, lip gloss, my overstuffed wallet, and finally found my card case and pulled out a business card. "Could you please contact its owner and tell him we found the hat and would like to speak with him? He can call any-time."

Spindly fingers clamped onto the card. "Valentine?" His bushy eyebrows rose. "As in 'Oscar Valentine'?"

"He's my father."

Preston smiled triumphantly.

The man flushed with pleasure. "Why didn't you say so in the first place? Oscar is one of my favorite clients. He's quite fond of the fedora, is he not?"

"Not for long," Preston snapped. "I doubt he'll ever come in again once he finds out how you treated his *daughter*. His *only* daughter."

I sighed dramatically. I might as well play it up. If it helped track down the owner of the Lone Ranger hat, why not?

"And her *closest friend*," Preston added, linking elbows with me.

Okay. That was pushing it.

The shopkeeper hurriedly pulled a slip of paper from beneath the counter. In spidery penmanship he scrib-bled a name. He checked an old-fashioned Rolodex and jotted down an address as well. He slid the paper across the counter.

Jeffrey Denham-Foster with a Randolph address.

With a brittle smile, the shopkeeper said, "I don't know how much good it will do."

"Why?" I asked.

"Mr. Denham-Foster passed away a year ago."

That news certainly changed the direction of our investigation.

Preston glanced at me, then back to the man. "Was he married?"

"Why, yes. Lovely woman. Eva. They had three children together. Arnold, Matthias, and Linda."

I had the feeling, if asked, Pagano could provide birthdates. He wasn't kidding when he claimed a great memory.

"I'm quite sorry I can't be of more help. But please do give your father my best. Have a lovely day. And . . ."

"Yes?" Preston asked.

"If you come back," his smile turned to a snarl and he banged his hand on the counter, "remember no food or drink!"

The glass shook again as Preston grabbed the hat and my arm and steered me to the door. Outside the shop, she bent and picked up our coffees. She handed me mine, and I tossed it in a trash can.

"He's pleasant," I said, smiling.

She tipped her head. "I kind of liked him. I have a soft spot for crankypusses."

"I'll remember that."

Sipping her coffee, she frowned. "It's cold."

"Imagine." I started for my car and stopped short.

"What?" Preston asked, following my gaze.

My car sat at the curb, all four doors open wide. I quickly looked around.

"What are you looking for? Should we call the cops?"

"No use." My pulse raced. "I'm sure Tristan Rourke is long gone."

20

"How do you know it was Tristan?" Preston asked as Scarlett, my GPS, directed us from Medford to Roxbury. I'd lived in Boston and the South Shore my whole life, yet still couldn't find my way around.

"I just do."

"But how?" she pressed, tapping her fingernail on the console.

"I'm psychic, remember?"

"Not that kind. I've been reading up on psychics, you know."

I slid a look her way. Where was she going with this? She was leading me somewhere. "You have?"

"I'm just fascinated, especially now that I know your powers are real. Did you know a lot of psychic ability is hereditary?"

"Really?" I asked. "Because it was the lightning strike and the surge of electricity that gave me my abilities to find lost objects." I wasn't technically lying. I just left out the part where the surge had robbed me of seeing auras. The auras I'd inherited from my father.

"Was anyone else there when the surge happened?" she asked as she changed the radio station.

Though there was nothing overt in her tone, I heard the investigator at work. "My mother," I answered. "And I was on the phone with Marisol, who rushed right over from her house when the phone went dead."

I remembered it all too clearly. How the surge had knocked me clear off my bed. Mum had rushed into the room to check on me, and I hadn't been able to see her red aura. My colorful world had gone dark.

"I'm sure either of them would love to tell you all about that day."

She stared out the window, a frown tugging on her lips. Mine hadn't been the answer she had hoped for. It was obvious she suspected my father had powers. It was only a matter of time before she figured out he could see auras. Cutter, too. What would she do with the information?

When she didn't respond, I gratefully let it drop. "Did your shady contacts have any other information about Tristan?"

"Most were reluctant to talk about him at all."

"Yet they all knew who he was."

"Without a doubt." She shifted slightly to face me. "If it was Tristan who left your doors open, why would he do that? I don't understand."

I checked my rearview mirror. As far as I could tell, there was no one following us. I didn't feel relief. I felt duped. This was twice now Tristan had caught me off-guard. "I don't know."

He had every opportunity to be malicious. It would have taken only seconds to slash my seats. Minutes to steal the radio or the GPS unit. Instead, he had simply unlocked the doors and left them open wide.

In a way, it was more violating. As if he was declaring that not only could he find me, but also locks wouldn't keep him out. If it was a subtle threat, it worked. I was skeeved out.

I glanced in the mirror again. Still nothing.

Scarlett demanded I turn left in one hundred feet. She was bossy and demanding, that Scarlett, and woe to the driver who didn't do as she said. We were on our way to the location Preston's tipster had given her— the address for Tristan Rourke's underground head-quarters. We were scoping the place out, doing a quick drive-by to see if the tip held any merit.

"Do you know if this is a house or a warehouse?"

"Not a clue. Two hundred bucks will only buy so much."

I suddenly thought of the homeless man on the bench on the Common and the money he'd slipped into his glove. I hadn't seen him in a couple of days and made a mental note to check on him, make sure he had enough to eat.

I knew I couldn't save the whole world. And maybe I couldn't even help the homeless man, but I could try. I certainly had more than enough money sitting in my trust fund to be a benefactor. But first, I should ask if he wanted my help. Some people wouldn't—and I could respect that.

"About my expense report," Preston said.

"Were we talking about your expense report?"

Scarlett told me to turn right in twenty feet.

Preston ignored my question. "I think I should be

able to write off a new pair of boots. I was on the job when these broke."

The superglue wasn't holding. "But you weren't on the job for Valentine, Inc. The Lone Ranger has nothing to do with Lost Loves."

Raising an eyebrow, she said, "But if I weren't working the Lost Love cases, I never would have been downtown, ergo I never would have known about the Lone Ranger in the first place."

"Ergo? Did you go to law school when I wasn't looking?"

"Journalism law and ethics class."

She made a compelling argument. "We'll stop at DSW on the way back to the office."

Smiling, she said, "Now I remember why I like you."

"Because I have a company credit card?"

"Exactly."

Scarlett announced we had reached our destination. I drove past the storefront, banged a U-ey that had Scarlett pitching such a fit I had to turn off the GPS, and parallel-parked across the street.

I shouldn't have been surprised, but I was. I stared at the front of A Clean Start, the Laundromat owned by Tristan's grandmother, as a woman came out with a laundry basket full of something other than clothes. I squinted but couldn't identify the items. "What's in her basket? Can you tell?"

Preston pulled binoculars from her bag and trained them on the unsuspecting woman. "Groceries. Milk. Cereal. Soup. No clothes. You'd think with that being a Laundromat and that being a clothes basket there would be clothes. There's not even a sock to be seen."

I stared at the binoculars.

"What?" she asked.

"Do you always carry around an extra set of binoculars?" The other pair was back at the office, still sitting on the windowsill where I left them.

"I was a Girl Scout," she said, lifting one shoulder in a shrug. "I like to be prepared."

"You were a Girl Scout?"

"Don't look so shocked." She pointed. "Here comes someone else."

A young black man, early twenties, was headed into the Laundromat with an empty basket. Five minutes later, he came back out. The basket was full.

"What does he have in it?" I asked.

"Looks like two blankets, a loaf of bread, and a gallon of milk. Skim."

What was going on in that Laundromat? Was it a general store as well?

"We need to go in," Preston said. "Scope it out."

"Maureen Rourke knows what I look like. She'll never tell me anything."

"Okay, then. I'll go in."

"I don't think that's a good idea."

"Don't be such a nervous Nelly."

She was out the door and halfway across the street before I could even think to tease her about the phrase. Preston didn't seem the least bit intimidated. In fact, as she rushed in, the woman coming out gave Preston a wide berth. I couldn't blame her—Preston was a little scary herself.

The woman had one hand clamped tightly around a little girl's hand; the other was holding a paper sack with a loaf of bread sticking out of the top.

The mother looked both ways, held tight to the girl, and crossed the street. They passed my car, headed slowly toward an apartment complex farther up the block. The girl, maybe four or five, was dragging her feet through the slush.

On impulse, I jumped out of the car and jogged after them. I was closing in when the mother suddenly let go of the girl's hand, turned, and aimed a pepper spray canister my way.

"Stop right there," she ordered.

I skidded to a halt, nearly falling over with the sudden inertia. I swung my arms, teetered.

"I mean it!" she yelled, thrusting her hand forward. Her thumb was on the button, poised for squirting.

"She means it!" the little girl echoed.

My foot slipped on the slush and my feet slid out underneath me. I fell flat on my ass. The icy slush immediately soaked through my pants.

The little girl giggled.

Her mother still pointed the spray. Right. I was going to jump her now, armed with a snowball. "I come in peace," I managed to say, trying to find to find an elegant way to stand up.

The woman eyed me suspiciously but reached out her hand (I didn't *see* anything). She'd put the pepper spray away. "You scared the shit out of me," she said.

"Scared," the girl echoed.

"Shush, Nessie."

An icy drip slid down the back of my thigh. I didn't even want to check the damage.

"What are you doing chasing after me?" the woman demanded.

"I, uh—" It had been a completely stupid thing to do.

"Don't you know this is a bad neighborhood? You're lucky I didn't have a gun."

"Lucky," Nessie parroted, nodding her head. Jet-black twin pigtails bounced, brushing her shoulders.

It *was* a bad neighborhood. Yet I saw tiny gems of hope along the neglected street. New fencing, newer windows on some of the houses, and fresh paint covering gang graffiti.

"I'm sorry," I said. "I saw you come out of A Clean Start." A quick look at the storefront didn't show any sign of Preston, but I suddenly noticed how the building stood out. Bold paint, big windows, a bright airy feeling around it. The place fairly sparkled, which I supposed was a good image to have for a Laundromat. I wasn't so sure it was the best idea to stick out like a sore thumb, even if that thumb had just been manicured and painted with a fresh coat of polish.

"So?" she said.

I shrugged. "I don't know. It just seemed strange you came out with groceries instead of laundry."

"Why do you care?"

"Yeah, why?" Nessie asked.

She was the spitting image of her mother—her smooth skin a light brown, her dark eyes and lashes slanting slightly, her razor-sharp tone.

I couldn't very well come out and ask about Tristan Rourke. I stalled for time, but not only did my butt ache; it was now frozen also. I longed for home and a long bubble bath. I was fresh out of ideas of how to beat around the bush. "Do you know Tristan Rourke?"

The woman raised a paper-thin eyebrow.

"Robin Hood, Robin Hood," the little girl chanted.

I glanced at her, then at her mother. At the bag of

groceries and the pair's thin spring coats. It clicked. "Robin Hood? Robbing the rich to feed the poor?"

"You didn't hear it from me," the woman said.

Nessie smiled. A space was missing where a front tooth should have been. "Or me."

I smiled back. "Does he only provide groceries?"

"Clothes. Food. Blankets. Cash. In some cases, tuition."

"And what does he get in return?"

"I can't say I know." She started forward, stopped, turned. "This may still be a bad neighborhood, but a year ago, two years ago . . . It was hell on earth."

"Hell," Nessie said, nodding.

The woman tsked at her.

As they walked off, Nessie looked over her shoulder and waved at me. As I waved back, I felt a presence behind me. I spun just as the man reached out and grabbed me.

21

Sean gripped my upper arms. His eyes were a dark, stormy gray. "What are you doing here?"

Adrenaline zipped through my body, leaving my skin prickling. I drew in a deep breath and said, "Scare a girl to death, why don't you?"

"I'm sorry." He let go of my arms. The warmth of his handprints slowly ebbed. "I got your message about Tristan Rourke. I didn't think I'd find you here. This isn't a safe area."

"So I've heard." Now that I thought of it, why was I even here? How had I let Preston talk me into this? I was off this case. Sean might still be on it, but I had better things to do. Like take my bubble bath and soak away my worries.

His gaze swept my body, lingered on my lower half. I'd like to think he was taken with how nicely my pants fit, but I knew what he was looking at. "I slipped in the slush."

He opened my trunk, pulled out a beach towel, and

handed it to me. I wrapped it around my waist before I slid into the car. Sean slid into the passenger seat.

"Preston's inside the Laundromat. She's intent on uncovering Rourke's underground headquarters."

"Who is he, Batman?"

"More like Robin Hood."

Dark eyebrows dipped in question. I explained what I'd found out, which seemed big—but when broken down and examined closely wasn't all that much.

My teeth were chattering. I wished I had no modesty—I would have slid off my pants completely, but explaining why I was half-naked to Preston when she returned wasn't something I wanted to do. I started the engine, turned the heater on full blast.

My stomach hurt. I glanced at the Laundromat, willing Preston to come out. A little telepathy would be nice right about now. What could possibly be taking her so long? As I watched, a young woman walked into the shop, two little boys each holding a hand. No laundry basket.

It was really quite remarkable what Tristan was doing. A one-man welfare system. A criminally misguided philanthropist. Who would have thought?

"Lucy?"

"Hmm?" My teeth chattered. My rear end was freezing.

"Are you okay? You look a little pale."

A car pulled up in front of the Laundromat as I turned and looked at him. I wasn't okay. I was getting mad. Really mad. "Why couldn't you walk away from this case?"

He opened his mouth, then snapped it closed. His

eyes targeted something over my shoulder. I turned to take a look.

Agents Thomas and St. John were staring back.

The sun was dipping in the sky as I made my way home. A plane flew along the horizon, its taillights blinking.

Preston had finally emerged from A Clean Start five minutes after the FBI agents had asked Sean to answer a few of their questions. Downtown.

That was two hours ago, and I still hadn't heard from him.

I parked along Main Street in Cohasset Village and ran into my favorite little bistro to pick up my take-out order. I was tired, I was hungry, I was grumpy, and all I wanted to do was eat, take my bath, cuddle with Grendel, and go to bed. Alone.

Sean never had the chance to tell me why he'd taken Meaghan's case, and I wasn't even sure he was going to at all. He must have a good reason, and I wanted to know what it was.

Thankfully, I'd been able to drop Preston off at Valentine, Inc., instead of hitting the shoe store. Maureen Rourke apparently took one look at Preston when she walked through the doors of A Clean Start and deemed her worthy of help. Preston's haircut (which was choppy enough to look self-inflicted), the coffee-stained coat, and the broken heel had been enough to grant her a pass through the doorway next to the vending machine for detergents and softeners.

A back storeroom had a set of stairs leading to a warehouse under the shop that would make Wal-Mart jealous.

"You would not have believed it," Preston gushed as

I drove her back to the office. "It was part flea market, part Whole Foods, part Bank of America. What really amazed me is that people only took what they needed."

Preston had come out with a new pair of shoes (flats), a coat, and twenty bucks for a haircut. No one had asked her any questions or suggested payment in any form.

"Are you going to write about it?" I asked.

She bit her lip. "I don't know."

If she did, it would be a major scoop. At the same time it would be taking away something so many people obviously relied on, even if its origin was a bit on the iffy side.

It was a hard decision.

I turned into Aerie, wondering when I'd hear from Sean. It seemed odd to me the FBI only wanted to speak to him, but Preston speculated it was because he was the licensed investigator. Whereas I wasn't.

The scent of herbed chicken barley soup drifted from the seat next to me. It had been an impossibly long day with no lunch.

I crested the hill, followed the bend, and Dovie's house suddenly appeared as if out of nowhere. It was a grand estate, absolutely gorgeous even at night. Uplights highlighted the classic architecture, the simple elegance of Dovie's pride and joy. I loved the Craftsman elements of her sprawling manor. The stonework, the wide eaves, the numerous windows. I was surprised to see a car in the driveway and even more shocked when Dovie opened her front door and started flailing her arms to catch my attention.

Looking longingly at my little cottage on the bluff, I turned the wheel into Dovie's circular driveway, parking behind a dark Mercedes I didn't recognize. I left my soup on the seat and yelped when my door flew open.

"Thank God you're here," Dovie said, yanking on my sleeve.

"What's wrong?" I hurried after her as she jogged toward the house. "Is it Rufus?"

"Rufus is fine. He's upstairs, locked in my room because he wouldn't behave himself."

"He didn't take too kindly to the vet?" I asked, wondering how kindly Dovie had taken to the vet.

"No, no. The vet was fine." She colored a bit. "It's because Rick and Jemima Hayes are here. Christa's missing. She never showed up at school this morning."

I followed Dovie through the double doors and closed them behind me. I smelled a hint of garlic in the air as we walked down the hall and into the kitchen. From here, I could see my cottage down the lane, the front lights on, just waiting for me to come home. It was filled with the same charm as Dovie's house. The stacked stone, the wide eaves, the huge windows. My place had the added benefit of a wraparound porch that was simply heaven on summer days.

Home.

There was nowhere I'd rather be right now.

Jemima and Rick sat at the kitchen table, and each had a mug of coffee in front of them. I looked around, half-expecting to see Em, but I quickly remembered she was on her way to Hawaii.

I bit back a jealous sigh.

Sinking into a chair, I said, "What's going on?"

"Christa never showed up at school today. She's not

answering her phone. Her car is gone. We don't know where she is," Jemima blurted.

"I'm sure she's fine," Rick said, petting his wife's hand.

She snatched it away, set it in her lap.

"She's a teenager," he said. "Didn't you ever skip school as a teenager?"

I looked at my watch—the numbers were blurring, my eyes were so tired. "What time does her play practice start? Has anyone checked to see if she showed up?"

Jemima lifted an eyebrow. "How do you know she has play practice?"

"She told me. This morning. When she called to ask if she could come over and see Rufus after school."

"She called you?" Dovie asked, sliding a mug my way. It was my favorite mug, the one that read: "National Sarcasm Society. Like We Need Your Support."

"About nine or so." I sipped from the mug. The coffee was piping hot—just the way I liked it. "She said she had a late start."

"Well!" Rick boomed. "She didn't have a late start today. I think that proves Christa skipped. She'll come home eventually."

Jemima looked at him as though he had three heads. "She's never skipped before. And even if she did today where is she now? Why didn't she turn up at play practice? Why hasn't she answered her phone?"

Dovie rested a hand on Jemima's shoulder. "I'm sure everything will be all right. Lucy, can you do a reading?"

I was tired. So tired. And the coffee hadn't kicked in yet. But I couldn't say no. "Sure."

Rick's chair scraped the floor as he pushed away from the table. "This is nonsense. She's almost eighteen. She'll be home soon. You baby her too much. We should go. They're not going to hold our dinner reservations."

Dinner reservations? He was thinking about going out to eat at a time like this? Even if Christa had played hooky, which was entirely likely, she'd never done so before and Jemima had every right to be worried.

"Actually," Jemima said, glaring at him, "I'm starting to think I didn't baby her enough."

"Whatever," he said. He took up a spot near the back door and looked out at the ocean. "Just hurry it up."

Talk about a baby.

"This will only work if Christa has something on her that you've given her as a gift. Jewelry, a cell phone, that sort of thing."

Jemima frowned as tears gathered at the corners of her eyes. "I don't know what she was wearing today. How could I not know what she was wearing?"

I didn't want to answer, so I said, "Cell phone?"

"Mac bought it for her," Jemima said.

"IPod?"

"Mac."

"Watch?"

"She doesn't wear one."

"Class ring?"

"She doesn't own one."

Rick sniggered from the corner. I was glad Em wasn't here to see it.

Dovie said, "Her car?"

Jemima brightened. "It's Rick's old car."

"Then I can only probably get a reading from Rick."
Great. Fantastic. A wonderful way to cap my day.

"No thanks," he said.

Jemima stood, squared her shoulders. She was wearing a long suede skirt and a pale blue wraparound sweater. Her hair was twisted and clipped in an updo, showing off a small hummingbird tattoo at the nape of her neck.

Dovie came and stood by my side.

"I suggest," Jemima said to her husband, "you rethink your stance."

He faced her. "Or else?"

He was saved from her answer by the ringing of a cell phone. Jemima snatched it out of her pocket, stared at the screen, and burst into tears. "Where have you been?" she cried as she answered. "Where are you now?" A beat later she said, "Home? You're at home?"

Rick rolled his eyes.

Jemima said, "We'll be right there."

Rick was already on his way to the door. Jemima gave Dovie a quick hug. "Thank you," she said.

"Did she say where she's been?" Dovie asked.

Jemima smiled. "Shopping in the city with her girl-friends. I could kill her if I wasn't so relieved."

Dovie showed them out, closed the door, and said, "Good riddance."

My soup was probably cold by now. Thank goodness for microwaves. I was going home and not coming back out till morning. I had one hand on the door, ready to make a quick escape, when Dovie cleared her throat.

"I have a favor to ask," she said.

Something easy, I silently begged. "Oh?"

"I have a date tonight." She did the cha-cha around the foyer. "With the cutest doctor from Marisol's clinic. He's a bit younger than me—not much," she was quick to point out, "and I thought why the hell not?"

"That's great! Are you going dancing?" Marisol would be gloating the next time I talked with her.

"Dinner and dancing and then," Dovie waggled her eyebrows, "who knows."

I stuck my fingers in my ears. "Lalalala." First my parents, now this. I couldn't take much more. "What's the favor?"

Dovie looked up the stairs. "Rufus. I'll take him out before I leave, but he'll need a walk around nine."

Maybe my plan for Dovie to adopt Rufus had been ill thought out.

"And I'm not sure when I'll be home." More eyebrow waggling. "So he may have to go out again around midnight."

Definitely not my best idea. "Why don't I just bring him home with me now?"

Dovie's eyes lit. "Perfect! Why hadn't I thought of that myself?"

She wasn't fooling me.

22

Rufus tugged me along and for a while I wasn't sure who was walking who.

Who. Whom? Where was Preston when I needed her? Scratch that. I couldn't handle Preston right now. I really just wanted some alone time. Now that the caffeine was kicking in I wasn't as tired, so I thought about indulging my love of musicals dragging out my DVD of *Seven Brides for Seven Brothers*.

Dusk settled early this time of year. The bluffs were in shadow, while the setting sun danced along the water as Rufus did his business.

My cell phone rang, and I thought for sure it was going to be Sean with an update. It wasn't—it was Marisol, and sure enough, she was gloating.

"You should have seen Dovie and Dr. Kearney, Lucy. Your father couldn't have planned it any better."

"He would be proud."

"Well, I can't see auras, but I know people. They're perfect for each other."

"Maybe so." I didn't want to set my hopes as high as

Marisol's. I'd been down this road before with my grandmother. "Have you heard from Em?"

Rufus tugged at the leash. He led me down the long drive toward the main road, sniffing his way along the lane and stopping to mark every bush in sight.

"She called from the airport before her flight took off. She sounds happy."

"I don't like her going alone."

"Me, either," Marisol agreed, "but it might do her some good. She's been having a harder time adjusting to single life than I thought. Has Aiden asked her out yet?"

The driveway was lined on both sides with woods Dovie's landscapers kept from encroaching onto the gravel. Flowers and trees had been added over the years to accentuate what Mother Nature had already made beautiful. In the spring, crocuses, daffodils, and tulips would be the first colors to show against the dull browns and greens left by a long winter. "Not yet."

"What's he waiting for?"

"I'm not sure. Maybe a sign from Em."

"This could go on forever. We need to push this along. Let me think on this. I'll get back to you."

She hung up, and I stared at the phone. Before I knew it, she'd be asking my father for a job.

Rufus stopped and marked the trunk of a beech tree. He pressed on, dragging me behind, and as we neared the end of the driveway I nearly fell over Rufus when he stopped short, freezing mid-step. Then I heard it. The snap of a twig to my right. Rufus barked. I squinted, trying to make out any forms in between the shadowy trees. My heart beat hard against my ribs.

After a long minute, Rufus licked my hand, set his

nose to the ground, and led me away. I was being paranoid again, that was all. Twigs snapped in the woods
all the time. There was nothing nefarious about a squir-
rel scampering from tree to tree.

Along the main road, two mailboxes sat along the
edge of a small crescent cut out of the woods—a safe
pull-off for the mail carrier. Rufus investigated the area
around the black posts as I scooped the mail from my
box.

While Rufus sniffed around, I picked through bills
and catalogs and several handwritten envelopes to
me—probably requests for my services. I opened one of
the letters. It was a request from a teenaged boy to find
the diamond necklace he had "borrowed" from his
mother so his girlfriend could wear it to a costume
party. He had gone dressed as a sugar daddy and she his
trophy wife. I smiled but knew I couldn't help the boy
unless he was willing to confess to his mother—I'd
need to do the reading on her.

Tucked in between two letters was a postcard with a
picture of the Old North Church on the front. It had a
Boston postmark.

MISS YOU! WISH YOU WERE HERE! SEE YOU SOON!
—CUTTER

The smart-ass had mailed it before he left town.

Laughing, I tugged Rufus away from a poison su-
mac tree. Though it was winter, the oil could still rub
off on his fur. "Come on, Rufus. Let's head back."

I heard revving sounds as a car barreled down the
road, its engine roaring. I dove for Rufus as the car
lurched to a stop two feet from where I cowered,

sending bits of snow flying into the air along with my mail.

Rufus licked my chin as I shook with fear, with anger.

"Are you crazy?" I shouted as the driver opened the door. Then I couldn't say anything at all.

"Don't look so scared, Ms. Valentine. If I wanted you dead, you'd be dead by now."

"I thought that wasn't your style?"

Smiling, Tristan Rourke said, "It's not, but it sounded good, didn't it?"

He walked over to me, patted Rufus's head. "Cute dog."

Rufus flopped onto the snow and rolled onto his back, obviously hoping Tristan wasn't opposed to giving him a belly rub.

Grendel would have held out. He had a lot more pride.

Tristan crouched and obliged the dog. Rufus's tongue hung against the side of his muzzle in ecstasy.

I glanced at the car, an older-model black Chevy, trying to memorize the license plate number. Just in case I made it out of here alive.

"Don't bother," Tristan said, crossing his arms. Muscles bulged. He wasn't wearing a coat. "It's stolen."

"Why am I not surprised?"

He laughed and scooped up my mail, leaving Rufus wriggling in the snow trying to stand up.

Handing me the stack of mail, Tristan said, "I don't have long."

"Why have you been following me around?"

"I want Meaghan's information."

As if I was going to hand it over to him when he

was wanted for murder—despite what she thought she wanted. She wasn't thinking straight. Love could do that to a girl. Luckily, I wasn't obligated to share the information. She was no longer a client of mine.

"Maybe you should turn yourself in," I suggested.

"Why?"

Good question. If he turned himself in, he was going to jail. For a long, long time. That wouldn't hold much appeal to me, either.

When I didn't say anything, he added, "I'm not guilty, Ms. Valentine. I didn't run over Spero, though I'd like to thank the person who did."

"There's an eyewitness."

He shrugged. "That person is mistaken."

Not a chance.

"Now, about Meaghan's information . . ."

"No," I said.

"I don't want to do this the hard way."

I took a step back.

He sighed. "Didn't I tell you violence wasn't my style?"

"I didn't believe you."

Rufus tugged on the leash. He was eager to get on with his walk. I heard an engine in the distance, drawing closer. I wouldn't mind a bit if it was a police cruiser.

Tristan heard it, too. He jumped into his car, rolled down the window. "I always get what I want, Ms. Valentine. I'll be in touch."

Unfortunately, I believed him.

He drove off, and the car I had heard coming never materialized. I let Rufus walk me back to the house.

We were almost to my front door when Rufus froze again, his ear cocked, his head tipped to the side in doggy concentration. I tried to pick up on what caught his attention, but I could only hear the crashing of the waves against the bluff.

Suddenly Rufus bolted. I lost hold of his leash as he darted off toward the woods on Dovie's side of the lot. He was barking and wagging his tail as he galloped along. I dropped the mail and gave chase but was winded by the time I reached the top of my lane. I watched Rufus run down the driveway, and in a blink he was out of sight. I knew I couldn't keep up with him. I went back for my car. And three hours of frantic searching and many tears later, I had to admit to myself I'd lost him.

23

Grendel was sleeping atop my head when I woke to the sound of the phone ringing. It had jarred me awake from the most awful dream—I had lost Rufus.

I sat up, rubbed my eyes. They were crusty from salty tears.

Right. It hadn't been a dream.

I rolled to my right, quickly grabbed the phone from its base, hoping someone had seen the message I'd posted on craigslist last night about a missing golden retriever. "Hello?"

"Uva," Raphael said. "It's me."

I focused on the clock. It was just after seven. I'd slept for only an hour. "What's wrong? Did something happen?"

"Your father needs you to come in to the office as soon as possible."

"Why?" I had a dog to find. If this wasn't important . . .

"There's been a break-in and Oscar wants you to check and see if anything is missing."

There was a tight edge to Raphael's voice. I knew he hadn't told me everything yet. "What else?"

There was a long pause. "There was also a break-in at the penthouse. The Vermeer is gone, the Gandolfi, too."

I sat up. "Tristan Rourke."

"We think so, yes."

I knew so. I rubbed the sleep from my eyes. I'd only had an hour's rest. "I'll be there as soon as I can."

Taking a quick shower, I let my hair air-dry to save time. I fed Grendel and Odysseus and grabbed the LOST DOG poster I'd made of Rufus last night. I needed to make copies and hang them on every streetlight around town. But as I gathered all my things, I couldn't help but wonder if I would be wasting my time.

It seemed to me Tristan Rourke had been on a stealing spree last night.

Had it extended to dognapping as well?

It certainly wouldn't be the first time.

Suz was sitting at her desk when I came into the office, her eyes red rimmed and puffy. "I set the alarm last night."

I gave her a hug. "It's not your fault. Really. Tristan Rourke isn't a criminal mastermind for nothing. Our alarm system is child's play to him. Is my father here?"

"He's at his penthouse. He wants you to go there as soon as you look around here."

I did a quick scan of the front room. Nothing was out of place. Even the binoculars were still sitting on the windowsill exactly where I left them yesterday. In my office I could tell someone had gone through my files, but nothing was taken.

I knew what Tristan was looking for. And it was in my satchel.

Meaghan's file.

I went over to my corner desk, pulled out the bottom drawer, and grabbed a large envelope. I slipped Meaghan's file inside, addressed it to Marisol. In the little kitchenette off the hallway that also housed the Xerox machine, I made a hundred copies of the LOST DOG flyer. There was a pit in my stomach that ached so badly I didn't even think about drinking a cup of coffee. I was operating on pure adrenaline.

Suz was still at her desk, sniffling. I said, "Did you find anything missing?"

"No. I probably wouldn't have known someone was in here except for the alarm company called about a sensor being tripped."

It was unusual that Tristan would have been so careless. Usually no one knew he'd been in or out until they realized valuables were missing. Which made me suspect he'd tripped the alarm on purpose. To let us know he'd been here. That we couldn't keep him out.

I gave Suz another hug and climbed the stairs leading up to SD Investigations on the third floor. It was just after eight, and as I hoped, Andrew, the office assistant (he hated being called a receptionist), was just arriving.

When he spotted me, he said, "Sean's in his office."

"He is?"

"You didn't come up to see him?"

I suddenly felt the pull from Sean's office, iron to a magnet. "No, I came up to see you."

His eyes widened and his chest puffed a bit. "Me?"

I pulled the envelope from my bag and slipped him

a twenty. "Can you mail this for me?" I hadn't wanted to involve Suz just in case Tristan ever approached her for information. This way she wouldn't have to lie.

He looked at the twenty, then at me, a brazen look in his eye. "How about instead of money—"

"I'm not kissing you," I said.

Frowning, he sat. "It was worth a try."

I smiled at him. He was gutsier than I had ever given him credit for. Because if Sean had overheard him, he'd be out of a job. And most likely maimed. But Andrew was young, early twenties, and still had a lot to learn. He'd come to work at SDI during a time when Sam and Sean hadn't been able to keep a receptionist thanks to a pesky hex. They'd learned the hard way not to mess with curses.

I headed back to Sean's office. I had received a text message from him late last night that he'd finally been released from questioning and he'd tell me all about it this morning.

I stopped at his doorway, leaned there for a minute just watching him work on his desktop computer. He wasn't what *GQ* would consider handsome, with his broken nose and strong chin, but there was just something about him that radiated sex appeal, a special kind of aura. Maybe that's why I'd been so attracted to him. And maybe it was why when I touched his hand I could see images of our future. Because I sure as hell couldn't figure out why that happened, and I'd spent many nights trying.

He glanced up, caught me staring at him. In a flash he was out of his chair, rushing over to me. He cupped my face, his fingers strong, sure, and warm. "What's happened? You've been crying. This isn't about me not coming over last night, is it?"

"Such ego," I cracked, though I could feel tears welling again.

"Then what?"

Where to start? "I bumped into Tristan Rourke at my mailbox last night. I lost Rufus. Valentine, Inc., was broken into last night, my father's penthouse, too, and his Vermeer and Gandolfi are missing."

Sean swore, then said, "Rourke?"

"He's looking for Meaghan's information because I wouldn't give it to him. The paintings have to be a bargaining chip."

"And Rufus?"

"I was walking him, and suddenly he bolted. I don't know if he's wandering the streets of town or if Rourke stole him, too." I remembered the way Rufus had rolled over to offer up his belly for scratching. The shameless mutt. "I searched well into the morning. There was no sign of him. I have posters to hang, but I have to go see my father."

Sean closed his laptop. "I'll come with you."

I wanted to sag in relief but felt I should be stronger, put up a fight. "You don't have to; you're probably busy. . . ."

"I'm coming."

"Okay."

Fifteen minutes later, we were at the penthouse. Dad was pacing; Raphael was watching him. I didn't see any police presence. I took the mug of coffee Raphael offered, and said, "Where are the police? Shouldn't they be dusting for prints or something?"

My father raised a dark eyebrow. His brown eyes burned with fury. He waved his hand, dismissing the notion of police with one swipe.

I walked over to the mantel. The Vermeer was indeed missing. Sean had taken a mug of coffee and was about to sit on the couch. "No!" I shouted.

He hovered in a half sit as though he realized he was about to sit on a porcupine.

"Not the couch," I said. "The chair. It's much more comfortable."

Raphael chuckled. My father continued to glare. Sean switched seats.

"Nothing was taken at the office," I said to my dad. "Rourke riffled through the files but didn't find what he was looking for. Meaghan Archibald's file was at home with me."

I blew across the mug but didn't drink. My stomach was in knots, twisting and turning, churning and burning. The rhyme had me thinking of the homeless man again. My mind had wandered to him a lot lately. I took it as a sign I was supposed to help him. Later, after we sorted out this mess, I'd look for him.

"I don't know whether he came here looking for the file or specifically looking for your artwork, but it doesn't really matter at this point, does it? I'm glad neither of you were home. Rourke insists he's not violent, but there's a dead man who might not agree."

"Dead?" my father gasped.

"The house was empty?" Sean asked.

I hadn't had time to tell him about all the moving out going on around here. "Dad moved in with Mum yesterday."

"And I moved in with Maggie," Raphael said, refilling Sean's mug from the coffee press. "It was good timing on Rourke's part."

"How did he get past the alarm?" Sean asked.

My father growled. "The security issue will be addressed later today. The bigger picture is my missing artwork."

"Did you call the police?" I asked. "What did they say?"

"The police have not been notified," my father said stiffly, running a hand through his hair. "I'd rather not involve them if I can help it."

I sat on the arm of Sean's chair. I wasn't going anywhere near that couch. "Why?"

"Red tape. Besides, I have you. We'll do a reading, find the paintings, have them returned, and everything will be settled and forgotten."

I set the mug on a side table. "Were the paintings insured?"

My father scowled, breath blowing through his nose. He reminded me of the milliner in Medford at that moment. Such bursts of temper couldn't be good for their blood pressure.

"Lucy Juliet," my father said through clenched teeth. "You'll do a reading?"

My head was pounding. Not enough sleep, too much worrying about Rufus, now this . . . And I never did get my bath. "Since you asked so nicely." I walked over to him, held out my hand. He knew the drill.

Slowly, he placed his hand on mine. I waited for the dizziness, the images. None came. I drew my hand back and said, "Which one were you thinking about?"

"Both."

"Let's try again. Focus only on the Vermeer."

Still nothing. My father's hand was turning clammy. I let go of it. "Nothing," I said, wincing.

"What do you mean nothing?"

I shrugged. "I didn't see anything. You own the paintings; therefore, I should be able to get a reading from you. The only time I see nothing is when someone is deliberately not thinking of the item or—" I stared at my father. He had the good grace to stare at the ceiling. Raphael had busied himself in the kitchen, suddenly deciding the wine bottles on the rack all needed to be turned.

"What?" Sean asked.

"The objects don't belong to the person. Dad, where'd you get the paintings?"

"I don't really see where that matters, Lucy Juliet."

"They're stolen property?" I sank onto the couch and leaped off the moment I realized it, as though my rear end had caught fire. I was going to have to throw these jeans away. Great. Another pair of pants ruined.

"You don't have to sound so disdainful. It's a common practice."

"Insurance?" Sean asked.

My father gave a short shake of his head. "I don't understand, Lucy. If I paid for the paintings they should belong to me, no matter the provenance."

"Don't blame me that my abilities came with a conscience."

"What are we going to do?" Dad dragged a hand down his face. "Those paintings are worth millions."

I didn't want to lecture about buying from legitimate sources.

"Rourke wants Meaghan's information. He'll make a trade," my father said softly, testing the waters.

I thought it fairly obvious that was Rourke's plan all along. I hadn't wanted to bring it up, because I didn't want to give in. It was essentially blackmail. Or extortion. I never could remember the difference.

The three of them looked at me.

"No," I said. "No way."

My father said, "I expected nothing less from you." He kissed my forehead.

"We should go," I said to Sean. There wasn't anything we could do here.

My father walked us to the door. "When Rourke contacts you, and he undoubtedly will, give him my number. It's time I dealt with him myself."

I said I would but immediately pictured my father making deals with Rourke for more stolen paintings.

Sean pressed the button for the elevator. "Lucy?"

"Yeah?"

"What's with the couch?"

24

Sean drove me home. Dad had closed the office for the day. I hated to disappoint clients, but I was glad for the day off. I fought a yawn as I asked Sean about the FBI questioning.

"They left me in a holding room for hours by myself. Head games."

Sean had told them all he knew about Rourke, but they hadn't believed him and had accused him of holding back.

"They want me out of their case and proved just how far they're willing to go to prove they have more power."

"What are you going to do?" I asked.

"My job."

"Do you think Tristan is innocent?"

"I don't know what to believe, Lucy. I'm just looking for the truth. It might not be what Meaghan wants to hear, or it may just be the best news of her life."

My cell phone rang, and I fished around in my bag until I found it. Preston's name flashed on my screen. I answered because I hated the silence stretching between Sean and me like elastic pulled too tight.

"Guess where I am," she said, sounding too bright and perky for my foul mood.

"Jail."

"Ha. Ha. I'm in Randolph. I just met with Eva Denham-Foster for tea."

I tried to place the name, and then it clicked. "The hat."

"Right. Well, it turns out her sons cleaned out their father's belongings after he died. She doesn't have a clue to what they did with them."

"So one of the Denham-Foster sons could be the Lone Ranger?"

"Exactly. Believe me when I tell you they have enough money to be throwing it around. I drank out of a teacup rimmed in twenty-four-karat gold. Can you believe that? I'm glad you and your family aren't that pretentious."

Twenty-four-karat gold was a long way from my sarcasm mug.

"Anyway, I'm off to meet with Matthias Denham-Foster. Did you want to come along? Are you busy?"

"Kind of."

"Kind of?"

"I lost Rufus," I said. "I need to put up flyers."

"You what?"

I couldn't repeat it again. The tears were welling. Sean reached over and placed his hand on the back of my mine. Little zaps of electricity tickled my fingers, but there were no visions this way—only when our palms touched. The tips of his fingers massaged my knuckles. It was soothing. And just like that the elastic tension between us went slack.

"I'll come right over," Preston said. "I'll help."

"You don't have to. Really."

"I want to."

How could I argue? "Okay."

I searched for any sign of Rufus's copper tail as we drove toward Aerie. As soon as Sean parked in front of my cottage, Dovie was out her back door on her way down. I didn't know how to break the news to her.

I unlocked the door, scooped up Grendel, and held him close. Sean met Dovie on the walkway and they whispered back and forth.

Dovie rushed through my front door, took one look at me, and opened her arms wide. I set Grendel down and went willingly, and no sooner was I wrapped in a tight hug than I burst into tears.

There were a lot of mumblings of "there, there" and "poor thing." Before I knew it, I had drunk two cups of tea and was lying down on the bed, a cool towel on my head, Grendel at my feet. The last thing I remembered before I fell asleep was Sean kissing me gently and telling me not to worry and to trust him.

As I drifted off, I realized there was no one I trusted more.

I woke to knocking. Someone was at my front door.

Suddenly wide awake, I sat up. Tristan Rourke probably wouldn't knock, so I let out the breath I was holding. I couldn't get his words out of my head.

I'll be in touch.

Yeah. *After* his little crime spree.

Did he have Rufus? Because as much as I wanted to

deny it, I'd probably trade Meaghan's information for Rufus in a hot second. Which made me question my every moral fiber. Integrity? Did I really have any?

The knocking continued. I pushed back the covers, checked the time. It was just after one. I'd been asleep for close to three hours. Where was everyone?

I peeked out the door and saw Aiden standing on the porch. I let him in and didn't even care when he said, "Whoa, what happened to you?"

"Don't ask."

I spotted Rufus's rubber chicken on my hearth and nearly broke down again. "Coffee?" I squeaked.

"Sure."

I poured the water into the system and went to brush my teeth and comb my hair. I corralled my curls into a claw clip.

By the time I was done, Aiden had already poured his coffee and was teasing Grendel with one of his kitty toys—a feather at the end of a long stick. Grendel was in heaven.

Aiden was dressed in his suit and tie—his standard work uniform. His shoes were gleaming perfection. I'm not sure how he managed that with all the snow and slush outside. Sunlight spilled into the room, and I could hear the drip, drip, drip of melting snow from the eaves. Maybe spring would come after all. I had begun to harbor doubts.

"Official visit?" I asked, grabbing a mug of coffee for me. I should really have eaten something but still lacked an appetite.

The feather swished from side to side. Grendel thumped after it, reaching out with extended claws to grab hold. "Sean called. He asked me to swing by and check on you. He said he had some things to wrap in town but would be back with Thoreau by suppertime."

My head was fuzzy with not enough sleep and plenty of worry. I was having trouble remembering how I'd found my way into bed in the first place.

"I heard you had a visitor yesterday." He let Grendel catch the feather for a second before pulling it away.

"Tristan Rourke." I sipped the coffee. It burned the back of my throat, made the ache in my stomach worse. I put it down. I told Aiden everything that had happened in the last twenty-four hours, right down to the fact that my father had bought paintings from the black market.

"I'm just going to pretend I didn't hear that."

"Tristan said he'd be in touch. I'm sure he wants to swap the paintings, and possibly Rufus, for Meaghan Archibald's phone number and address."

"If Meaghan *wants* to meet with Tristan, why not?" He'd had a long talk with Sean if he knew Meaghan was in Tristan's corner. *I* hadn't told him.

"Technically, I shouldn't be involved at all anymore. She's no longer my client. It's not my place to make any kind of trade."

He arched an eyebrow.

"Fine," I said. "I'm trying to protect her. She's so googly-eyed over seeing him again, she's completely overlooking the fact that he's wanted by the FBI. And is wanted by the police for killing a man."

"Don't you think that's her call? She's old enough to make her own decisions. Protect herself."

He was right, but I didn't want to admit it.

"I have good instincts, right?"

He smiled. "The best."

"I completely believe Tristan is a criminal mastermind."

"But?" Grendel swatted at the feather to remind Aiden he'd stopped swinging it.

"I don't know if he's a killer."

Aiden leaned forward. "The motivation is there. As is the witness."

"I know. That's why I'm having a hard time with it."

Blowing out a thin thread of air, he said, "I trust your instincts, Lucy. Let me talk with the detective in charge of Spero's case. See if there were any other witnesses."

"Thanks," I said. "Have you heard anything else about Mac?"

He chuckled. "It took you long enough to ask."

"I'm tired. Synapses aren't firing right."

"The investigator on Mac's case admitted he never followed up on Christa Hayes's report about the phone call she'd overheard the night before Mac went missing. He thinks Mac killed himself by jumping off the bluff near his house and considers the case closed, though he hasn't made an official announcement."

"Why does he think that? Does he have any evidence?"

"Beyond Mac having a terminal illness, Rufus was found wandering *inside* Mac's compound. The front gate was closed, and the property is fenced. If Mac had taken Rufus for his usual walk and disappeared along the way, there would have been no way Rufus would have been able to get back up to the house on his own."

I tried to process this. "Mac disappeared from his *own* property."

"Right."

"Do we know for certain Mac had even taken Rufus for a walk that day?"

"There were several sightings of Mac and Rufus, and the family housekeeper also verified Mac had taken Rufus out. They had a scheduled routine."

"When Rufus came back without Mac," Aiden said, "the housekeeper knew something must have happened."

"So, let's get this straight. Mac takes Rufus for a walk, comes back to the house, and jumps off a cliff?"

Aiden let Grendel have the feather. He swatted it a few times before growing bored and walking away. "That's the investigator's theory."

"Was the house ever processed?" There could be evidence inside, though I hated thinking Mac had met with a violent end.

"No. The local police never suspected foul play."

Rick Hayes was hurting for money—would he go so far as to hire someone to kill Mac? Push him off a cliff? "What do you know about Rick Hayes?"

"Why?"

I explained about the insurance policy, Christa's inheritance, and Rick's TV show.

He whistled low. "I don't know much, Lucy. Washed-up rock star—that's about it. I'll share your information with the lead investigator. Along with that phone call Christa overheard, it might make him change his mind about declaring the case closed. I finally got my hands on Mac's phone records, and using the information Christa gave you, I was able to track the number to Fred Ross."

Fred was Mac's poker partner, not to mention a

pillar of the community. He and Dovie had been friends for years.

"I wanted to go pay him an informal visit," Aiden said, "verify Christa's story. It's a loose end I want to tie up. Did you want to come along?"

Technically, this wasn't Aiden's case. He was going above and beyond to help me out. "Definitely."

Ten minutes later, we were heading to Fred's house. At the bottom of Aerie's drive, my heart caught in my throat. A LOST DOG sign was taped to my mailbox post. As we drove, I saw signs everywhere. Tears clogged my eyes, stung my nose. Sean had been busy. And I had a feeling he had help from Dovie and Preston, since neither had been around when I woke up.

Aiden tapped his hand against the curve of his steering wheel. The car smelled strongly of wintergreen, thanks to the mints he popped into his mouth every other minute.

Mr. Ross lived a couple miles down the road, right across the street from Mac. I thought about the day he'd disappeared. It was amazing anyone had seen him walking Rufus. These weren't well-traveled streets— not this time of year, at least. All too often, no one ever saw anything, heard anything. People had an annoying habit of minding their own business. It was as if Mac had gone out of his way to be seen—or maybe it had been his way of saying good-bye.

I dropped my visor, blocking the sun. Beams reflected off the snow, making it sparkle brilliantly.

Aiden tossed another mint into his mouth and offered me one from his Tic Tac container.

"No, thanks." With the way my stomach hurt, I might not ever eat again.

He glanced my way, then looked back at the road. Again, he glanced my way, then looked at the road.

"What?" I asked.

At forty-two, Aiden had been with the Massachusetts State Police since graduating from Boston College with a criminal-justice degree. It wasn't luck that had propelled him to the rank of Detective Lieutenant, head of his own unit. His hunches were legendary, his work ethic unquestionable. He was extremely loyal—something I'd learned firsthand over the last few months. And it wasn't like him not to come out and say what he was thinking. Which had me believing whatever was on his mind was more of a personal nature.

"Nothing," he said.

"Something," I countered.

"It's just that . . ."

"What?" I was too tired for this. Bone-aching fatigue had settled in. I had too much on my mind, and I needed to get some of it sorted out before I went into a coma.

Finally, he said loudly—as though it wasn't a big deal at all, "I haven't seen Em around in a while."

Ah. Em. Now his hesitation made sense. "She's been busy with school, and now she's on spring break. She left for Hawaii yesterday."

Aiden stared at me. The car swerved before he yanked the wheel hard to the left. I clutched the door handle.

"Sorry," he mumbled. "When will she be back?"

"Nine days."

Lost in thought, he turned into Fred's estate, which was located on the inland side of the street. The stone house, which technically should be called a mansion, sat tucked into surrounding woods, looking every bit like a storybook cottage on steroids. The paved driveway narrowed into a small bridge that spanned a swath of frozen marshland before widening into a courtyard in front of the house.

Fred Ross greeted us as we got out of the car. He gave me a kiss and asked for Dovie as he led us into his home. Dark interiors and hand-hewn wood gave off an impression of a hunting lodge as we followed Fred down a wide hall and into a kitchen that overlooked the backyard pool area that been closed off for winter.

Small finches sat on a feeder just beyond the window as Fred offered us something to drink. Aiden and I both declined. A fire roared from a fieldstone fireplace in the family room just off the kitchen. Fred motioned for us to sit on the sofa. He stoked the flames and took a seat in a high-backed chair near the hearth.

"You're here about Mac?" he asked. "Have there been any new developments?"

Small gold-rimmed glasses perched on his beak-like nose. Wrinkles jogged from the corners of his eyes, his mouth. Thick folds creased his forehead and his neck, disappearing beneath the white collar of a turtleneck beneath a checkered sweater. His watery brown eyes were bright, intelligent. Thin white hair striped the top of his head, combed back into a neatly trimmed style. The barest hint of white stubble whispered along his jawline, his chin.

"Not really," I answered.

"We're here tracking a loose end," Aiden said. "Mac's granddaughter, Christa, overheard him on the phone the night before he disappeared."

"He was telling someone he'd do what he pleased,"

I said, "and for that person to mind his own business. That person was you, wasn't it?"

Fred nodded, smiled. "I remember. Mac could be a stubborn old geezer."

"What had Mac been referring to?" I asked, smiling at Fred's affectionate tone.

"Same old argument we'd been having for months. His health."

Aiden said, "The cancer?"

"Mac wanted to die on his own terms, and not go through with the treatments his doctor recommended. I didn't like that decision."

The *Globe* was open on the coffee table. The Lone Ranger's antics had big headlines. Preston was probably seething with jealousy. "You were trying to convince him to do the chemo?"

Fred smiled again, revealing a set of big teeth that had to be dentures. "I was nagging him like an old woman. Mac didn't take it too kindly. Told me he'd do what he pleased and I should mind my own business."

It corroborated what Christa had told us.

"I hate like hell that was our last conversation."

"How was his relationship with Jemima?" I asked.

"Mac's the quiet type," Fred said, "but he'd get to talking about Jemima every so often. The relationship was strained at best. He gave her money every month so she could pay her bills. He didn't like having to support Rick, but he didn't want to see Christa suffer because of Jemima's bad taste in men." His glasses slipped and he pushed them back up his nose. "Mac wasn't real crazy about that husband of hers. Never had been. Always thought Rick had a hold over her she couldn't break free from."

"What do you think happened to Mac?" Aiden asked.

"I've been working that over in my head since he turned up missing." A log shifted in the fireplace, sending sparks up the flue. "I miss my friend and want to blame someone for his being gone, but I can't help but feel, deep down, that Mac . . ." His voice trailed off.

"Took his own life?" Aiden asked.

"I think whatever happened," Fred said, "it was Mac's choice."

25

"Do you have a few more minutes?" I asked Aiden as I pulled my seat belt across my lap.

"To do what?"

"Fred's sweater reminded me of something."

"A checkerboard?"

"Ha. Ha. No. Christa mentioned Mac had been wearing a hideously ugly sweater the day he went missing. He bought it from a local consignment shop."

"I'm not following, other than you made the leap from one ugly sweater to another."

"Consignment shops track their inventory, right?"

He started the car. "Right."

"Then the shop has a record of who owned that sweater before Mac." I adjusted the visor. "I might be able to get a reading from the previous owner on the whereabouts of that sweater now."

"Might?"

"Clothes are tricky. It all depends on whether my ESP will recognize the sweater had more than one owner. I've never tried to do a reading on an item from a consignment shop before. I don't know if it will work, but I know it definitely won't unless I try. I need to get the name of the person who owned the sweater before Mac."

Aiden swung the car around, drove across the narrow bridge back toward the main road. "I don't think the shop will willingly give out that information."

I gave him a wide smile.

He rolled his eyes. "Of course. That's why you wanted me to come along. I feel so used."

I laughed. "A badge goes a long way in convincing someone to impart information."

"All right," he said. "Where is this place?"

"I'm not exactly sure. Christa mentioned it was in Hingham. How many consignment shops can there be?"

"Wait a sec." He pulled off to the side of the road. From the backseat he pulled forth a thick portfolio. Thumbing through folders, he said, "I have Mac's file in here somewhere." He pulled it out, opened it.

"What are you looking for?"

He thumbed through police reports, statements from Mac's doctor, Mac's phone records, witness statements, bank statements, and finally pulled out a sheaf of paper stapled together. "Mac's credit card bills." His index finger slid down page after page. "Here," he said, tapping. "Early December. 'I'll Take Seconds Consignment.' Mac spent just under one hundred dollars."

I was looking at the statement over his shoulder. "That's a lot of money at a consignment shop."

"In that area, it might be an upscale consignment shop. I know right where it is, just a couple blocks from my place." He pulled back onto the road, drove well over the speed limit.

That's right. He didn't live far from Hingham Center, in a dilapidated old Victorian he was slowly putting back together. "How are your renovations going?"

"Slow. I have some vacation time I need to take or lose forever, so I've placed an order for hardwood flooring. As soon as it comes in, I'll be calling in favors from friends to help me lay it." He glanced at me. "And stain it. And varnish it."

"Okay, okay. I'll help." He'd done more than enough for me. "And I can probably wrangle Sean to help, too. Maybe Cutter if he's back in town. Marisol can swing a mean paintbrush, though if Butch will be there, she might suddenly have the flu."

Marisol had dated Butch, Aiden's roommate, for a month or so before Butch broke it off with her. She hated being dumped.

"Butch moved out."

"When?"

"A couple of weeks ago. His family decided to expand their chain of markets and sent him to North Carolina to oversee the construction and running of the new store there."

"Will you look for another roommate?" I was thinking of Sean. If he wouldn't move in with me, at least he could be a little closer than the city.

"I don't think so."

Well, there went that idea.

"Butch and I went way back," he said. "College buddies. Having anyone else there would be strange."

His cheeks colored slightly, and I had the sudden

feeling he was thinking about Em. Marisol was right. We had to do something soon to push them together.

In Hingham, Aiden took the farthest exit off the rotary. The town center was filled with every kind of business, from bookstores, to boutiques, to several coffee shops. We parked in a diagonal slot in front of shop with I'LL TAKE SECONDS written in bold font on an awning above a wide glass window. Written on the window itself, in small letters, was A CONSIGNMENT SHOP. I supposed the qualification was needed to avoid confusion with a clock shop—or a really good diner.

A bell jingled when we entered and a woman behind the counter looked up from her book. "May I help you?"

"I hope so," I said. "We're looking into the disappearance of Mac Gladstone."

"The man with the dog," she said, nodding. "I've been reading about the case. So sad. What brings you here?"

"Well, the day he went missing he was wearing a sweater he bought from this shop. We're hoping to find the original owner of that sweater."

The woman placed her book down, creasing the spine. "Oh my." I put her to be early fifties, and I wasn't sure if it was because she'd been reading, but she had a librarian air about her that reminded me of Abigail from the Thomas Crane library. Intelligence shone in her eyes, and she carried the same don't-mess-with-me attitude that Abigail did. Unfortunately, Aiden didn't have dimples to sway her.

"There are several problems here. First, I don't keep records of those who *make* purchases, only clients who leave items for consignment." Her eyes widened. "And second, even if I did know the original owner of the sweater Mr. Gladstone purchased, I couldn't possibly give out personal information belonging to that client."

I waited patiently for her to finish—quite a feat, as I was eager to get the information and go. I looked around for Aiden. This was where he needed to step in. He was standing at a rack of clothes, fingering a Hawaiian print shirt. I coughed. He looked up and the fabric slipped from his fingers.

Striding over, he introduced himself and let the woman examine his badge. He provided the dates Mac had been in the store and the fact that he'd used a credit card for his purchases. "There should be a trail, either electronic or paper. Or both."

By the time Aiden was done, she was blushing to the tips of her frosted brown hair. He might not have the power of dimples, but he had a no-nonsense cop look about him that terrified many people into complying with his wishes.

"I can return with a warrant if you prefer," he added gently, "if it would ease your conscience."

Her hand fluttered over her chest. "There's no need for formality. As this is a police request, I'm more than happy to do my part. It'll take just a moment."

When she turned, Aiden flashed me a triumphant smile. I thought he enjoyed throwing his power around.

The woman—her name was Madeline—alternated between tapping on her computer and checking a thick logbook.

I leaned toward her. "If it helps, I heard the sweater was absolutely hideous. Deep orange with confetti-like colored shapes all over it."

She lifted her head from her computer. "*That* sweater?"

"You remember it?" I asked.

"Hard to forget. It was early December and a woman came in with all kinds of ugly clothes. Her brother had just passed on and she was looking to unload his wardrobe. There was a mound of items on the counter I just couldn't accept. I have a reputation, you know."

Aiden and I nodded so she'd keep talking.

"About the time I was telling her I couldn't take any of her items, a very handsome, distinguished man came in. He saw the sweater on the counter and straight off asked if he could buy it. I certainly wasn't going to turn down a sale, but I can't express how shocked I was when he sorted through the entire pile on the counter and bought several of the items from that lot, including an equally ugly sky blue sweater with purple stripes, a ratty coat, and worn-out sneakers that barely had any sole left."

I held in a smile. Mac really must have wanted to get under Jemima's skin.

"I had a dickens of a time telling the woman I couldn't take the rest of her clothing. She simply didn't believe me when I said no one would buy them."

"Do you have the woman's name?"

Madeline flipped through the logbook until she found what she was looking for. "Orlinda Batista."

"Do you have an address?" Aiden asked, pulling out a notebook.

"Only a phone number," she said, reading it off the book.

Aiden jotted it down. "Thank you. We might be in touch if we need any more information."

"If I can help," she said, her eyes bright, "I'll be glad to."

She was so sincere I almost expected her to salute.

"Can I ask why you need to see the woman?" she asked. "How does the sweater factor in?"

Aiden glanced my way and must have seen the hesitation in my eyes. "Sorry, ma'am. That's confidential."

Her lips formed a little o, and she pressed her hands to her heart again.

Outside the shop, Aiden glanced at his watch. "I have to go back to work, and I need a little time to track down the address that goes with this phone number. Are you free tomorrow?"

"I'll clear my schedule if I have to."

I just hoped Orlinda Batista's palm held the energy I needed to find Mac. Unfortunately, I was losing hope he was alive.

26

As soon as Aiden dropped me off at home, I dialed Marisol to run my plan past her.

"You're brilliant," she said, her voice light with laughter. "It will work. It has to work!"

I hoped it didn't backfire. "So, whoever talks to Em first has to get the information out of her. Deal?"

"Deal. How did Dovie's date go?"

My phone beeped with call-waiting, and I let it go through to voice mail. "I haven't talked to her yet." I explained about Rufus and the break-ins.

"Didn't you say you found Thoreau by finding his leash? Can you do the same for Rufus?"

"I can't. Mac bought Rufus's leash. I remember Christa mentioning he special-ordered it."

"Well, if it's any peace of mind, I microchipped him yesterday. If someone finds him and brings him to a local vet's, they'll be able to track him back to me."

"You'll let me know if someone calls?"

"Right away."

I didn't feel much relief. I had the sinking feeling Rufus wasn't running loose in the streets.

I'll be in touch.

I hung up with Marisol, and suddenly cold, I turned the heat up another two degrees. I made sure all my doors and windows were locked and the alarm set. Grendel watched me from atop the fridge as I poked around for something to eat. I nibbled on a cold slice of pizza, but my stomach wasn't in it. In fact, it was getting worse. At this rate I was going to have to see a doctor.

My phone chimed that I had a voice-mail message waiting—I'd forgotten about the call that had come in while I was talking to Marisol.

It had been from Sean. "Ms. Valentine," he said, causing warmth to chase away a lingering chill. "Bad news, good news. Bad news is I'm stuck in a traffic nightmare heading out of the city. Good news is I'm on my way to you. I should be there in an hour or so."

Just enough time for a bath. Finally.

Grendel hid under my bed while I ran the water and dumped in bath salts. I lit candles and turned the lights off. I sank into the water, letting the heat work its magic on my muscles, my stress, my worries.

I thought about Mac and what might have happened to him. I had pretty much ruled out any kind of blackmail scheme. The money he'd been withdrawing every month had to have been going to Jemima and Rick, to keep them afloat. It seemed more and more likely he'd killed himself. He made sure Christa was taken care of financially, and he made sure Rufus had his morning walk. He probably assumed Jemima would let Christa keep the dog, and that had been a poor supposition on his part.

Wind buffeted the cottage. The old wood within the walls creaked and shifted. Water splashed as I sat up, listening, straining to hear any noise out of place. The creaking had been louder than usual, but after listening intently for a moment, I relaxed. Tristan Rourke had made me completely paranoid.

I closed my eyes and wondered how Preston had fared with the Lone Ranger's hat. She was absolutely tenacious when she was tracking a story. I sank deeper into the water as I worried about her discovering the truth about the auras. I hadn't called Cutter yet—a mistake on my part. I'd do it as soon as I got out of the tub.

I heard another sharp creak and sat up again, every sense on alert. After a few seconds of listening to the wind, I sank back into the heat of the water. This bath wasn't as relaxing as I thought it would be.

Focusing on a water droplet stubbornly clinging to the curved faucet, I let my head fall back onto the bath pillow. Candlelight flickered against the travertine tiles, and I allowed myself to remember a vision I'd had just before Christmas. It had been of Sean and me, him in a fancy black suit, me in a white sleeveless dress. A tropical flower had been tucked behind my ear, and my curls had been styled so they flowed over my shoulders. It had been a wedding—I was sure of that. It was all I had seen—and it had yet to come true. Between that vision and the one I'd had yesterday of us in Hawaii, my concerns about our future rose on the thin spirals of steam from the tub, vanishing somewhere high above me. I wasn't sure how we'd get there, and I had a feeling we had quite a few roadblocks ahead—but we *would* get there. Now if only I'd be able to stop worrying about what came *after*.

Using my toe, I dropped the lever to release the water from the tub. I dried off, moisturized, and wrapped my hair in a towel, turban-style. I grabbed my robe from the back of the door and was grateful to have the night alone with Sean. I'd try to block out the strains and stresses of my life right now and just focus on us.

I blew out the candles, opened the bathroom door, and screamed.

Tristan Rourke was sitting on my bed. Grendel was in his lap, and I could hear his purrs from across the room. Apparently, I'd been wrong. He had no pride at all. Not even a tiny iota.

"Did you have a nice bath?" Tristan asked.

I kept my back pressed to the wall. I looked to my left, out the bedroom. The alarm was off and the front door was open. "How'd you get in?"

"I'm a man of many talents," he said, scratching under Grendel's chin before setting him aside and standing up.

I was glancing around for some kind of weapon when Tristan said, "I think you know what I want. Are you in the mood to trade?" He kept his distance, which was good, because the only weapon I could lay eyes on was Grendel's feather-on-a-stick. Which would do me no good whatsoever unless I wanted to tickle Tristan to death.

"Your father has excellent taste in art, by the way." He chuckled.

"What's so funny?"

"I wonder if your father knows who originally stole those paintings."

I gasped. "You?"

"I'd call that making a full circle, wouldn't you? Now how about a trade? The paintings for Meaghan's file."

"What about Rufus?"

He cocked his head. "Rufus? I only took the Vermeer and the Gandolfi."

"The dog," I clarified.

"What dog? Oh, you mean the sweetheart from the mailbox yesterday?"

"That's him."

"Sorry. If the pooch is missing, it's not by my hand. Can't you do your little magic thing with your hands and find him like you did the other little dog?"

"It's complicated."

"Too bad. The file?" he asked.

A flash of light caught my eye. Headlights. A car was turning down the lane. Sean.

"I'm sorry. I don't have that information anymore."

"I'd hate to sell those paintings. . . ."

I bit my lip. In my head I heard my father saying they were worth millions. "Can I think about it?"

I could now hear the crunch of tires on the snow-packed lane. Tristan heard it, too. He sprinted to the front door and looked back at me.

"One more day, Lucy Valentine. I'm losing patience."

Then he was gone, out the door and down the steps. I ran to the doorway.

Sean had just opened the car door when Tristan went running out. He looked at me, then at Tristan, and ran after him. Thoreau barked from the safety of the car. I grabbed my cell phone from the counter and dialed 911 as Sean chased Tristan toward the bluff.

I could hardly believe my eyes when Tristan reached

the edge, bent down, and disappeared over the edge into the darkness. Sean skidded to a stop before falling after him.

He was breathing hard when he met me on the porch.

"What happened to him?" I asked, still seeing him going over the cliff in my mind's eye.

"He had a rope anchored to the bluff and a boat waiting for him below. He rappeled down the side of the cliff. I've never seen anything like it outside a Hollywood movie."

I didn't question the relief I felt—I didn't like Tristan, but I didn't necessarily want to see him dead, either. "The police are on their way." It would be too late to catch Tristan. He'd be long gone by the time the police could contact the Coast Guard.

Sean was pale as he took me in his arms, held me close. "When I saw him coming out the door . . ."

Suddenly I was flying backward over the threshold. I landed with a bone-jarring thud. Worse, I watched in horror as Sean flew in the opposite direction, across the porch. He landed in a snowbank just beyond the steps.

Stunned, I couldn't move for a second. It seemed as though I was watching in slow motion. Then my brain kicked in, and I realized what had happened. Sean had been shocked, his heart zapped by his implanted defibrillator. I scrambled to my feet, tripping in my haste to reach him. An overwhelming sense of loss and grief sat heavy on my chest, crushing. I fought to breathe normally. In, out.

This. This had been my vision.

I couldn't lose him. I couldn't.

I sent frantic pleas to every deity known to man. God, Buddha, the fates, the Tooth Fairy. Anyone who might be able to help me. To save him. To let us share a life together.

Together.

The sirens in the distance sounded to my ears like angels singing as I knelt in the snow next to him. I didn't even know I was crying until the tears dripped onto his face.

"You better not be faking, Sean Donahue."

He struggled to sit up. "Or else what?"

"I don't know. I'd have to kiss you to death or something."

"Good way to go."

His voice was quiet, so quiet. I said, "Keep still."

He reached up, swiped at the tears on my face. "I'm okay."

How could he say that? Didn't he know what happened? Hell, *felt* it? His heart had stopped. If not for that shock, he could be dead right now. Dead. I shuddered and tried valiantly to put the word out of my mind, but grief fluttered in my chest.

"Help me up," he said softly.

"I think you should lie still. The police are almost here." I could hear the sirens growing louder.

"Lucy, I'm freezing. Please. And your lips are turning blue."

Me. He was worried about me at a time like this. I didn't even feel the cold. If I was shaking, it wasn't because I was only wearing a robe. . . . It was the fear. The damn fear.

"Please," he repeated.

Grabbing hold of his forearms, I pulled. I helped him up the steps and into the chair next to the fireplace. He was heavy. I hated that the term "deadweight" came to mind. I used the collar of my robe to dry more tears. I had to stop crying. This wasn't the time to fall apart. I had to be strong.

"I just need to sit for a minute," he said.

"You need to go to the hospital. I'll call an ambulance." I looked around for my cell phone.

He grabbed my wrist. "No. I'm okay. I just need to call my doctor and transmit the reading. Remember? We talked about this."

I drew in a shaky breath. We had talked about it. Months ago. He thought I should know what happened during a shock and the common procedure afterward. If he had another shock in the next twenty-four hours, he'd need immediate medical attention, but for now he was right. He just needed to sit and get his bearings. And I needed to calm down.

Ha! Like that was going to happen. But as I looked into his eyes, I knew I had to fake it. For his sake.

It's just . . . I had never really expected him to have a shock. On the surface he was so healthy, so alive. Yet just underneath . . . a time bomb lurked. And it had just reminded me that Sean was living on borrowed time.

27

I was afraid to sleep.

Afraid that if I closed my eyes, when I opened them again Sean would be gone.

Gone, gone.

The forever kind of gone.

It was illogical—I knew he'd be fine at least for the foreseeable future. During my panic earlier, I'd forgotten about my other visions. The beach, the hammock. The white dress, the black suit. They had yet to be fulfilled. It gave me a small measure of relief. But then what? What if there were no other visions after those came true?

I glanced his way. He slept, looking blessedly peaceful for a change. I eyed his bottle of prescription medicine on the night table. He'd taken something to help him relax, to sleep, to keep torturous thoughts away. Lucky guy.

Checking the clock on my side of the bed, I saw it was just after 2:00 A.M. It had been a long night. An hour after the Cohasset police arrived at my cottage, the FBI showed up (I was beginning to really dislike Agents Thomas and St. John), then Aiden and a couple of state police investigators.

There had been so many questions, I'd lost track of what I answered. Thankfully, everyone had left Sean alone for the most part to rest. One thing they all agreed on was that my cottage wasn't safe. I'd given in after an hour of trying to explain that I didn't think Tristan Rourke would hurt me. No one listened.

I nixed all talk of hotel rooms and safe houses and went to the one place that felt as much like home as my place.

Mum's.

She'd welcomed Sean and me and our menagerie with open arms and big smiles. There was nothing she liked more than houseguests, no matter the reason we were staying.

There was twenty-four-hour surveillance on the house, from land and sea. Tristan Rourke would have to be crazy to try to break in.

I expected he would try.

Moonlight slipped through the crack in the drapes. It was both sweet and disturbing that my mother had left my room as it was the day I moved out. My walls were covered mostly with Broadway show posters, but there were a couple of bands, too—Pearl Jam, Journey, Bruce Springsteen. I had eclectic tastes, even as a teenager.

I looked up. A yellow Aerosmith concert poster had been stapled to the ceiling above my bed, and my gaze traced the font, just for something to do, to keep my mind from wandering.

Sean coughed, rolled, and settled in again. I watched him carefully, monitoring the rise and fall of his chest.

My own chest squeezed so tight it hurt to draw in a breath. I couldn't keep up this vigil. It wasn't healthy—mentally or physically.

I tossed off the covers, slipped on my robe and my slippers, and almost tripped over Grendel and Thoreau snuggled together on a dog bed at the foot of the bed. I peeked in on Odysseus, but he was making a nest and was completely covered in pine shavings.

I went in search of something to drink. Water, milk, bourbon. Something.

Downstairs, a light glowed in the kitchen. I followed it and found my father leaning over the counter, a fork poised over a half-eaten New York cheesecake.

Guilt colored his olive skin tone. "Lucy Juliet. What are you doing up?" He glanced at the cheesecake as if just seeing it for the first time, kind of an oh-what's-that-doing-there look. I was waiting to see how he'd explain it away, but he must have decided he'd incriminated himself enough already.

Never mind that I rarely ever saw him eat sweets. He'd been a health nut his whole life, but he was currently on a strict diet. Low fat, low sodium. All in an effort to strengthen his heart. It hadn't been very long since his near-fatal heart attack (what was with the men in my life and their hearts?). How long had he been sneaking treats in the middle of the night? This little discovery could explain a few things.

He didn't try to make excuses. "Fork?"

"Of course."

He slid one across the counter. I sank the tines into the cheesecake. "Mum's going to kill us."

"Only because we ate it first. I found it hiding behind two cartons of soy milk."

So much for her sticking to her newfound diet plan. "I'll be sure to replace it tomorrow."

"Good thinking." After a minute of silent eating, he said, "I'm glad you're here. You'll be safe."

I didn't bother to argue my safety. My father would be as hardheaded as the police. Maybe more so. I hadn't mentioned to the police about Dad's missing paintings. I only told them Tristan wanted Meaghan's file. I ate another bite. "Tristan won't be put off by the police presence. He seems the type up for a good challenge."

"He wouldn't dare break in here, not after what he pulled at the penthouse."

Again, I didn't argue.

Dad's brown eyes softened. "How's Sean feeling?"

"Okay." I set my fork down.

"I like him," he said.

I heard something more. "But?"

"I worry."

I wasn't sure he was worried about Sean's health or our relationship. Or both. I didn't ask for clarification. It didn't matter. "I love him."

My father's fork paused halfway to his mouth. "That's half the battle."

"Only half?" I asked.

"Only half."

"What's the other half?"

"It's for you to figure out."

"Is this like when I was little and needed a definition for homework and you'd make me look it up?"

He laughed, a deep, throaty chuckle. "Just like that."

"I hated that."

"I know. But you learned."

"Not really. Raphael always told me."

Rolling his eyes, he said, "I should have known. That tactic won't work this time. You have to learn on your own. It won't be easy, Lucy Juliet. But I have faith. There's something between the two of you."

"Love conquers all?" I offered.

"We shall see."

I watched him as he rinsed his fork, put it in the dishwasher. He looked happier than I'd seen him in a long time. Maybe love would conquer all with him and Mum, too, though I knew better than to get my hopes up. Mum was right. *Life is about living, not about constant worrying.* He caught me staring at him and smiled. My smile. Cutter's smile.

As Dad hid the remainder of the cheesecake, I took a glass from the cabinet, filled it with filtered water from the fridge. The big dinner was coming up, and I still hadn't had a chance to talk to Cutter about Preston. "Have you talked to Cutter lately?"

"His name is Oliver."

My father refused to acknowledge the nickname. I had a feeling it had something to do with not liking that his son carried another man's surname.

"Yesterday," Dad added.

"Really?" I asked, surprised.

He lifted an eyebrow. "We speak often."

"You do?"

"Of course. We have our differences, but so do you and I. The love," he said softly, "is still there."

"Conquering all?" I teased.

He walked over and hugged me, resting his chin on the top of my head. I wrapped my arms around him, suddenly glad I was here. I ought to thank Tristan—he'd given me an unexpected gift. I wouldn't take it for granted. "Things will work out just fine, Lucy."

"Promise?"

"I am nothing if not a man of my word. I am a man of honor. Of integrity."

Smiling, I bit back a snide comment about receiving stolen property. "Don't forget modest."

"How could I?" He winked. "Now get some sleep. I have a feeling it will be a long day tomorrow."

An expected visit from Tristan, possibly finding out what happened to Mac, looking for Rufus, warning Cutter, not to mention worrying about Sean.

"Long" didn't begin to describe it.

28

An hour dragged by. I knew every nuance of that concert poster. Hartford Civic Center. 1986. My mother had taken me—my first concert. I'd been in kindergarten. She thought I should be initiated into the Aerosmith fan club at an early age.

Thoreau snored. Even Odysseus had gone to bed.

I stared at the glowing clock. Three thirty-six. I lay on my side, watching Sean. He had become restless—his medication must have worn off. I almost wanted to wake him up to take another pill, but I didn't think he'd appreciate that too much.

I was slowly driving myself crazy just lying here, so I slipped out of bed as quietly as I could. I needed something to occupy my thoughts other than Sean's breathing patterns. Grabbing my laptop, I headed into my walk-in closet and closed the door behind me. I turned on the light and settled in on the floor.

Sitting cross-legged, I started with Facebook and the South Shore fan page. I'd posted on there about Rufus. So far no one had seen him. I checked the notice I put on craigslist, too. Nothing. If Tristan hadn't taken Rufus, where was he?

I thought about Rufus's leash and suddenly had the sickening thought that maybe it had been snagged on a tree. He could be in the woods somewhere, just waiting for someone to find him. Pain ripped through my stomach, and I pressed my hand against where it hurt most. It didn't help, and I had to wonder if I really was getting an ulcer.

Trying my best to ignore the image of a stranded Rufus, I clicked through my e-mail. I sent a note to Cutter about needing to change our dinner plans—and why—and added that I needed to talk to him about Preston and her snooping *before* the dinner.

I checked Facebook again, in case anyone had spotted Rufus in the last couple of minutes. No one had.

I clicked over to Google and plugged Rick Hayes's name into the search box. No one around here seemed to know much about him, but over a million matches popped up. The first entry was Rick's personal Web site, which was under construction.

The second was a Wiki entry. It contained the usual bio information—born in 1962 in New Jersey. Started singing in high school. Had little success until a song of his was chosen to use as a popular sitcom's theme song but never again had another hit.

He'd been married four times—and divorced four times—before Jemima. Once as a teenager to a woman named Francine. That had lasted two years. No children. Then Patricia came along. That relationship lasted two years, no kids. Then Linda—two years, no kids. Then Esmeralda—four years, no kids.

At thirty-one, he'd met eighteen-year-old Jemima

Gladstone. It was no wonder Mac and Betty hadn't liked him—not with his track record with women. Considering he only had one relationship that lasted longer than two years, it was amazing that he'd been married to Jemima for almost twenty. I wondered if Christa had anything to do with that.

I noticed several citations referencing old teen magazines. I looked up at the top shelf of my closet. There were stacks and stacks of those magazines collecting dust. My mother had never thrown anything of mine away. Was there anything in those pages that would tell me more about Rick than the Internet could? I stood and grabbed as many magazines as I could hold. I set them down and peeked out the door to make sure I hadn't disturbed Sean.

He had kicked his feet out from under the covers, and a pillow covered his head, his arm flung over the top of it to hold it down. He looked so incredibly pale in the moonlight.

I closed the door and dropped to the floor. I paged through old magazines, looking for any sign of Rick Hayes. I found several articles, but there was nothing in them I hadn't learned online. There were, however, a ton of old pictures. I checked the dates on the magazines— most were early to mid-nineties.

I tried to focus, but every time I heard the bed squeak I had to stop what I was doing and peer out at Sean. Make sure he was breathing. It was a surefire way to lose my mind.

After the fourth time, I broke down and did something I told myself I'd never do—I Googled implanted defibrillators and the aftereffects of a shock. I read through story after story of people who felt as though they had been kicked in the chest. There was a whole site dedicated to people who had experienced inappropriate shocks (when the implant fires for no reason) just because they stood too close to a microwave that wasn't grounded correctly or swam next to a pool light that had electrical issues. Threats were everywhere (cell phones, iPods) and reading about them only served to increase my anxiety.

Life is about living, not about constant worrying.

I vowed never to do a search on Sean's condition again.

Suddenly I jumped as the closet door opened. I let out a strangled squeak.

Sean stuck his head in. "What are you doing?"

"Trying to remember how to breathe. You scared me."

He sat on the floor next to me. "Do you need mouth-to-mouth?" he asked, flashing a sleepy grin.

Just like that I was all hot and bothered. "Maybe."

I'd once promised never to treat him any differently because he had a heart condition. I was slowly realizing just how hard it was to keep that promise. Because even though I longed to have my way with him, a nagging voice in the back of my head kept wondering if it would be safe. Especially so soon after he had a shock.

But I'd *promised* him. So I tried to pretend everything was okay.

"It's kind of cozy in here." He glanced around at the shelves, the built-in dressers. "I think this place is bigger than any bedroom I had growing up."

He rarely talked about his growing-up years. "Did you always share a room with Sam?"

"No. Why aren't you sleeping?" Sean asked, stretching out beside me.

I noted the change of subject. I let it go. "Too much on my mind."

"Me?" he asked softly.

I didn't want to out and out lie. "Some."

The corner of his mouth twitched. "Just some?"

I teased back. "I have a lot going on." He'd be upset to know just how much I'd been worried about him. "What are you doing up?"

"I heard noises. So I investigated. It's what I do."

"Is that so?"

"It is. I might be a little off my game today, a bit slower than normal, but sometimes," he said softly, his gaze lowering to my lips before looking at me straight on, "slow is better. Don't you think?"

Oh. My.

He leaned in. I met him halfway. His lips brushed mine, tempting, teasing. I gently nipped his lip with my teeth.

I was quickly lost in the warmth of something that felt so incredibly good that I was trying desperately to silence the warning bells in my head.

As he pulled me atop him, we fell backward with a loud thump.

"Shh! Shh!" I whispered, giggling. "My parents!"

He kissed his way along the skin behind my ear, down my neck. Tipping my head back, I moaned softly.

Sean suddenly froze.

"What?" I asked.

Then I heard it. Knocking.

My mother's voice floated through the door. "LucyD?"

Sean lowered his head to the floor with a strangled sigh. I scrambled for the door, tugging on the hem of my shirt, straightening my lounge pants. I felt the color on my cheeks as I pulled open the bedroom door. "Mum?"

She eyed me as she tied her robe. "I heard something."

I noticed Thoreau and Grendel didn't so much as lift their heads at the intrusion. Tristan Rourke wouldn't meet much resistance with the two of them on guard.

"Oh. Well. Right." I coughed. "That was Sean. Investigating."

"LucyD," my mother said, fighting a smile, "normally I wouldn't be checking on bumps in the night coming from the room of a young couple in love, but there's a criminal on the loose, and the noise came from your closet. I worry!"

Craning her neck, she peeked in the closet, as if she didn't trust me that Tristan Rourke wasn't in there, lying in wait. Sean waved.

She waved back. "Why is your laptop on in your closet?"

No mention of Sean at all. "We're, ah, working."

Her eyebrow arched. In a sugary voice, she said, "Is that what they're calling it now?"

I smiled. "You just couldn't resist."

She wiggled her eyebrows. "Trauma cuts both ways, LucyD. That's all I'm saying."

As she walked down the hallway, I swear I could hear her mutter, "Therapy."

I closed the door, sank back onto the floor in the closet. Sean still lay where I left him, a huge smile on his face. "Your mom's room on the other side of the wall?"

I nodded.

"Figures," he said. "The curse?"

"I thought you were having doubts about its existence."

"Temporary insanity." He ran a hand over his face. "Guess that puts my investigating on hold. Rain check?"

"Sure." I was actually grateful for the reprieve. "How are you feeling?"

"I was better a couple of minutes ago."

I seconded that. For a while there I had forgotten I was worried sick.

"What are you working on? Tristan Rourke? Did I tell you I'm meeting with Mary Ellen and Catherine tomorrow morning?" His brow furrowed. "*This* morning. Meaghan begged them to meet with me. She's convinced Mary Ellen is mistaken in IDing Tristan."

I supposed it was possible. Catherine, especially, had been terrified Tristan Rourke would seek revenge. Maybe fear had influenced what Mary Ellen had seen, too. I bit the inside of my cheek. Aiden probably hadn't had time to check on other witnesses in the case. . . .

Sean turned the laptop screen to face him. With a swipe of his finger, he cleared the screen saver.

Oh. No.

His eyes narrowed and his lips thinned into a grim line.

"I, ah—" I suddenly knew how my father felt with that cheesecake. There was no explaining the Web site away.

Sean closed the screen and looked at me with such tenderness I could have melted into a puddle. "Come here."

I crawled over to him, fell into his open arms. He held me so tight I could barely breathe, but I didn't care. My cheek was pressed to his chest, and I could hear the reassuring beat of his heart. *Wump, wump. Wump, wump.*

"You know if you have questions you can ask me, right?"

His voice echoed around his chest, mixing with the *wump, wump.*

"Luce?" He nudged my chin. "Right?"

I shook my head. "You don't always answer my questions. You pick and choose."

Wump, wump.

"Not about my heart," he answered. "I've always been completely open with you about that."

I love you, Lucy Valentine.

I lifted my head. "I know. But about other things. Your childhood, for one. Your years as a firefighter. Why you couldn't walk away from Tristan Rourke's case."

Wump, wump. "I know," he said. Here in the closet, with its dim light, his eyes glowed, almost unnaturally. "And I'm sorry."

I waited him out, hoping for more of an explanation.

He twisted one of my curls around his finger. "Sometimes it's easier to just lock it away."

"Lock what?" I was pressing. He didn't want to talk about it; I could tell by the way his voice grew tight. I put my head back on his chest. *Wump, wump.*

"The pain. I took Rourke's case because I wanted to believe he was innocent. I wanted to believe because we have a lot in common."

"You do?"

"To an extent. I was a foster kid once, too. I had my fair share of trouble. My juvie record is at least ten pages long. I was kicked out of more homes that I can remember before finally deciding I could do better on my own."

My jaw dropped. I lifted my head again and stared at him. He wasn't teasing. His eyes were troubled. No wonder he'd been acting strangely all week. It was a wonder Sean hadn't run Spero down himself after the hellhole comment he'd made the night he was killed.

"I met Sam on the streets."

"You mean he's not . . . your brother?"

Sean twisted another of my curls around his finger, let the hair slide free. "Not biologically, no. But that hardly matters in here." He tapped his chest.

Of course I'd noticed he and Sam didn't look alike, but I never dreamed they weren't really related . . . I just thought they took after opposite sides of the family. "How did you end up together? With the same last name?"

Sean yawned loudly. "It's a long story."

I suspected he faked the yawn to get out of telling me. But I didn't push. I couldn't. There was such pain in the depths of his eyes it made me ache to the center of my soul. What kind of hell had he been through? No wonder he kept it all locked up. "Some other day?"

He cupped my face and kissed me. "Thank you," he whispered, "for understanding."

I fussed with the magazines so I wouldn't start crying again. Sean picked one up, grinned. "These yours?"

My stomach hurt and my chest felt tight, but I managed to return his smile. "Will it lessen your high opinion of me?"

"Possibly."

I batted my eyelashes. "Then they're all Marisol's."

"I thought so." Smiling, he thumbed through one of them. He now seemed wide awake. "What were you looking for?"

"Rick Hayes."

"Find him?"

I pointed to a stack I'd set aside—the issues that had articles on Rick. "But I feel like there should be more." I realized I wanted him to be guilty simply because I didn't like him and I wanted someone to blame for Mac's disappearance. But there were no skeletons in Rick's past. It didn't mean he was innocent, but it made proving him guilty that much harder.

I hated admitting that might be because he wasn't guilty.

Fred Ross's words floated through my head. *I think whatever happened, it was Mac's choice.*

Now that Sean was wide awake, it would have made perfect sense to move the magazines and laptop into my room, where there was abundant space to spread out. But I liked this closeness, his knee touching mine. I could pick up the faint scent of his toothpaste, could still taste his kiss on my lips.

I glanced at him.

Home.

All my life my home, my heart, had been with my mum. Now . . . I felt it shifting, making room to include Sean. Here, tucked away in this closet, the air moist, warm, I felt safe. Loved.

He looked up, caught me staring. Seemed to know what I was thinking. Smiled.

I smiled back, wondering how long I could keep us in here, instead of facing the world outside.

Not long, I knew. So I was determined to enjoy it.

Sean flipped a page. He held up the magazine. "Who drew the heart around Mark Wahlberg?"

"Marisol."

"Ri-i-ght," he said, drawing the one syllable into three.

"I'm not kidding! He's not my type."

I smiled at memories of Em, Marisol, and me crowded together on this floor. We'd spent hours flipping through the pages of these magazines, declaring who was going to marry whom. Marisol still had dibs on Mark Wahlberg—a proclamation renewed when he posed for those Calvin Klein underwear ads a few years ago. For a fleeting second, just for that memory alone, I was glad my mother never threw anything away.

"Who did you have a teenage crush on?" Sean asked.

"You first."

He skimmed the magazine as he said, "No one."

"Liar."

"All right." He smiled. "Wonder Woman."

"No pressure there for me."

He laughed. "Now you."

"Dewey Evans."

"I think I just fell in love with you all over again."

Though it was said lightly, my heart melted. I was so lost in mush and gush that I jumped when Sean said, "Whoa!"

"What?"

"Look." He spread the magazine in front of me and tapped a picture.

It was a photo of Rick and his fourth wife, Esmeralda, taken on the red carpet at the 1989 Grammy Awards. Rick hadn't changed much over the past twenty years. I suspected he may have had some work done on his face. A lift here, a tuck there. "What?"

"Do you recognize her?"

Her? Esmeralda? I scanned her flawless face, her long dark hair, her emerald eyes. She was gorgeous, but I'd never seen her before.

Sean said, "Shorten her hair."

I still didn't know who it was.

"Put her in a housekeeper's uniform and give her a British accent."

My eyes widened. "Esme!"

"Interesting, don't you think, that Rick's fourth wife is now working as his family's housekeeper?"

Very interesting—but did it have anything to do with Mac?

Sean suddenly tipped his head, listening. "Is that your phone?"

Sure enough, I heard the *Hawaii Five-O* ringtone. I jumped up, ran for the night table where my phone was charging next to the little box of trinkets where Mum had found her ring. "Aiden?"

"Sorry, Lucy, I know it's late. I mean early. But I have news I thought you'd want to hear."

Sean sat on the edge of the bed. Dark smudges colored the skin under his eyes. I pressed my hand into my aching stomach again.

"What kind of news?" I asked, my heart racing. It was four in the morning. Nothing ever good happened at four in the morning. It was the worst time for a phone call.

"The Boston Police Harbor Patrol responded to a distress call from a small boat taking on water near Thompson Island. It was Rourke's boat."

Suddenly four in the morning was my favorite time of day to get a call. Unless . . . "He didn't get away, did he?"

I could practically hear Aiden's smile. "Not this time. Boston police have him in custody."

29

"Have you slept at all?" I asked as Aiden drove. We were on our way to see Orlinda Batista, the woman who had brought Mac's hideous sweater to the consignment shop.

Dark gray clouds crowded the sun out of the sky. It was just past nine. I was operating on pure adrenaline and caffeine.

"Did *you*? You don't look like you did."

"Such flattery," I said, sipping from my Dunkin' latte. "Stop. I'm blushing."

He popped an orange Tic Tac into his mouth and smiled. "I got in a couple of hours on a cot at the office. You?"

"About the same," I lied, knowing he'd worry if he knew I hadn't slept a wink. "How much did you tell Orlinda about me?"

Orlinda Batista lived in Hingham, but we were meeting her at her office in Plymouth. She was a psychologist who was squeezing in our visit between patients and had made it clear her time was limited.

"The usual. How your abilities work, what we're hoping to accomplish. She readily agreed—she'd heard of you before and seemed eager to meet you."

I was eager to meet her, too—especially if she could help me find out what had happened to Mac.

Sean had hitched a ride with my father into the city for his meeting with Catherine Murphy and Mary Ellen Spero—the meeting Meaghan had set up in hopes of clearing Tristan's name. Now that he was behind bars, would Meaghan back off? Or double her efforts?

The shock Sean experienced yesterday now presented a new problem—he wouldn't be able to drive for a while. When he remembered that fact this morning, he'd been in such a grumpy mood I was glad when Aiden called about going to see Orlinda.

"Any Rufus sightings?" Aiden asked.

"Not a single one." Again, the image of Rufus stuck somewhere, his leash snagged, came to me. I tried to shake it loose, but it wouldn't go away. I could see him, sitting there in snow-covered woods, trapped, straining on his leash, his pink bandanna the only color amid brown tree trunks and startling white snow.

A sob caught in my throat. I bit my lip hard and tried to focus on anything else, but my mind wouldn't cooperate. I kept seeing that bandanna as if it were glow—

"Oh!" I cried, straightening. Coffee sloshed.

"What's wrong?"

I smiled so wide my cheeks hurt. "Nothing. Something is finally right. I can find Rufus! Or I think I can. I'd forgotten he was wearing a bandanna."

"Wouldn't Mac have bought that for him?"

"No, Christa bought it. I remember Jemima saying something about the color."

"Do you want me to turn around?"

It was tempting, but we were so close to Orlinda's office now and we wouldn't be there long. Plus I had a bigger problem. "Christa's probably in school. I'll have to wait until she gets out."

"Why don't you see if Jemima will call the school and arrange for Christa to get out of class for a couple of minutes to meet with you?"

It was a good idea. Christa wouldn't want to wait— she was probably worried sick about Rufus (I knew the feeling). I dialed Jemima, but no one answered. I left a message for her to call me back and why.

I could barely contain my excitement and finally— finally—some of the weight I was hauling around lifted from my shoulders.

Orlinda Batista's office was in an old three-story house that had been converted into a medical office building on Route 44, a few blocks from Plymouth Harbor. Original wooden floors sloped as we found Orlinda's office on the first floor. A receptionist checked us in, while a couple who were already waiting checked us out, probably wondering what we were being treated for. I could imagine the guesses, what with Aiden's no-nonsense cop look and my look-what-the-cat-dragged-in appearance.

It wasn't long before we were called back, earning us disgruntled looks from the other couple, who obviously put a lot of faith in the first come, first served motto.

"Please have a seat." Orlinda Batista remained behind an old metal desk stacked high with medical charts. She studied me as we came in, and I tried not to flinch under the scrutiny.

Around sixty or so, she had an earth-mother look about her with plump cheeks, kind blue eyes, shoulder-length wavy brown hair, purple tunic, and colorful beaded necklace. There was no offer of a handshake, and her wheelchair caught me off-guard. "You're here about Mac Gladstone?"

"As I explained on the phone, he's missing," Aiden said, holding out my chair for me. I sat.

"I don't know if this will work," I added. "I've never tried to read energy from a consignment shop item, but I wanted to try."

Orlinda rolled away from her desk. The wood floor squeaked under her wheelchair as she stopped next to my chair. She smiled kindly. "I think, Lucy, there is more to your abilities than you're aware."

I shifted in my seat, suddenly uncomfortable with the way she was looking at me. "Oh?"

She glanced at Aiden. "I'm sorry, I hate to rush, but my time is limited. Are you ready?" she asked me, holding out her palm.

"Think of the sweater you brought to I'll Take Seconds, the ugly orange one with the colored confetti."

Her eyebrows dipped. "Ugly? I knitted that sweater."

Aiden coughed and bent his head to hide a smile.

"I, ah—"

She burst out laughing, a loud booming bark that sounded like a sea lion. One of her bottom teeth was charmingly crooked. "I'm kidding. Sorry," she said. "I find so little humor in the day."

I couldn't help a small smile.

Orlinda held out both her hands to me.

"I only need one," I said.

"Take both," she said softly but insistently.

I took both.

Dizziness mixed with relief mixed with anxiety (would I see Mac?) as images raced in my head. It took me a second to sort them out as they flashed between locations, sort of a slide show on fast forward. Orlinda was obviously thinking of more than one item.

One of the visual slides was very clearly Mac's orange sweater in a pile at a Goodwill shop downtown. The other was a black coat hanging in the closet of an expensive Beacon Hill hotel room, and the other was a pair of sneakers on a man walking a dog up the cobblestoned streets around the hotel.

I tried to pull my hands away, but Orlinda held on tight. "Wait," she said in a whisper. "Relax. Breathe, Lucy."

She closed her eyes and held on to my hands. My palms warmed under her touch and tingles went up my arms, down my sternum, and pooled in my stomach.

"There." She opened her eyes.

Aiden said, "Did you see anything, Lucy?"

I stared at my hands, wondering what had just happened.

There were many things to work through, with not just what I had seen but also what I had just felt. There was only one thing I knew for sure.

Mac Gladstone was alive. And he had Rufus.

There was something else nagging me about that vision, but I was having trouble concentrating, with the tingles and all.

"I'm sorry," Orlinda said, "but I have other patients I must see to, and you have a long day still ahead of you. Don't overlook the obvious, Lucy, and you might want to cut back on the coffee."

She asked nothing of what I might have seen . . . yet I couldn't shake the feeling she somehow knew.

Aiden stood, a confused look on his face as he glanced between me and Orlinda. I followed him to the door.

"I'll meet you in the waiting room," I said to him.

He looked like he was going to protest but walked off.

"Orlinda?" I turned to her.

"Yes, dear?"

"I hope you don't mind my asking, but what happened to your legs?"

She smiled as though I had just passed some kind of Princess and the Pea test. "I was struck by lightning when I was twelve. It left me paralyzed." Her words hung between us.

"I'm very sorry." I tried to wrap my head around what she was saying between the lines.

"Don't be. Sometimes from the ashes a gift rises." She rolled forward and pulled the door open wide, dismissing me. "It was a pleasure meeting you, Lucy." Warmth glowed in her eyes. "I'm sure I'll be seeing you again."

It wasn't until I was back in the car that I realized for the first time in three days my stomach didn't hurt.

I was stuck on why.

Why would Mac disappear, leaving his family behind? And his dog, too—at least temporarily.

Aiden had gotten an emergency call and dropped me off at Mum's house. I was trying to figure out what to do about Mac. My first instinct was to drive into the city and find him and get some answers.

It was my second instinct, too.

But I fought against them. I needed time to think. To figure it out. Because I felt as though I was missing something big.

I let my thoughts drift to Orlinda Batista, but I didn't let them linger. What she had said—what she had done—wasn't something I had time to think about now.

Glancing out the kitchen's big bay window, I spotted Thoreau running through the snow. He sniffed his way along the fenced-in yard. The pool had been covered for the winter and the gardens looked tired, worn. Beyond my mother's music studio, the land dropped straight down into a dark roiling ocean.

I needed to pack. Now that Tristan was behind bars, it was safe to go home again. Although I was glad I'd be sleeping in my own bed tonight, I was going to miss being here. It felt safe. *I* felt safe. Loved.

Behind me, Mum stood, hip propped against the counter, scoring the skin of a grapefruit so she could peel it. She was whistling the Beatles' "Yesterday." Soft overhead lighting bathed the kitchen in a comforting glow. In here, my mother's style shone through. Concrete countertops, a soft red on the wall—the same color as her aura. High-end Wolf appliances, yet a secondhand kitchen table with mismatching chairs. It was as if the term "shabby chic" had been invented solely for her.

Opening the cupboard, I searched through the mugs. I finally settled on one that read: "I'm not a doctor, but I'll take a look anyway." I opted for decaf tea.

I lowered onto a counter stool and waited for the teakettle. Grendel was sitting in the window, keeping an eye on Thoreau while watching the seagulls.

"You're quiet," Mum said. "Are you still worried about Sean?"

"Just thinking."

"About Sean?"

"Mostly Mac." Reluctantly, I told her about my reading—the Mac portion of it, at least. I hadn't planned to, but I needed to get it out, talk about it.

Her knife stilled, and the grapefruit rocked on the counter. "He's alive?"

I nodded. "I think I need to go to that hotel and see if I can find him. Hear his side of things. The police have to be notified. His family. And I can't figure out why he did it—why he's continuing to do it."

My gaze settled on her hands as they set about expertly sectioning the grapefruit. She preferred to eat it like an orange, rather than to scoop it out. "Where's your ring?"

"I'm having it resized and cleaned."

"Where?" I asked.

Waving her hand, she said, "In town. You wouldn't know the place."

"Try me."

"What's with the questions, LucyD?"

"What's with the evasiveness?"

She smiled. "I'm not being evasive. I told you it needed to be cleaned."

"You and Dad didn't break up, did you?"

"There's time left today."

I froze, then smiled. She was teasing me.

"Stop worrying so much, LucyD."

Easy for her to say. "It'll take me some time to get used to."

"Understandable. But remember, it might not last. I don't want you to get your hopes up."

"Can you say 'dysfunctional'?"

She laughed.

My cell phone rang. I pulled it from my pocket.

It was Jemima and her voice sounded strained as she said, "Christa is absolutely refusing to do a reading, Lucy."

The kettle whistled, and I filled my cup. I watched in horror as Mum took celery, carrots, and an apple from the fridge and pulled a juicer from a cabinet. She *wouldn't. . . .*

"I don't know what to tell you," Jemima said. "I'm sorry. I'd really like to be of more help. I hate to admit it, but I miss that stupid dog more than I thought."

. . . She *would.* Mum dropped the celery and carrots in first. I couldn't watch. I took my mug over to the kitchen table. Grendel flicked an ear at me as a hello before turning his attention back to Thoreau.

Jemima sounded sincere, which took me by surprise. I didn't want to say anything about Mac—or Rufus at this point. Not until I knew more.

Mum whistled in between the mechanical pulses of the juicer.

"And Christa didn't mention why?" I thought for sure she'd want to help.

"No. It's strange, too. She loves Rufus and was heartbroken when she heard he had run away. She's never had any issues with your gift before now. Unless Rick has gotten to her."

There was an underlying bitterness when Jemima said her husband's name that I found interesting in light of what Sean had uncovered last night.

The juicer silenced and Mum walked over to the back door and gave a sharp whistle. Thoreau froze, cocked his head. Mum whistled again. Thoreau suddenly took off for the door, practically flying across the yard. His little paws sent snow shooting behind him as he bounded over the threshold and into Mum's arms.

I blinked. I couldn't believe what I'd just seen. It was exactly the way Rufus had acted the night he took off. Except I hadn't heard a whistle. . . .

Then I remembered the small silver dog whistle hanging in Mac's apartment and knew immediately it had been used the night Rufus took off. That's why Rufus acted so excited—he'd missed his master. That whistle meant he'd see him soon. But how did Mac know where Rufus was? And how was Mac getting around? Did he have a car?

I leaned back. Like a slap upside the head, everything suddenly made perfect sense.

But just to confirm, I said, "Can I ask you a favor, Jemima?"

"What kind of favor?"

Mum glanced at me as she dried off Thoreau's paws. *Jemima?* she mouthed.

I nodded.

She whistled low as she set Thoreau down.

"Can you go down to Mac's apartment and tell me if Rufus's dog whistle is still hanging on the wall?"

She didn't ask why, for which I was grateful. Grendel hopped down from the window, went over to Thoreau, and jumped on him. Subtlety wasn't one of Grendel's strengths. They tumbled across the floor.

"It's not," Jemima said. "It's in Christa's room—I

saw it in there this morning when I woke her for school. Why?"

There went my gratitude. I thought fast. "I just thought it might help in the search for Rufus," I lied. "I was going to walk through the woods today and thought he might be able to hear the whistle better than my voice."

Tell *me* I'm not a good liar. Ha!

"I didn't think of that, but I bet Christa had the same idea."

I rather doubted that. I bet it was in her room because she'd used it the night Rufus went missing. Mac had an accomplice. It was why Christa didn't want to do a reading with me. Because she knew I'd be able to find Rufus . . . and that he'd be with Mac.

"I can drop it off at your house," Jemima offered. "I'm on my way out. Or I can leave it with Esme."

Esme. Esmeralda. What to do, what to say?

"Lucy? You still there?"

"I'm here," I said. I was weighing what to tell her. "Can I ask you something personal?"

"That depends."

My call-waiting beeped. I let it go through to voice mail.

I wished I could see Jemima's face, gauge her reactions. "How much do you know about Esme?"

"Esme? The housekeeper?"

"Yes."

"Not much. Rick hired her about six months ago. She's a little lazy, but we haven't had any big issues. Are you looking to steal her away?"

She laughed. I didn't.

"You may want to look into her background," I finally said.

"Why?" Her voice was taut, on guard. "What do you know about her? Is she dangerous or something?"

I scrunched my nose. Why was I getting involved in this? I knew now Rick had nothing to do with Mac's disappearance. Whatever Rick was doing with Esme wasn't any of my business. And maybe it was all completely innocent. A woman down on her luck who needed a job; an ex-husband willing to help her out. Except Rick didn't strike me as the charitable type. He struck me as a manipulative, selfish bastard.

Softly I said, "I know her real name is Esmeralda."

I heard a sharp intake of breath. It was obvious Jemima was familiar with the name. "I have to go," she said, and hung up on me.

I dialed into my voice mail and cringed as I watched my mother sip putrid-colored juice. Her lips pursed every time the liquid touched them.

The voice-mail message was from Marisol. "Aloha, Lucy!"

I listened to the rest of the message, smiling. Marisol had done a great job getting all the information we needed from Em. Now to put the rest of the plan into action.

I jumped up and poured my tea into a to-go container.

"Where are you off to?" Mum asked. "Going to talk to Mac?"

I wasn't sure. "Maybe."

"You look like you're on a mission."

"I am." A mission to get Em and Aiden together

once and for all. "Can I leave the critters with you a little while longer?"

"Of course." She kissed my cheek. "Dovie's coming by later, so they'll get lots of attention."

I hadn't really had a chance to talk to Dovie since Rufus went missing—she would be relieved to know he was okay. "You can go ahead and tell her about Rufus and Mac."

"As if I could keep that kind of information to myself."

"Well, beyond Dovie, try. I'm not sure how to go about letting the world know he's alive. Or even if I should. He's a grown man who can do what he wants with his life."

"It's an unusual situation, to say the least, but Dovie will be glad to hear the news."

I grabbed my coat and my bag and headed for the door. "By the way, how did her date go the other night?"

"Fizzled. Surprisingly, Dr. Hot to Trot wants to settle down with a good woman by his side. Dovie was out of there before he could say 'retirement community.'"

I smiled, but it was just another instance of Dovie's commitment issues. Cursed by association, she had told me. I was beginning to believe it. I pulled open the door. "Tell her I said hi."

"Oh, LucyD?"

"Yeah?"

She poured the rest of her juice into the kitchen sink. "I don't suppose you know what happened to the cheesecake that was in the fridge?"

30

A bell jingled as I pulled open the door at I'll Take Seconds.

"You're back," Madeline said. She set her book down and stood up. "Did you find the man?"

"Not yet," I said uneasily. "But the information you gave us was extremely helpful."

"I'm glad to hear that. Is there something else I can help you with?"

"Actually, yes." I looked around. "There was a Hawaiian shirt in here yesterday . . . there it is." Picking it up, I smiled. It was perfect.

I laid it on the counter and pulled out my wallet. I'd already made a stop at the Triple A office. Everything was coming together nicely.

The bell jangled. I glanced over my shoulder and my eyes widened. "What are you doing here?"

"I was about to ask you the same thing." Preston carried a Filene's Basement bag. She spotted my credit card. "Are you *shopping*?"

"A present for Aiden."

"Big spender."

"It's the thought, right?" I signed the credit slip.

"I hope you think of *me* at Saks. No offense," she said to Madeline. "You do still owe me some boots, Lucy."

"I thought Maureen Rourke took care of you."

Preston swiped her bangs out of her eyes. "You're not getting out of buying me boots that easily."

Madeline handed me a receipt and a bag. "Thank you," I said to her.

Preston narrowed her eyes on me.

"What? Why are you looking at me like that?"

"There's something about you that's different."

"I noticed, too," Madeline said, nodding in agreement.

Preston looked at her. "Is it the hair, do you think?"

I touched my head. It was the same curly honey blond do I've had my whole life.

Her nose wrinkled. "I don't think so."

"It's not the makeup." Preston scrutinized my face.

"You two are going to give me a complex."

Preston snapped her fingers. "Your cheeks."

"What about them?" I asked as they heated.

"They have color."

"That's it," the woman said. "You look . . . healthy. Yesterday you looked a little pale, if you don't mind me saying."

"Sickly," Preston added.

"Gee, thanks." I hadn't looked that bad. Now this morning . . . I'd looked—and felt—like death warmed up, spit out. Until those tingles in Orlinda Batista's office. There was no explaining that, so I said, "What are you doing here?"

Preston plopped her bag on the counter. "Remember how I went to see Eva Denham-Foster yesterday about the Lone Ranger's hat and she sent me to see her son Matthias? Well, Matthias said he gave most of the things to *his* son, Craig, who didn't want them and gave them to his pastor for the church bazaar."

"You were busy yesterday," I said.

Madeline nodded in agreement.

"Not as busy as you." Preston crossed her arms. "I heard about the break-in and Tristan's arrest. Why didn't you call me?"

"When? In between finding Tristan in my bedroom, Sean's heart attack, or the FBI questioning?"

"Oh my," Madeline said.

The color drained from Preston's face. "Sean had an attack? Oh my God. I didn't know."

She rushed forward and threw her arms around me in a bear hug I found oddly comforting.

"Are you okay? Is he? Is he in the hospital? What happened? Did you freak out?"

"Preston, breathe!"

She gulped air.

"That," Madeline said, pointing at Preston, "is how you looked yesterday. Well, without the hyperventilating and the . . . are those hives?"

Preston scratched. "I get them when I'm upset."

"I looked that bad yesterday?" I asked.

Madeline nodded.

"Hey!" Preston cried, scratching her neck.

This time *I* hugged *her.* "Everything's fine. Sean's fine." Kind of. For now. "And you'll be your pretty self again as soon as the splotches go away."

Looking up at me, she said, "You think I'm pretty?"

"Yes." Smiling, I added, "What happened with the hat, Preston?"

She pulled it from the bag. The hives were already fading. "I went and talked to the church pastor, and he actually remembered the hat. When it was donated, he recognized the Medford Millinery tag and knew it would do better at a consignment shop than at the bazaar. He brought it here."

Madeline had picked up the hat. "It was right after Thanksgiving. I remember it well because it's not often we get custom-made hats in stock and I was thinking, ha ha, that I was *thankful* it would bring in a big profit."

"Do you recall who purchased it?" Preston asked.

Madeline looked at me, and chills slid down my spine. I knew what she was going to say before the words came out of her mouth.

"It was Mac Gladstone."

I found a parking spot on Beacon, not far from the office. I took this to be an omen that the rest of my day would be trouble free for a change. I fed the meter and crossed the street to walk the sidewalk along the Common perimeter.

Squirrels bustled about, mostly chasing after unsuspecting tourists with food in their hands. There were dozens of people roaming around, a good majority of them homeless. I paused along the iron fence and searched the crowd for anyone who looked like Mac.

Surreptitiously I looked over my shoulder. A car with dark windows had parked a block away. I'd picked up the tail as soon as I hit the highway. Agents Thomas and St. John weren't being very careful about following me, and I had to wonder what they wanted. Tristan was already behind bars. Unless he was now Houdini, he wouldn't be bothering me anymore.

As the wind whipped my hair into a frenzy, I drew the collar of my coat up and walked slowly along, wishing I suddenly heard the squeals of an excited crowd, saw twenty-dollar bills rustling along the ground like dried-out leaves.

Mac was the Lone Ranger.

It had been hard to believe at first. I thought I was going to have to take Preston to the hospital when she made the connection. Then, when I told her about my reading with Orlinda, Preston had broken out in hives again.

But the more I thought about it, I kept coming back to why *not* Mac? He was rich, dying, and living his final days the way he wanted—by giving his money away. When Rick Hayes found out what Mac had been doing, he was going to go, as Preston would say, apeshit. I was rather looking forward to that.

The hives had lasted until she received a phone call from the *South Shore Beacon* that sent her running for her car.

There had been a federal raid at A Clean Start this morning. SWAT teams, tear gas, the whole shebang. When no stolen goods were found, the FBI still closed the Laundromat until further notice. Preston was on her way to cover the protests that had broken out in Roxbury, where thousands of people had taken to the streets to support A Clean Start and its attempts to revitalize the neighborhood when no one else seemed to care.

The mayor had already held a news conference about working with the people to get the situation resolved as soon as possible, mentioning that A Clean Start had broken some zoning laws and lacked proper permits, which only fueled the crowd's fire. Preston couldn't wait to jump into the thick of things.

As I walked along, I pictured little Nessie's face and my heart hurt. What would the neighborhood do without A Clean Start helping them out? I held on to a tiny thread of hope that the protests would bring the kind of publicity the neighborhood needed. More people would want to help, to step up in Tristan's stead. I hoped via legitimate means.

I took one more look around. I didn't see Mac, and the homeless man who liked to rhyme wasn't around, either.

Tucking my head against the cold, I headed to the office. Suz was at the window, binoculars in hand. "I've been watching all day. No sign of the Lone Ranger. Teddy and I talked about it, and we're going to start saving the money I catch for a down payment on a house. We're tired of renting. "

"How much do you need?" Would Mac even make another appearance as the Lone Ranger now that he had Rufus? I imagined the rambunctious retriever chasing the pigeons in the park and smiled. He'd have a blast. But there was no disguising the coppery dog as a horse named Silver.

"About ten thousand."

I sat on the sofa. "That's a lot of twenties."

"I know, so don't expect me to give any more of it away to panhandlers."

"He wasn't panhandling. He was observing."

She set the binoculars down and turned. Her prepare-for-a-lecture scowl quickly faded when she took a good look at me. "Wow," she said. "You look great. Did you just get a facial?"

"No."

"Did you get lucky last night?"

"Suz!"

"Well, if not, then you must just be relieved that Tristan Rourke is in jail."

At first I was, but now . . . I wasn't as relieved as I should have been. Mostly for one reason only. Sean. Now that I knew why he took Meaghan's case, I wanted a happy ending for Tristan Rourke. Which was impossible. One way or another, he was staying in jail for a long, long time.

"I can't believe Meaghan Archibald is offering to post his bail," Suz said.

"She's what?" I couldn't have heard her right.

Suz grabbed the binoculars for a quick check of the Common and then turned back to me. "Well, you know how Andrew and I take our coffee breaks together?"

I nodded.

"According to him, Meaghan was waiting for Sean this morning when he opened the office. She'd heard Tristan had been arrested and demanded to know if Sean had proved him innocent yet. When Sean admitted he couldn't find any evidence to clear Tristan, she was on the phone in an instant, securing one of the best defense attorneys in the city to represent Tristan. Then she set off for the jail to see if she could visit him."

So much for my effort to keep them apart, protect her. "How did Andrew know all this?"

"Overheard it. The walls are apparently pretty thin up there."

I blushed. I'd have to remember that. "There's no way Tristan will get bail. Not with his history."

"I agree," Suz said, "but Meaghan is a determined woman. Plus, she has the money to back her up."

"She does?" I asked.

"Her adopted father is Martin Archibald. He's a doctor, but his family owns Archibald Industries, who, as you know, could give the Wal-Mart Waltons a run for their money."

I let that sink in. Meaghan had never said a word. "How did you know?"

"Andrew."

"He's just a font of information."

"Cute, too, with that little lock of hair that falls onto his forehead. Anyway, he was a business major at BU—he recognized the name and had a hunch. He Googled Meaghan, and sure enough there she was. She's an heiress worth billions."

The phone rang and Suz jumped up from her perch on the windowsill to answer it.

As I listened to her make an appointment for a new client, I thought about Meaghan and felt a deep sadness settle over me like a heavy blanket. In her case, love wouldn't conquer all. Life's little twists of fate were sometimes so cruel. If not for Meaghan's suicide attempt, she never would have met Martin Archibald and would not be one of the richest young women in America. If not for Anthony Spero lying to Tristan about Meaghan's "death," he never would have lashed out, which had earned him a stint in a maximum-security prison and fueled a career as a lifetime criminal.

One was adopted into a loving, wealthy family.

One became a criminal mastermind who robbed the rich to help the poor.

Love wasn't enough to bring them back together.

Maybe Preston was right—Tristan and Meaghan's story was more like Romeo and Juliet than I wanted to believe.

Suz hung up. She checked the Common again before saying, "Sean came down a little bit ago to see if you were in yet. He's in a bad, bad mood. Do you want some coffee?" Suz asked me on her way to the kitchenette.

"No thanks. I'm cutting back."

Her eyes widened. "One night at your mother's and now you've gone all health-food nut on me, too?"

"Not quite."

"Well, I might be gung ho for that Zumba class, but I draw the line at coffee," she mumbled as she walked away.

I heard footsteps on the stairs outside the door and jumped up, hoping it was Sean. I hadn't seen him since this morning and was suddenly desperate to lay eyes on him, maybe take his pulse.

I stuck my head out the door. Catherine Murphy was coming down the steps, one hand in an enormous handbag, rooting around the (seemingly bottomless) depths.

"Car keys?" I asked.

She smiled as she stepped onto the landing. "I can never find them in this thing. It might be time to down-size."

I leaned against the railing, held on to the newel

post. Up close, she looked pretty darn good for the week she'd had. "I'm sorry about Anthony."

"Don't be," she said, her lips thinning.

"I don't understand."

"It's terrible, but I'm glad he's gone. He was mean, abusive, and downright nasty. He made Mary Ellen's life miserable."

"Why did she stay with him? Why not get a divorce?"

"She took a vow," Catherine said simply. "For better or worse. She suffered through a lot of worse."

I couldn't help comparing Mary Ellen to Mum. Whereas Mum bailed on a relationship whenever things turned bad, Mary Ellen had stuck it out. Mum was happy. Mary Ellen had spent most her life unhappy. I decided I needed to reassess my definition of "dysfunction."

Catherine pulled out a set of keys from her purse, jangled them triumphantly.

"Did you come alone?" I looked up the stairs, fully expecting to see Mary Ellen coming down.

"Mary Ellen's at work."

"So soon?" I asked.

"We both went back yesterday. We can't find it in ourselves to mourn."

"What about a funeral?"

"Tony was cremated and his ashes will be scattered in front of his favorite pub. Appropriate, don't you think?"

I didn't think she was really looking for an answer. "How did the meeting with Sean go? Did you see Meaghan?"

She looked up the stairs, toward the SDI offices.

"Meaghan was gone by the time I arrived. Honestly, it was a waste of my time coming here, but I couldn't refuse Meaghan's request. I'm truly sorry for Meaghan, but there's nothing I can do to help her at this point. Tristan Rourke did Mary Ellen a favor as far as I'm concerned and I'm not necessarily of the belief that he should be punished for it, but there is nothing I can do to help him. The course that he's on is one of his own making. Stealing a car . . . running Tony over. Crime is in his nature. Maybe it's best for Meaghan it turned out this way. She can move on, find a nice boy to settle down with. Because with Tristan she'll be looking at a lifetime of pain. Men don't change."

But all of this really wasn't Tristan's own making, was it? It was a childhood that had a little boy stealing to survive. It was a man's cruelty that ripped the heart from a young man. It was a judge who showed no compassion. And from that pain it was a grown man out to avenge the happily ever after he'd been denied.

"I should go. I'm late for work." Holding out her hand, Catherine said, "I learned a long time ago that you can't save them all."

Maybe not, but I'd keep trying. I shook her hand. The images came quickly, telling me a story to which I already knew the ending.

"Are you okay?" she asked.

Slowly I pulled my hand away. "Yeah, just a dizzy spell. The earrings Mary Ellen wore the other night— the pearls—did you happen to give those to her?"

"For Christmas, why?" she asked suspiciously. "Are you looking to buy a pair?"

"Something like that," I mumbled.

With a sinking feeling, I watched her walk down the stairs and out the front door.

"I know that look," a voice said from behind me. Sean was standing on the third-floor landing, looking down at me. "What did you see?"

"A small pearl earring."

"Like the one Mary Ellen was wearing the other night?"

"Just like that one," I said softly, sadly.

"Where was it?"

"It's wedged in between the cushions of a black sedan at the BPD's impound lot." It made perfect sense—now. The car had been stolen in Quincy Center, not far from the library. Then I remembered the survival book on Catherine's desk—the area she shared with her sister. I'd lay odds there was a chapter on hot-wiring a car. All she'd have to do was call Anthony and tell him to meet her at the hotel and wait. . . .

Sean came down the steps. "The car that ran over Anthony Spero?"

"Yes."

"So it was Mary Ellen who ran him over?" He dragged a hand down his face.

"It looks that way, but my guess is Catherine was in on it."

His eyes were a dark gray in this lighting. Or maybe because he was still troubled . . . with Meaghan and Tristan, with his heart. "Why do you think so?"

"She was thinking about the earring—she had to have been for me to be able to see it. She knows it's missing—and it's weighing on her mind. I bet she's worrying it will be found in the car the police recovered."

I ran my hand over his cheek. Stubble scratched my palm. "We gave them the perfect opening to get rid of Anthony with the news that Tristan was out for revenge. He had motive, opportunity, and a criminal record. If I hadn't seen that earring, they might have gotten away with it."

"It seems against their nature to use Tristan as a scapegoat. Especially after everything Anthony had done to him."

"Catherine just mentioned that she thought Meaghan would be better off without Tristan. I think in a strange way she thinks she's protecting Meaghan by sending Tristan back to jail."

Just as I'd tried to do. And like me, Catherine was wrong. Meaghan's heart knew all along Tristan was innocent—of murder at least—and she had been willing to risk everything for the man she loved.

I should have trusted her, because I knew how she felt to take a risk for love. I leaned upward and gave Sean a long kiss. His arm curved around me, pulling me closer. His heart beat hard against mine. Reassuring.

"I'll be back in just a second."

Without looking back, I ran down the steps.

I had to do this. For that seventeen-year-old boy who thought he was responsible for the death of the girl he loved. For a love that still had a chance to conquer all.

I jogged down the block and skidded to a stop in front of a nondescript Ford. The window powered down.

Agent St. John said, "We've got to stop meeting like this."

I looked across at his partner, who smirked. I'd be very happy never to see them again. Maybe now I wouldn't have to. "I know who ran over Anthony Spero, and it wasn't Tristan Rourke."

31

Soft lights lit expensive artwork. Beautiful carpeting lined the hallway of the exquisite five-star hotel. I knocked on the door to room 223.

"What am I going to say to him?" I asked Sean.

Down the hall, a uniformed man with a housekeeping cart tried to blend in with the woodwork.

"Are you getting cold feet?"

"A little." I didn't really know Mac, but in a way I did. I could almost understand why he'd run away from home if the changes I'd seen in Jemima over the last couple of days were any indication. Maybe by disappearing he was teaching his daughter one last life lesson—that she was strong enough to stand on her own. "I miss Rufus. I'll be glad to see him."

I knocked again.

The man with the cart approached us. "Are you looking for the dark-haired gentleman? The one with the dog?"

"You've seen him?" I asked.

"Nice man, nice man. Good tipper." He smiled.

If he only knew just how free Mac was with his money.

"I was sad to see him go," the man added.

"Go?" Sean asked.

"Checked out about an hour ago. He was in quite a rush."

So close. "Do you happen to know where he went?"

"Sorry, no. You might want to check with the front desk."

Sean slipped him a folded bill and the man trotted off.

"Interesting that Mac would suddenly check out an hour ago," Sean said. "Coincidence?"

"Not coincidence. Christa."

I thought it was high time we had a talk with Christa Hayes. But as we approached Mac's estate, the street out front was crammed with TV crews and reporters standing around. There was no sign of Preston, which meant she was probably still in Roxbury.

"This can't be good." There were three police cars that I could see from here.

"No," Sean agreed.

A Cohasset patrolman manning the gate stopped me as I tried to head up to the house. "I'm sorry, ma'am, no visitors."

I flashed him my state police credentials—I didn't have a badge, but my ID was still impressive. I asked, "What happened?"

Looking unimpressed, he handed my ID back to me. "Some sort of domestic dispute. The captain has more details up at the house." He waved us through.

We found a place to park at the bottom of the drive. It was a long way up to the house, but I held back any suggestions about Sean staying put. I found I was getting quite good at faking the whole I-was-okay-with-his-health thing.

As we passed the police cars, my mind flew through theories. One of which was that Mac had come home and Rick had gone ballistic and killed him. I shared these thoughts with Sean.

"You have quite the overactive imagination."

It was a cool afternoon with a hint of spring in the air. The snow would soon be gone, and tiny crocuses would pop up through the frozen ground. I was looking forward to not being cold all the time.

The image of Sean and me in Hawaii came to mind, and I could practically feel the sway of the hammock.

"You're overlooking the obvious," he said.

I stumbled a bit, righting myself. It was the same thing Orlinda had said to me this morning.

Sometimes from the ashes a gift rises.

Who was Orlinda Batista? She was a psychic healer—that much I knew for certain. My stomach had never felt better.

Had it been fate our paths crossed? Destiny?

I think, Lucy, there is more to your abilities than you're aware.

I had the feeling she could help me understand my gift. Help me to learn why I saw visions of the future when I touched Sean's hand. And maybe, if I was really lucky, she could see my aura and I would know for certain if Sean and I were meant to be.

She was right—I would see her again.

"What's so obvious?" I asked, trying to pretend I

didn't already know. That I hadn't been thinking about it since I saw the police cars and heard the words "domestic dispute." That my telling Jemima about Esmeralda hadn't been the fuel for a situation that needed a response from so many cops.

Sean glanced at me. His color was a bit better, though that could have been from the exertion of climbing the steep driveway. I didn't want to think about how his heart was working extra hard right now. Mine was, too, which reminded me I should take better care of it. Exercise more. Maybe I'd take up running. Or one of those cycling classes at the local gym. Or even Zumba.

Sean must have heard something in my tone, because he put his arm around my shoulder and kissed my temple. "That Mac and Rufus came back and Rufus tore the place apart looking for his rubber chicken, which sent Jemima over the edge, and she threw her book of Tao out the glass window, which shattered into a million pieces, and—"

"You're humoring me."

"Yes."

"I'm okay with that." It was better than the image I had of Jemima taking a steak knife to Rick.

We crested the drive and suddenly my feet wouldn't budge. "Oh."

The house was bathed in bright lights as a construction crew set about hammering plywood over the missing windows. Windows that had been shot out if the bullet holes in the remaining windows were any indication. I was suddenly worried sick about Christa and Jemima.

I nudged Sean. Rick Hayes was sitting in the back

of a cruiser with a smug look on his face. Ha. See if I ever told him where his pink guitar pick was.

Looking around, I noticed the yard was a mess. Clothes everywhere. Books. A few guitars—all broken. My eyes widened when I spotted a Grammy award that had been sawed in half.

"Domestic dispute" might have been an understatement.

I tapped on the shoulder of another patrolman. "Where's Jemima Hayes?"

His jaw thrust toward the door. "Inside."

I let out a breath of relief. She was alive. Sean and I carefully picked our way over broken glass. We didn't have to look far for Jemima. She was sitting on the bottom step of the marble staircase. When she spotted us, she said wryly, "Come on in."

"Are you okay?" I asked.

Outwardly, she looked great. Her hair had been blown out and flowed over her shoulders. Her makeup was picture perfect, and she was dressed in dark jeans and a silky top. Her feet were bare, which I thought to be a little dangerous with all the glass around, but she didn't seem worried. In fact, she didn't even look like she'd broken a sweat over all this, but after that little showdown with Rick two days ago I knew better. She was just good at hiding her true feelings.

"I'm good."

"Where's Christa?" Sean asked.

"Staying the night at a friend's house. I didn't want her to be part of this circus."

This probably wasn't the best time to get into Christa's role in Mac's disappearance—or tell Jemima that

Mac was alive. I hoped he'd make that pronouncement himself. "Do you need me to call anyone?" Like a lawyer.

"No. Everything's been taken care of, but thanks for asking."

I sat next to her on the step. "What happened, Jemima?"

She was silent for so long I thought she wasn't going to answer. But finally she said, "I was blind. For so many years, I was so damn blind." A muscle in her jaw pulsed as she clenched her teeth.

"Rick?" I asked.

"Do you think he ever loved me?"

"I—" I glanced at Sean for help, but he'd wandered off. I saw him talking with a police officer near the door. "I'm sure he did."

She stared straight ahead, not really looking at anything in particular. "I want to believe that, but ever since Mac disappeared I've been seeing things a lot more clearly. The only things Rick really loves are money, fame, and himself. I was blind. A fool in love."

"What about Christa? He must love her."

Jemima picked at a fingernail. "I wish I could say that was true—for Christa's sake—but the only thing Rick sees when he looks at his daughter is dollar signs. I'm convinced now he only married me because I came from a wealthy family. And he got me pregnant to make sure he always had a meal ticket. My parents knew it, but I couldn't see it back then. I couldn't see it for a long time."

"It's hard to think those kinds of things about someone you love."

Her jaw clenched, unclenched. "After I spoke with

you this morning, I went into his office and snooped around. Turns out Esme is one of the producers on Rick's reality show. I found notes about a future episode where it would be revealed to me the housekeeper was actually one of my husband's ex-wives. It was all for the ratings, Lucy. So I did what I needed to do. I tossed everything he owned outside and changed the locks."

"The Grammy?"

A hint of a smile ghosted across her lips. "A nice touch, don't you think?"

"Hit him where it hurts?"

"Exactly."

"Where was Esme?"

"Supposedly out shopping, but I doubt it was a coincidence she and Rick came home within minutes of each other. Neither could get in, of course. When he called me and I confronted him, he didn't deny any of it. Do you know what he did?"

"What?"

He went back to his car, called a camera crew, and waited for them to arrive. Then he took out the gun he keeps in his glove compartment and started shooting up the house, ranting and raving like a lunatic, screaming about how much he loves me and how heartless I was being. Thankfully I was upstairs, or I could have been hurt. Not that he'd care."

"It's all on tape?"

"The police confiscated the camera, but I suspect there will be footage on every entertainment news program tonight. Rick has been arrested, but he'll be out in a day or two. His popularity will soar. He'll be famous again."

"And you?" I asked, hearing the sadness in her voice.

As she looked at me, I saw her eyes filled with hurt, anger, and grief. "Me? Well, I'll still be in love with an asshole, won't I?"

32

The next morning, I sat behind my desk watching Sean. Ordinarily I wouldn't be working on a weekend, but because of the unexpected day off this week, all the appointments missed that day had to be rescheduled for today.

In light of all that had happened this week, my parents' big dinner tonight had been moved to next weekend. I had a sneaking feeling they'd rescheduled because of me—sensing I needed some time to recuperate after a rough week. I appreciated that more than they could know, even though it didn't stop my father from insisting I come into work today.

Sean leaned over the conference table as he wrote notes on various files. If I tried hard enough, I could see the rise and fall of his chest with each breath he took.

He tossed the pen on the table. "Will you stop?"

"Stop what?" I could play innocent really well when I had to.

"Staring at me like that."

"Just admiring the view." Flirt, flirt, pretend everything's going to be okay. All in a day's work.

"Lucy."

"Sean."

"I'm *fine*."

Yeah, right now. "Why, yes, you are. Mighty fine." Inwardly I cringed. That sounded worse than I thought it would. Way too cheesy. Maybe I wasn't as good at pretending as I thought.

He groaned and shook his head.

"I'm working on it," I said softly.

"I know." He crossed over to me, pulled me out of my chair, and kissed me. I relaxed in his arms and simply enjoyed. No thinking, no worrying, just feeling. No need for pretending with that one.

There was a knock on the already-open door. "Sorry to interrupt," Aiden said, not looking sorry at all.

I reluctantly let go of Sean. He went back to the table, gathered up his files.

"Good news or bad news?" Aiden asked, sitting on the edge of the table.

"Good?" I could use some good news.

"I got a call from the flooring store. My hardwood has come in."

"Woo-hoo," I said dully.

Aiden laughed.

Sean said, "What am I missing?"

"You didn't tell him?" Aiden asked.

"I've been a little busy," I countered, and explained to Sean about the renovations at Aiden's. "If that's your good news, then what's the bad news?"

"Catherine Murphy and Mary Ellen Spero have skipped town."

I sank into my chair.

"The Boston police found the earring just where you said it would be. By the time they secured a search warrant, they were gone. Cleaned out their bank accounts, packed up, and left."

Catherine must have known that earring would be their downfall. "Any leads yet?"

"Not yet. It's just a matter of time before they turn up."

Sean said, "What does this mean for Tristan Rourke?"

Aiden covered a yawn with his hand, then said, "The DA is beside himself. Rourke was released on bail an hour ago. The FBI couldn't find any solid evidence Tristan is behind the art thefts, and so the only thing they could hold him on was breaking into your house, Lucy. The judge had no choice but to set bail, which Meaghan quickly posted. "

So, Tristan was out. He and Meaghan were together. There might just be a happily ever after in their future.

"Why are you smiling?" Aiden asked me.

Sean said in a syrupy voice, "Because love conquered all."

"I'm sorry, I'm a sap." Speaking of. I pulled a box out of my satchel. "I got you a little something. As a thank-you for helping out with Mac's case. Marisol helped pick it out."

Aiden stood, took the box. "Oh, well, if Marisol helped . . ." He lifted the box top, separated the tissue paper, and pulled out the Hawaiian shirt. He bent down and picked up the piece of paper that had fluttered out of the box.

Sean kept his head down, suddenly focused on aligning his files just right, but I could see his smile. He might just be coming down with the Love Conquered All syndrome himself.

Aiden glanced at me, a question in his eyes.

"The flight leaves tomorrow morning. The hotel information is still in the box. Everything's been taken care of. You've been working so hard lately. We thought a vacation was in order and knowing how *stubborn* you are, we thought you might need a little push in the right direction."

He was quiet for so long I thought he was going to protest. Finally, a smile pulled at one corner of his mouth, then the other, and then went straight to his eyes. "I'd better get home and start packing. Thanks, Lucy," he said softly. "And thank Marisol for me, too." He shook Sean's hand and headed for the door before stopping and looking back at me. "Don't think you're getting out of helping with the floors."

"I wouldn't dream of backing out of our agree—" My voice caught as a woman stepped into the doorway. "Hello."

Meaghan Archibald said, "Hi."

Why hadn't Suz buzzed me to let me know?

Aiden looked between us, smiled, and said, "I'm on vacation," as he walked out.

Sean walked over to the door and said, "Come on in."

Meaghan wore a simple white T-shirt and UMass sweats but made them look as good as any designer outfit. She had a large backpack slung over her shoulder and set it on the floor as she sat down. "I can't stay. I just came by to say thank you. If you hadn't seen that earring . . ."

I wondered how she felt about Mary Ellen and

Catherine. Whether it was anger or compassion. After all, they had been victims of Anthony Spero, too.

Meaghan stood up. "I should go. Tristan is waiting for me downstairs. The past is completely behind us now. Today is a new day. The first day of the rest of our lives. Together." She smiled, glowing. "I think it was kismet the way everything worked out. Now with my family's money Tristan and I can help others—legally," she said with a wink. "Maybe everything worked out just the way it was supposed to."

"Good luck," I said, knowing they had a long road ahead, kismet or not.

"Lucy, I don't need luck. I have love." She walked out.

Sean said, "Wait!" He grabbed her backpack. "You forgot this."

Looking over her shoulder, she said, "I know," and kept on walking.

Sean set the backpack on the table and unzipped it. I peeked inside.

Two paintings were covered in Bubble Wrap.

The Vermeer and the Gandolfi.

My father was going to be a happy man.

"I'll put these in the safe upstairs," Sean said, slinging the backpack over his shoulder. I followed him to the empty reception area. No sign of Suz.

"I'll wait until he's done with his consultation to tell him the good news."

"Why the frown?" Sean asked.

"It just feels like he shouldn't be rewarded. Those are stolen paintings. Someone is missing them. It just doesn't feel right."

"I'm not sure I like that look in your eye, Ms. Valentine."

I smiled. "I don't think my father will like it, either."

Footsteps pounded on the stairs and the office door banged open. Suz stuck her head in. "The Lone Ranger is back! Hurry!"

Mac.

Sean looked at me. "Go! I'll wait here for you."

I took off running, hating that Sean had to stay behind. Hating that he knew he'd slow us down.

"Did you see him, Suz?"

Her long dark hair streamed behind her. "No, but look." She held up a fistful of twenties. "I'd been watching for him, but then Aiden came in and I was sidetracked, and by the time I made it back to the window there was chaos on the Common. I got down here as soon as I could."

People were running around chasing money, pushing and shoving. Suz dove back into the fray.

I frantically looked around for Mac but didn't see him. Someone pushed me aside as they chased a twenty. I took a quick jog around the heart of the chaos. Mac was gone.

As I started across the Common, I spotted the rhyming homeless man sitting on a bench watching me with a smile.

"Is this seat taken?" I asked, motioning to the spot next to him.

He shook his head. A black trash bag sat on the ground between his legs. I didn't see a thermos today, but he was wearing the same holey knit hat, the same black coat.

"I—" I blinked.

He tipped his head, waiting for me to finish my sentence.

That black coat. It was the same one I had seen hanging in the closet of a swanky hotel room during my reading with Orlinda Batista.

I couldn't believe it had taken me so long to put it together. That's why my reading with Orlinda had been nagging at me. I'd recognized the coat in the closet but hadn't been able to make the connection.

Now I had to make sure.

"It's been a long week," I said. "Really long. You see, I have this talent for finding lost objects. Sometimes it comes in handy, and sometimes it's a pain. There are all kinds of rules. For example, my father lost some valuable artwork this week. Priceless, really. But I couldn't help him find it, because it didn't really belong to him. That's a long story in itself. Have you ever lost anything?"

He nodded, watching me warily.

"Then you can understand," I said brightly, taking his cold hand in mine. I felt the wave of dizziness as my vision took me from Boston Common, to Roxbury, to a well-maintained street, to a gray house with black trim and lacy white curtains in the upstairs windows, inside to a basement with a hidden trapdoor that led to a secret warehouse packed with Bubble-Wrapped canvases.

I pulled my hand back, focused through the dizziness. "It's harder for me to find people. Part of the rules. Plus, it doesn't help when the people don't want to be found. They dress up in a costume, or use an assumed name at a hotel, or pretend to be a rhyming gimpy homeless man."

"Lucy!" Preston ran up the path. "There you are. Sean said the Lone Ranger was here. Did you see him? Was it Mac? Is he still around? Does he know what happened with Rick yesterday?"

"Preston, breathe!"

She sucked in a lungful of air but didn't take her eyes off the crowd.

"He's not out there," I said.

"How do you know? Did you search the whole crowd?"

"Preston, have a seat. I want you to meet someone, a friend of mine."

Her gaze flashed between me and the man on the bench. She held up her hands. "Whoa, I don't have any extra cash, so don't think I'm giving any away. I work hard, you know."

"Sit, Preston. Please."

"You know, Lucy, you should have called me about what happened with Rick Hayes. I missed a huge scoop. The protests were just about over by then. My boss is hopping mad and my front-page story went to the sportswriter."

"I might have a bigger scoop for you."

Interested, she motioned for me to scoot over. I made room for her.

"Like what?" she asked.

The man looked helplessly at us.

"First, introductions," I said.

Preston sighed. She stuck out her hand. "Preston Bailey."

The man looked at me, then held out his hand. "Mac Gladstone."

In the distance I saw a coppery-colored blob chasing pigeons while someone tugged helplessly on his leash. Rufus was taking Christa Hayes for a walk. And he was, in fact, having a blast.

Preston fell off the bench.

I looked down at her. "Mac and I were just discussing that it was time to go home. Right, Mac?"

"Yes, it's time. This was my last hurrah."

Suz walked over and looked at Preston on the ground as if it were a common occurrence. "Only sixty dollars. How am I going to save a down payment on a house with sixty dollars?"

Mac stood up and handed her his trash bag. "This might help."

"Uh," she threw me a help-me look, "thanks?"

Preston was still stunned. The rapid-fire questions would come as soon as the shock wore off.

"You might want to open it," I said to Suz.

Holding it at arm's length, she said, "I think I'll pass."

"I'll open it!" Preston lunged.

"What's going on?" Suz held it out of Preston's reach. "What's in here that's so exciting?" She untied the plastic strings and looked inside. The color drained from her face. "Oh. My. God."

"There should be about five thousand in there, give or take a bit," Mac said. "The last of my stash. Is that enough for a down payment?"

Suz stumbled over her words. "What? I mean who? *Why?*"

"Because you cared enough about a homeless man to give him money."

Suz winced. "I can't keep this. I only gave you that money because Lucy made me feel guilty." Reluctantly she held the bag out.

He pushed it back toward her. "But you still gave it. And any friend of Lucy's is a friend of mine."

"I'm a friend of Lucy's," Preston chirped.

Mac laughed, then sobered. "Yeah, but you stole my hat. She," he motioned to Suz, "didn't steal my hat." Mac took a small silver whistle from his pocket and blew into it.

Rufus suddenly stopped chasing pigeons and headed our way. Christa chased him. He barked happily as he reached us. His tail wagged as he sniffed and licked in greeting. Christa hung back until Mac motioned her near. He put his arms around her shoulder. "We're going home, kid."

Mac, Christa, and Rufus walked ahead of us. They were going to gather Mac's things from his new hotel room and head back to see Jemima.

I was impressed Preston didn't ask if she could join them because I had a feeling Jemima wouldn't have welcomed the media. There was time enough for questions, for answers, for figuring out the whys and hows.

Suz walked next to me, hugging her trash bag. Preston glanced over at her and pouted. I put my arm around her. "Look on the bright side."

"What? The scoop?" She smiled halfheartedly. "I guess it *is* a good scoop. It's not a five-thousand-dollar scoop, though."

"Not that scoop. I have another one. A huge one. The biggest of your career, Preston. National—no, international headlines."

Her steps faltered. Her lip quivered. "What is it?"

I motioned to a bench, and we sat. I looked her straight in the eye. "There's a condition."

Her jaw dropped. "You're kidding."

I wasn't. At all.

"What kind of condition?"

"I want you to stop looking into my family's past. Stop trying to figure us out. Let it be."

"But—"

I cut her off. "And I want a promise that if you ever do learn anything about us you won't write about it. That you'll keep our secrets—all of them—safely tucked into your heart, just as my family as tucked you into theirs."

Tears swam in her bright blue eyes. "That, Lucy Valentine, is better than any old scoop."

I smiled. "So you don't want to know what it is?"

"Are you kidding?" She bounced with excitement. "Spill! And while we're at it, can I get a company credit card, too?"

"Now you're pushing it."

We linked arms as we walked back to the office. If I planned everything just right, Tristan Rourke could get a fresh start, Mac's paintings would be recovered, my father would get a little life lesson, and Preston Bailey, roving reporter, would get the scoop of a lifetime and I could stop worrying about her so much.

All I had to do was see a woman about some laundry. . . .

33

Later that afternoon, Maureen Rourke opened the door with a smile on her face. It didn't fade when she recognized me. "Lucy Valentine. Yours be a name I'm hearing a lot these days. We owe you a debt of gratitude, we do."

"Not at all." I glanced at the street. The black Ford with tinted windows sat idling a few houses down. "Come for a walk with me?"

She looked between me and the car and said, "Let me get my coat."

We headed in the opposite direction of the car. The curtain in an upstairs window of the house next door to Maureen's fluttered. It was a three-story house, gray with black trim. The basement had a secret trapdoor leading to an underground hideaway.

"Has Tristan been living next door to you all this time?" I asked.

She didn't bother denying it. "There's a secret tunnel that runs between the houses."

I stopped, looked at her. "I think we both know the

FBI won't leave him alone until he's proven innocent of those art thefts. And we both know he's guilty."

Her eyebrows shot up.

"But here's the thing," I said. "If all that artwork in Tristan's basement is found, oh, say, in an abandoned warehouse on the outskirts of town . . . Tristan might just have a chance at a normal life. The life he's always wanted."

"I'm listening," she said.

So I told her my plan.

A week later, a rubber chicken flew through the air. Rufus chased it, Thoreau nipping at his tail.

Dinner was cooking and there were a lot of people gathered to celebrate my parents being back together. I admit to some doubts they'd still be together come tonight, but they proved me wrong. And then they surprised me by accepting Jemima Hayes's request to hold the shindig at Mac's house.

The front windows were still boarded up, but the rear of the house—where the party was being held—was as beautiful as ever.

I watched Christa's face as she sat on the couch between Dovie and Mac and flipped through the album Dovie had put together for her. Inside were dozens of old photos of Betty Gladstone that Dovie had rounded up from her collection of pictures and from friends as well. There seemed to be a story with every photo. Pipe tobacco scented the air as Mac puffed away. No one dared tell a dying man that smoking was bad for him.

Across the room, Rufus dropped a drool-covered chicken in Sean's lap for him to throw again. He obliged.

I stood off to the side and watched as Maggie, Mum,

Jemima, and Suz (Teddy was working) shared the kitchen, laughing and chatting as they put dinner together. My father and Raphael sat on the stainless-steel Fritos, heckling.

Cutter looked at me from his spot on the hearth. I raised my glass to him in a silent toast. He had Preston on one side and Marisol on the other. Cutter smiled. He loved every second of the attention—maybe he wasn't so different from Dad after all.

I jumped when Raphael appeared by my side. "Sorry, Uva, didn't mean to startle you."

"I was lost in thought."

"Good thoughts or bad?"

I sipped my wine, glanced at Cutter. "Good."

Raphael followed my gaze. "Ah. It's good to have him here. Did you warn him about Preston?"

"I did, but I don't think we need to worry about her trying to dig up our secrets anymore."

"She's making quite a name for herself."

"Yes." Two of her stories—one on Mac's disappearing act and stint as the Lone Ranger and one about a raid on a Nashua, New Hampshire, warehouse where millions of dollars of priceless art pieces were recovered—had been picked up by the Associated Press. And she was currently working with Tristan and Meaghan on an article about the launch of their Clean Start Foundation, whose mission was, among other things, to revitalize impoverished neighborhoods and mentor foster children. I'd just received an invitation to their wedding, which was three weeks away. They weren't wasting any time.

"Has Dad forgiven me yet?" I asked.

His Vermeer and Gandolfi had been in that ware-house and were now back with their rightful owners. It had taken me quite a while to convince him it was the right thing to do. He still wasn't totally buying it.

"No."

"He will."

"Undoubtedly."

When Mac's paintings had been recovered, Mac had bought them back from the Mayhew, and both were now hanging above the fireplace. Jemima carried a platter of appetizers into the living room. She patted Christa's head as she passed and gave her father a kiss on his cheek. Rick was due back in court next week. Jemima had been right about his star rising in the wake of the shooting. I couldn't turn on the television without hearing his name.

Mac had admitted he left in a last-ditch effort to show Jemima what was truly important in life and that it wasn't too late to turn things around. By the glow on Jemima's cheeks, she had taken the lesson to heart. Mac had, too. He started chemotherapy in two days.

"Any news on those librarians?" Raphael asked.

"Not a peep. They could be anywhere by now."

"Could you find them?"

"Maybe. Depends on what they took with them."

He eyed me carefully. "Do you want to find them?"

I patted his cheek. "I think you know the answer to that."

He kissed my forehead and went to help set the table.

"I've been spurned," Sean said, standing next to me. He motioned to Rufus.

Rufus had switched allegiance and dropped the

rubber chicken in Dovie's lap. She gave him lots of attention before she tossed the chicken again. He charged after it. I caught the look she shared with Mac over Christa's head. It was full of affection.

My father came over and clapped Sean on the back. "Did you tell Lucy the good news?"

"What news?" I asked.

Sean said, "I haven't had a chance yet."

"What news?" I asked again, looking between the two of them.

"Even though I had a new security system installed, I'm not fond of my penthouse sitting empty. I knew Sean was looking for an apartment, so I offered him my place, rent free."

"And he said?" I prompted.

"I move in next Monday," Sean said. "I'll be living in Raphael's old quarters."

"Isn't that great news?" my father asked.

I drained my wine. "Wonderful."

"It is; it is," my father said. "By the way, Lucy Juliet, do you know why I would have received a complimentary fedora from Dominic Pagano with a note expressing his apologies if he offended you and your dear friend?"

"Maybe."

My father grinned. "He's a creepy little man, isn't he?"

I laughed. "The creepiest."

After my father wandered off, Sean said, "Are you really okay with me living at your father's place?"

I smiled at him. "As long as you don't ever expect me to sit on the couch in the living room."

"I'm sure it will be short-term. Just until . . ."

Right. The fear. "I know."

"Did you tell my father about Thoreau's leaking issues?"

Sean grinned. "No."

"Then you may be evicted sooner than you think."

"I think I'll bring him to work with me more often. Marisol said it was probably separation anxiety causing his issues."

"You think Grendel taught him?"

"Definitely. Your cat is a bad influence." Sean nudged me with his elbow. "Are you sure you don't mind?"

I really didn't. I finally understood the saying "home is where the heart is." It didn't matter where he lived. Wherever he was would always feel like home. "I'm sure."

Cutter headed our way. "I need a drink. I think I just agreed to adopt a cat from Marisol, and I think I have a date with Preston next week to see the Rembrandt exhibit at the Museum of Fine Arts. If this keeps up, Dad will have me making matches within the month." He strode off toward the wet bar.

Dad. I smiled. Maybe they would figure things out on their own after all.

"I thought Preston made a promise to you. . . ."

"She did."

"Then why the date?"

I looked at her. She was staring after Cutter. "I think she likes him."

"Ah." Sean laughed. "The way things work out sometimes."

"I wish Em were here. She'd love this." She and

Aiden had extended their vacations a few days and weren't due back till the middle of the week.

"As much as you'd love being where she is?"

"Not *that* much. I mean, she is in Hawaii, after all. But I do miss her."

There was a twinkle in Sean's eye. "Do you want to go visit her?"

"What are you talking about?"

He slid two plane tickets from his coat pocket. "A flight leaves tomorrow. Do you want to be on it?"

My heart jumped for joy. "Just try and stop me."

"Why would I do that?" he asked. "You see, I had this vision. . . ."

"You did not."

"It was clear as day. Let's just say there was a private hula dance involved."

I punched his arm. "I liked my vision better."

Sean and I were sharing a hammock tied between two palm trees, overlooking ocean so beautifully blue it stole my breath. Vibrant green islands dotted the horizon. A sailboat swayed, anchored just offshore. Sean turned his head, looked at me, a smile in those pearlescent eyes of his. Our bodies were nestled, skin on skin, my hand on his chest, my bare leg draped over his, his arm around my shoulders pulling me closer, tighter. He leaned in, his gaze on my lips, his intent crystal clear. . . .

"What was your vision?" he asked, pulling me in for a hug.

"Oh, you'll see."

"Will I like it?"

"I guarantee you're going to *love* it."

"Were you in it?"

"Of course."

He cupped my face and kissed me. "Then I already do, Ms. Valentine. I already do."

Everybody Loves Lucy Valentine!

"Lucy is someone whose adventures you'll want to
follow again and again…"
—Charlaine Harris

Don't miss Heather Webber's

TRULY, MADLY
ISBN: 978-0-312-94613-5

DEEPLY, DESPERATELY
ISBN: 978-0-312-94614-2

**AVAILABLE FROM
ST. MARTIN'S PAPERBACKS**